ABOUT KILLER SMILE

He's a covert operator. A killer built by the U.S. Army. He's tasked with taking out his dream girl—and not on a date.

Targeting Nicole should be simple, since she hates his guts. Sebastian The Dentist—yes, a *real* freakin' dentist, don't make it scary—has wanted Nic since they first locked horns. He's not sure why they're enemies, but knows there's more to the sweet daycare owner than crayons and cardigans. But discovering her secrets lands them both in danger they'll dodge only by working together.

Between awkward wedding dates and puppies with no personal space, Sebastian and Nic get closer. They're also close to discovering if Nic's dead associate may not be so dead.

If Sebastian can stop her from hating him long enough to eliminate the threat, they might just fall in love. But only Nic can stop him from hating himself.

3

ASSASSINS
in Love

KILLER SMILE

USA TODAY BESTSELLING AUTHOR

TAWNA FENSKE

KILLER SMILE

ASSASSINS IN LOVE BOOK #3

TAWNA FENSKE

KILLER SMILE

Assassins in Love book #3
Sebastian and Nicole's story

For Dr. Andy Engel, DMD.
A decade of urging me to write a dentist hero finally pays off.
Thanks for sticking things in my mouth.
And forgiving me when I make terrible jokes.

CHAPTER 1

Target: Code name Rogue

Assignment date: Thursday, October 5

Job details: Target to be eliminated for the slaying of Danny "Duck Toes" DeCosta. Female subject will wear a red dress. Considered armed and dangerous. Location and details provided upon acceptance of contract.

*D*r. Sebastian LaDouceur, DDS, stares at the incoming memo. He's on his encrypted tablet, which he won't normally check at work.

Work at the *dental office*, which is just one of his jobs. The Dentist is a busy man.

He reads the words again, surprised The Union pinged him. He's taken fewer contracts lately to focus on pediatric dentistry. Who knew there were so many kids needing checkups and tartar scaling?

As he scans the note again, two words catch his eye.

Female target.

Interesting. They know he doesn't typically target women, so this one must be big. He heard of the hit on Duck Toes DeCosta. Doesn't know much besides the shooter used an M24 sniper rifle from 900 feet. A clean shot, one Seb admires in principle.

He types a message back.

MORE DETAIL REQUIRED. Time? Target profile? Price?

THE LAST ONE doesn't matter. Seb doesn't do this for money. His covert work for Uncle Sam's Army left him with a disdain for terrorists and rapists and other lowlifes he's asked to eliminate. These side jobs are a hobby.

Not like Dante and Matteo, who've mostly done dirty work for the Dovlanese government. Seb's a freelancer. A gig worker, as the cool kids say.

His front door chimes, and a guy walks in, gripping his jaw. "You've gotta help me, man!"

Sebastian taps the tablet into lock mode. "What's the problem?"

"Oh, hey—you're the dentist." The guy drops his hand. "Saw your billboard on Eighth and Main. Can you squeeze me in?"

Seb's not taking new patients today, but the guy looks desperate. "What's going on?"

"I've got this big hole in my tooth." He bares his front incisors like a spaniel subjected to non-consensual butt sniffs at the dog park. "See?"

"First bicuspid?"

The guy runs his tongue over his teeth. "Whasssat?"

"Left top. Three back from the central incisor." Sebastian peers in the guy's mouth. Solid, sharp cuspids. Some enamel discoloration indicative of a coffee habit. He scans the suspicious spot and nods. "That'll require an extremely specialized extraction technique."

"Extraction?" The man uncurls his lips. "I've got a date in three hours. I can't have her thinking I've got rotten teeth."

Sebastian slips a hand in his desk drawer. Finds a pack of plastic toothpicks with soft, bristled ends. "Congratulations, sir." He hands off the pack of picks. "I declare you an honorary dentist."

The guy stares at the packet. "Is that some kind of pill I should take?"

"Toothpicks." Has he never seen them not made of wood and stacked in a pink box? "That's pepper on your tooth. Use the mirror over there to get it off."

"No shit?" He pivots and stares at the mirror. "Huh." He pops out a pick and starts on his teeth. "I swear I brushed."

"Pepper's stubborn." A glance out the window gives Seb a second glimpse of stubborn. Matteo and Dante in Teo's 1973 Alfa Romeo Spider. They've got the top up and their eyes glued on Sebastian's guest.

Flipping them the bird, he checks his patient's progress. "All good?"

"You're a lifesaver, man." The guy pockets the pack of picks and makes for the door. "If I get laid tonight, I owe you."

"Wonderful." He leans back in his chair and waits for the guy to go away in his Tesla. The second he's gone, his buddies have their car doors open.

"Afternoon, gentlemen." He hooks his hands behind his head as his pals stride through the clinic entrance. "You here for a complimentary tongue scraping?"

Matteo leans on the counter. "A fucking comedian."

Dante scans the waiting room. "Where's your receptionist?"

"Terri's at lunch." Seb drops his chair legs to the floor. "Which means she can't slap me for calling her Terri." It's her name, but not one he gets to call his grandma. "Need her to schedule you for a denture fitting?"

Matteo glares. "You can stop the comedy routine any time."

Not really. It's kind of his thing. He's mulling another crack when Dante leans in and lowers his voice. "Last chance to join the Svenson job. Shouldn't take more than an hour."

"I thought you'd gone straight." Dante's a farmer now, and Teo took a job for some computer firm. "No more killing bad guys for money?"

"No killing." Dante cracks his knuckles. "Just talking."

A talk from big, bald Dante could scare anyone to death, so it's kinda the same. "Good plan."

"And we're not making money." Matteo hands him a ski mask. "It's a pro bono job."

The mask is a nice touch. Necessary, since Seb's face decorates billboards all over town.

"While I appreciate the anonymity, I'm out." He shoves the mask back. "I've got a gum graft at two."

Teo lifts a brow. "Performing or receiving?"

"Performing." He does a lot of that. "Maybe the next job?"

"Later this week." Dante scrubs his bald scalp with one big hand. "Drinks with a guy who sticks kittens in a sack and throws them in his pond instead of getting his cats spayed."

Grounds for murder in Dante's book. Seb can't blame him. The big guy loves animals.

As usual, Teo will pull the reins, insist they *talk* instead of slipping cyanide in the target's beer.

It's nice how his pals complement each other. "Which night?"

"Depends." Dante looks at Matteo. "Which night were Jen and Nic doing that fancy charity thing?"

Teo shrugs. "I'll ask Renee. They're all going together."

Sebastian rests a hand on the darkened tablet. It buzzed ten seconds ago, so The Union must've answered. "Can I let you know? I might have something going on this week."

"Busy guy." Dante thumps the counter with a meaty fist. "I'm making elk chili next Friday night. Come by at five."

His week's perking up already. "Will everyone be there?"

Matteo shares a scowl with both of them before jerking a thumb at Dante. "Just because this asshole's marrying one sister doesn't grant you permission to date the other."

Seb stifles a snort. Nicole Bello needs no one's permission for anything. "One of these days, she'll stop hating me. Then I'll be at all the family dinners."

"Dream on." Teo heads for the door. "Let us know which night you're free for the kitten guy."

"Will do." He watches his buddies march out. One bald and brooding, one dark and scowling. Both big as hell. If anyone's casing his clinic, they look like the weirdest couple to ever book a tandem cleaning.

Grabbing the tablet, he taps in his passcode. Waits for the message to appear.

TARGET IS a **female operator with 18 confirmed kills. Further details forthcoming only with signed contract.**

SEBASTIAN SNORTS ALOUD THIS TIME. He's been at this too long to take a job without more intel. He taps his favorite poop emoji, followed by a blue tyrannosaurus, a balloon bouquet, and a smiley face with oversized teeth.

It's meaningless crap and not code for anything, but The Union guys will spend hours deciphering its hidden message.

NO SHAREY, **no signy.**

HE'S BARELY SET the tablet down when his door bangs open. He looks up, and his heart heaves into his throat.

"God, you're a jerk."

As his heart simmers down, a different part of him wakes up. "Afternoon, Nicole." He gives her his best dentist grin. "You look lovely today."

It's true, though her scowl suggests she doesn't like hearing it from him. "How many times do I have to ask you *politely* not to let your patients park in my lot?"

"Politely?" He pretends to ponder. "Once would do it."

She huffs out a breath. "Seriously, LaDouceur. My families need to get in and out of my building as quickly as possible. They can't trek across the lot every time some douche in a Porsche shows up late for his teeth whitening and parks in front of my daycare."

Nicole Bello runs a childcare facility for families in hiding. Moms fleeing abuse or dads in witness protection. A remarkable gig, and she's remarkable for running it.

Doesn't mean he won't mess with her. "Much as I'd love to be the first dental clinic in Oregon to have valet parking, that's not in the cards. I put up a sign. What else do you want?"

"They're not getting the message from your stupid sign." Nic blows blonde hair off her forehead. "Make it *bigger*."

This bickering sends conflicting signals to his libido. "You want it *bigger*, huh?"

"God, you're a pig." Nic folds her arms. She's wearing one of her teacher dresses with a thick cardigan, but he sees the swell of her breasts behind the fabric.

He'd see them if she wore a suit of armor.

"Seriously, Minty Fresh." Her eyes soften, but her voice stays sharp. "It's a safety issue. I need you to take this seriously."

The fact that she said "seriously" twice means he shouldn't joke around. "*Seriously* seriously, or just *sorta* seriously?" He tips back in his chair. "Because there's a difference between—"

"Between me speaking plainly to you—business owner to business owner—versus me involving the police?" She grits her teeth. "Is that serious enough for you?"

Yeah, that'll do it.

He sets down his chair. "You know I'm just messing with you." He ordered the new sign last week. "M'lady wants it bigger, she'll get it bigger. It'll be up by the end of the week."

Her face softens like her eyes. Green eyes the color of sea glass or ocean waves or the little jade roller Terri uses for her face cream.

Thinking of his grandma helps make his hard-on go down.

"Thank you." Nicole rests her hands on the counter, and he does his best not to look at them. Not to wonder what they'd feel like trailing down his chest. "I don't mean to be a hard-ass. It's just really important."

Sebastian nods gravely. "All asses are important. Particularly yours."

Nic flings her arms up. "You're hopeless."

"Not true." He lifts one brow. "I'm very hopeful you'll go out with me tomorrow night."

"No."

"Wednesday night?"

"Sebastian—"

"Okay, okay." He rests his arms on the counter.

Is he seeing things, or did her eyes just flick favorably to his biceps? "Thursday night, and that's my final offer."

"Well, *that's* a relief." She backs toward the door. "Even if I wanted to—which I don't—I have plans Thursday."

"What sort of plans?"

"None of your business."

"Tuning your harp to play hymns with the angels?" He dials up the wattage on his grin. "Renewing your license to drive me wild with desire?"

Nicole snorts. "Do lines like that ever work for you?"

"Dunno." He grabs a paperweight off the counter. He's got no papers to anchor but wants to watch her ogle his arms as he throws it from one hand to the other. "I save all my best stuff for you."

"Please." Nic's eyes flicker.

He tosses again.

Another flicker.

She licks her lips. "If that's your best, God help the women who get your lousiest."

"There's only you, Nicole."

Another toss.

Another flash.

A roll of those green eyes. "Goodbye, LaDouceur."

She shoves out the door, and he sits up to watch her walk from his clinic to her car across the lot.

Wait. Not to her car. To the dry cleaner two doors down. He stares through the window as she hands them a ticket, then waits while the clerk shuffles in back.

Seb's not kidding about the date. From the instant he laid eyes on Nicole Bello, he wanted her. The fact that she hated him on sight may be a motive.

Sebastian loves a challenge.

But he loves her fiery personality more. Her beauty, her brains, her fierce love of family. He even loves how she tells him off. It's a game he enjoys, and deep down, she enjoys it, too. He's almost sure.

The dry cleaner comes back with a plastic-wrapped garment on a hanger. Sebastian squints to see it. A dress? Not one of her teacher dresses. This one looks slinky. Something long and curve-hugging and…

Red?

She swings through the door with the bag over her arm, and he follows her with his eyes. Stares as she slings the dress into her sensible Volvo. She checks the mirrors and buckles her seatbelt like a fine, upstanding instructor of young minds.

As she drives away—hands at perfect ten-and-two on the wheel—Sebastian feels his arms prickle.

Dragging his eyes to his tablet, he shoves it aside. Wiggles the mouse for his desktop computer and toggles past the patient portal. In the search bar, he plugs in "charity benefit events." Three clicks later, he's on the website for the chamber of commerce.

It's the silliest hunch he's ever had.

But as he scans the listings, he can't lose the tingle in his gut.

CHAPTER 2

"*Y*ou want more bubbles?"

Nicole shakes her head and sips her virgin cider. "I'm good, thanks."

Her sister tips the bottle of champagne to Renee's glass as Nic swallows her lukewarm drink. She swapped the contents of her flute when Jen and Renee ran to the restroom.

Not that she doesn't like booze.

But her gut says to keep her wits sharp tonight. Her gut's rarely wrong, so she's swilling this non-alcoholic crap. "I wonder where that guy is with the bacon-wrapped shrimp?"

Jen shrugs and sets down the bottle. "Maybe we ate them all."

"They were damn tasty." Nic's distracted as she scans the crowd. Is that a gun on the hip of the waiter with the canapes?

No, it's a bar towel.

Or the woman in the green cocktail dress—what's she slipping in that mug? Poison or roofies or—*no*. It's fucking Sweet-n-Low.

"You okay, Nicole?"

She snaps back to Renee. "I'm great!" Resettling in her seat, she lifts her champagne flute. "Just wondering who won that helicopter tour in the silent auction."

Renee makes a wistful face. "I lost out on the necklace."

"Seriously?" Nicole huffs. "Some asshole outbid you?"

It's Nic. She's the asshole.

"Probably best." Renee shrugs. "I couldn't afford it, anyway."

Exactly why Nic placed a secret bid. "It would have been great for your wedding." And now it's a great birthday gift. She'll give it to Renee at family dinner next Friday.

Shifting to Jen, Nic smooths hair off her sister's temple. "I love you in an updo like this."

"Yeah?" Jen pats the poofy bun. "I don't look like I have a bagel on my head?"

"Even if you did, bagels are delicious." She fixed Jen's hair herself, so it's totally stunning. "But you don't have bagel head. And the bonus is you're showing off those killer collarbones."

Jen's got a gorgeous athletic physique. Not that Nic's lacking in the bod department. She's rockin' this red dress, if she can say so herself.

"I'm so glad we're all doing this." Renee's smile shifts to sheepish. "I always wished I had sisters."

Nic sets her glass on the table. "I'd have offered you mine if I'd known."

Jen snorts. "She tried to sell me once."

"*Sell* you?" Renee looks horrified.

"She was six and I was ten." Nic remembers well. "Grandma Nondi said we couldn't have a pet tiger because tigers weren't good around defenseless little kids."

Jen takes it from there. "Since Nic's never been defenseless in her life, she knew Nondi meant me."

"I tried to put an ad in the paper, and I felt bad right away." Nic still feels guilty. Protecting Jen has been her job since their parents died. "I cried and gave you all my Starburst."

Jen's patting her hand now. "And you broke open your piggy bank to buy me the stuffed pig I wanted."

She also beat up Tommy Cline for calling Jen "Piggy Pancake Butt." Whatever that meant, the little asshole never said it again.

Scanning the crowd some more, Nic sips from her glass. "I still want a pet tiger."

The ladies keep chatting, but she's back to being distracted. Distracted and… edgy. Her fingers find the knife strapped to her thigh, and she strokes the blade through the sheath. It's tough to be armed in a gown this slinky, but this isn't her first rodeo. There's a Glock 43 in her beaded handbag, but that's more difficult to grab. Besides, swanky black-tie affairs aren't the place to bust out firearms. Not without solitude and a silencer, neither of which she has. A girl can only do so much.

Rustling in a potted fern whips her gaze to the corner. She squints at the tall plant across the ballroom. Is someone watching her?

"—isn't that right, Nicole?"

She blinks back to their conversation. "Say again?"

Jen bumps her arm. "Mom's wedding dress. You're the one who kept Nondi from tossing it."

"True." Her peripheral vision slips back to the fern. *Red hair, mustache, muscular build.* She's seen that guy before. Where?

"Our grandmother brought it from Dovlano." Nic drags her focus to Renee. "This was before our parents died. Before Teo got us to America to live with Nondi."

Jen spins her flute on the table. "We were little when we found the dress in a closet. Nondi wanted to burn it, but Nic stopped her."

"She'd forgotten she even had it." Nic remembers it like yesterday. The fury in their grandma's face wasn't about the dress. "We convinced her one of us might want it someday."

A little light leaves Jen's eyes. "Nondi agreed, since she'd lost the ring. Her great-great-great-*great* grandmother's diamond that got passed down for generations."

Renee touches her engagement ring, and Nic knows what she's thinking. "The one from Teo came from Nondi's father," she explains. "This other one was older. It passed through the female line. The Italian side of the family."

"Always to the eldest daughter," Jen adds.

"It was on our mom's finger when she died." Nic's throat gets tight. "It wasn't enough for the assholes to shoot her. They had to take the ring, too."

"How awful." Renee's eyes go glassy, and Nic takes note. Is she weepier than normal? "They never caught whoever did it?"

"Nope." Nic looks at Jen. "Our parents ran with some bad people." She's not sure how much Teo shares, so she shouldn't overstep. "When the mob's involved, Dovlanese police don't work too hard tracking down killers."

Jen's frowning now. "They didn't even care our parents left three kids behind. We were kinda on our own after that."

"That's so tragic." Renee dabs her eyes, and Nic decides she's definitely more emotional. Pregnant? Could be. Might not even know yet, based on the champagne.

But Nic's got a sense for these things. A new niece or nephew will be awesome.

First things first. Time to ditch the dark cloud she's cast over girls' night. "Anyway," Nic says, "Jen's wearing Mom's wedding dress, and it looks great on her."

"And you're wearing her veil." Jen pats Renee's hand. "She would have loved you."

Nic's throat gets tight again. "You really are perfect for this family. And for Teo." Not that Nic's jealous. There's no time in her life for relationships, and besides. Her track record's not great in that department.

But she's thrilled for her brother and her sister and really—

"Thanks." Renee sniffs. "You guys are the best."

Nic's chest feels tight now too, so she looks back at the fern in the corner. The guy's not there, so maybe she imagined him.

Time to find out.

"I need to visit the ladies' room." She stands and slings the beaded bag over her shoulder.

"Want company?" Renee moves, but Nic sets a hand on her arm.

"No, stay." Wincing, she touches her belly. "Those crab puffs made me gassy. Kinda need some privacy, you know?"

"Of course."

Nothing like fake flatulence to score a solo bathroom run. "I'll be right back."

Jen gives a supportive sister smile. "Text if you need us."

"Thanks." Nic hustles through the crowd, cataloguing guests. In a small town like this, she knows nearly everyone. She waves to the Gibsons, who have a farm next to Jen. Smiles at Pete and Sam Porter, who own the car dealership where she bought her Volvo. Good guys, Pete and Sam. Never questioned the bullet-proof windshield she requested.

There!

The creepy redhead steps back from the fern, ducking deeper into shadows. One of Danny Duck Toes' men? Or maybe a guy from The Union. Neither group loves her much right now. Nic can't really blame them.

She slips a hand in her bag and touches the Glock. Should have brought the silencer, but it's too late now. If she has to take him out, the knife's a better pick. Quiet, efficient, lethal.

Just like Nicole.

Slipping past the ladies' room, she heads for a dark hallway. There's a second restroom down here, so if anyone spots her, she'll say it's for privacy. With a steadying breath, she swings a glance behind her.

Footsteps?

No, that's the grandfather clock beside the boardroom. This

community center holds tons of antiques. Even a Dovlanese vase Nondi donated before she died.

Heart pumping, Nic scans the clock. It's nearly nine, so if she has to bail, that's an easy excuse. She's got parent meetings in the morning.

With her pulse flooding her ears, Nic clicks her heels down darkened concrete and turns the corner. Office doors line both sides of the hall, but most are locked. She scoped it out earlier. Steadying her breath, she hurries past the soda machine.

"Hey there." Sebastian LaDouceur steps into her path. "Going somewhere?"

Her mouth falls open. His blue eyes glow in the red light of the soda machine. That definitely shouldn't be sexy. "What the hell are you doing here?"

"Me?" He gives his infuriating dentist grin. "Buying all the sugared soda to save the teeth of future patients."

Good Lord. She has to get him out of here. The man's annoying, but she doesn't want him dead.

Much.

Crossfire could make a mess of that pretty face.

Unless he's been sent by The Union? Anything's possible. Nic fingers the clasp on her purse. "Seriously, Minty Fresh—why are you here?"

He's smiling as he shifts around her and... *crap.* Now he's wedged between her and the end of the hall. If someone starts shooting, Seb's in the way.

Not good.

"I'm here for the event." He shoves his hands in his pockets and leans against the soda machine. "Big night for charity."

She raises one eyebrow. "You're a donor?"

"Absolutely. Very passionate about the... cause."

The man has no clue.

Doesn't mean he deserves to die. "If you're so passionate,

you'd better get back out there." She tips her chin back toward the ballroom. "They're about to auction off the grand prize."

"Is it something you want?"

"Uh…" She's clueless, too. "Absolutely. I'm very much a fan of —" What kind of charity is this, anyway? "Endangered cats."

"Endangered cats?" It's his turn to execute the single-brow lift, and damn if he doesn't do it better. "Are they auctioning one off?"

Why are they having this conversation?

And are those footsteps she's hearing? She can't see with the dumb dentist in her way.

"Sure." Wait, no. "I mean—they're auctioning the chance to name one." They're still talking about endangered cats?

Seb's grin gets bigger. "A chance to name an endangered cat, huh?" He shifts again, so he's in her personal space, and she definitely shouldn't like it. "I'm thinking Andy."

She frowns. "What?"

"Andy for an Andean Mountain Cat." He folds his arms and makes his pecs do nice things beneath that tailored suit coat. "Fewer than fourteen hundred of them left in the world, mostly due to habitat loss at high altitudes."

"Huh." She needs to get rid of him. "That's… tragic." She tries to move, but he's big and beastly and blocking her way.

"Probably Borris for the Borneo Bay Cat." He's getting into it now. "Fewer than twenty-two hundred left, thanks to deforestation and palm oil plantations in Borneo."

"Fascinating." She pushes past him. Almost makes it when he calls after her.

"Or Danny," he says. "For the tiger."

Nic freezes. Turns back to Seb.

A coincidence, right? She licks her lips. "Tiger?"

"Yeah." Sebastian shrugs. "I hear they make great pets."

She shifts her stance. Lets her fingers find the weapon. "Why Danny?"

His eyes, sharp and steady, give nothing away. "Tigers have

webbed toes." He shifts again, broad shoulders blocking her view down the hall. "Read an article about some mobster. Danny 'Duck Toes' DeCosta." His chuckle has an edge. "I guess the guy had webbed toes—syndactyl, it's called in humans. Kind of a rare trait."

Nic's heart kicks up. Suspicion, not attraction. So what if Sebastian has the broadest shoulders she's seen? She's cataloging the threat, not admiring the view. This must be a coincidence, right? All the stuff about tigers, the mention of DeCosta—

"This Duck Toes guy—he did his mobster thing barefoot or something?" She's conscious of how close he is. How big. Her fingers find their grip on the gun. "That's weird."

"His wife started the nickname." Another shrug as Seb leans on the soda machine. "She vanished a few months ago."

Nic holds her ground. Doesn't break eye contact. As she licks her lips, his eyes flick to her mouth. "I need to get to the restroom. Girl problems." She's careful as she pivots, not turning her back on him for a second. "I hope I've got tampons."

It's the quickest way to send a man running, but The Dentist doesn't move. Just plants a hand on the wall, bracing with one arm. One muscular, chiseled arm that—

"I thought it was gas."

Nic halts. "I beg your pardon?"

"Crab puff, wasn't it?" He shrugs and shifts his weight on the balls of his feet. "But hey, hopefully you've got room in your purse for tampons. That Glock takes up a fair bit of space."

Her mouth goes dry. "What the f—"

Zing!

Sebastian pounces, taking her to the ground. There's another *zing*, and his hand cups her head as they hit the floor behind the Coke machine.

She struggles as a window shatters, glass raining down from where she stood just seconds ago.

A silencer. Someone's shooting with a silencer.

Her body keeps fighting as her brain catches up. Did Sebastian just save her?

Or maybe he's the enemy. Uncertainty swirls with lust in the pit of her stomach. Shoving him off, she goes for the blade at her thigh. It's easy to reach with her gown ripped to hell.

Sebastian tilts his head. "The knife and not the gun?"

She spits hair out of her mouth. "What the fuck?"

Grinning, he gets to his feet behind the pop machine. Extends a hand to help her. Nic hesitates.

"I'm not after you." His eyes glow with something dark and dangerous. "But someone is."

For some stupid reason, she believes him. Lets him hoist her to her feet as he draws a gun with the other hand. Nic's brain reels as she tries to tug her hand back.

"Who *are* you?"

Still gripping her left hand, he draws it to his lips. "Dr. Sebastian LaDouceur, DDS." He brushes a kiss on her knuckles, and she shudders. "We've met."

Not like this. Never like this. He's her brother's buddy, her annoying neighbor. And also—

"You're with The Union." She'd pegged him as an operator. An ex-military renegade, and yeah, she's checked him out.

Not in *that* way.

Nic yanks her hand free. "Did you take a contract on me?"

"No." The growl seems sincere, and so do his eyes. "Absolutely not." Seb sticks his head out from behind the soda machine. He's frowning as he stares down the dark hallway. "Shot came from over there, yeah?"

"Yeah." Nic shifts closer, not sure why she's trusting him. She *isn't*. But his body's a good blockade, so she slides behind him and—

Zing!

Another shot zips past. She grunts as Seb drags her back against the wall. Against his body, which is thick and hard and—

"Let go of me." She doesn't need a damn bodyguard. Especially not one this hot and solid and— "Do you seriously have a stiffy right now?"

She feels every inch of it with how he's pressed against her.

"I'm flattered." He grabs for the bulge and—okay, yeah. A pocket pistol. Beretta Tomcat.

She's got one just like it. "Nice piece."

"You should see the stiffy." He shoves it back in his pocket and takes aim with the Walther.

"Who the hell brings *two* guns to a charity event?"

He's too busy muttering to answer. "Shoulda brought a lock pick."

"What for?" She draws one from her purse.

It's Sebastian's turn to blink. "You bring a pick set to charity events?"

"*This* shocks you, but not the Glock?"

"Good point."

Another zing, this one closer. Whoever's got the silencer isn't messing around.

"Jesus." He scowls at the end of the hallway. "It's too risky to return fire. If someone's out there—"

"Yeah." Someone like Jen or Renee, coming to look for her. "You're thinking we bust into one of the offices and hope for an outside door?"

"Second one from the left." He nods down the hall. "It's the bookkeeper's office."

"How do you know this?"

"We dated a while back."

Nic grits her teeth. "Of course you did." It shouldn't annoy her. Neither should the memory of their first meeting. He doesn't remember since Nic was disguised, but she's never forgotten his words.

"*Forget the petty shit you think you know, and get your ass back in the bathroom, ho.*"

Sexist, verbally abusive asshole. That's Sebastian LaDouceur. What lurks behind the charm. It behooves her to remember.

Gulping, she rejoins the present. "Cover me while I get the door open."

He frowns but doesn't take his eyes off the end of the hall. "Keep your head down."

Like she doesn't know that.

But she bites back the snark and crawls to the door he indicated. Another zing sends her flat to the floor.

"You okay?" His voice sounds strained.

"Peachy." She belly-crawls the rest of the way, heart hitting her ribs. Her gown snags on a nail sticking from a baseboard and she curses.

"You've got great legs."

Gritting her teeth, she yanks her hem free. "You're not seriously hitting on me right now."

"Seriously," he agrees. "But only seriously and not *seriously* seri—"

Another zing slaps his mouth shut. A bullet pings the planter near her head, and Nic yelps.

"Fuck." She pops to her knees and jams the pick home. A twist to the right and she's in.

"Go, go, go!" Sebastian shoves after her, slamming the door shut behind them. They face each other across a big maple desk. They're both breathing hard.

His blue eyes glow green from the exit sign. Sebastian nods at the side door. "Get back to your table."

"What about you?"

Footsteps thunder down the hall. Someone tries a door in the distance. "I'd like to talk with our friend."

She's no stranger to that kind of talk. "I want information."

"And I want you safe."

Like that'll happen. The steps thud closer. Someone's tossing the office next door. Nic draws the knife from her thigh.

Sebastian's jaw clenches. "Under the desk."

She dips her eyes to the dark space. A good spot to stage an ambush. To eavesdrop. "Both of us?"

"Trust me, it's big enough for two." He shoves her toward it, and she doesn't fight him.

Just hikes up her dress and ducks beneath the maple monstrosity. "And you know this *how?*" Never mind, she doesn't want to know. He's not answering, anyway. She turns and sees him crawling in after her, gaze on her ass.

"Eyes to yourself, Minty Fresh." She's all the way under, and he's right—it's huge under here. Someone shouts in the room next door.

"Bookkeeper's husband showed up." Seb sounds entirely too cheerful about it. "Had to hide under here for an hour."

"You're a pig." She already knew this.

"If it makes you feel better, I didn't know she was married." He's got the Walther in his fist as he settles across from her. Foot steps hit the hall. More than one set?

Nic looks at Seb. "Still a pig."

"Oink." His knee bumps hers, and she draws back.

Gets her gun out, but the blade stays clenched in her fist. The door bangs open, and Nic holds her breath. Two sets of oxfords —one brown, one black—slip through the slab of light on the floor. She grips the knife tighter. Seb's watching her, pistol in his fist. His doesn't have a silencer, either.

Dammit. She wasn't prepared for this tonight.

Seb's watching her. When she meets his eyes, he frowns and shakes his head.

What?

She's not expecting a response, but he catches her calf and squeezes. Heat arcs up her leg and explodes between her thighs.

You. He mouths it, and she frowns.

Me?

Somewhere behind the desk, a man speaks. "Where'd the bitch go?"

"Dunno, but I need a body to claim the cash."

She winces. Seb has a point. It's her they've come to kill. If her head pops up, they'll shoot on sight.

Brown loafers cross the office. "She's alone?"

"Her friends are back at the table."

They haven't seen Seb, which means they shot blind down the hall. *Assholes.* They could have killed an innocent bystander.

Seb taps a finger to his lips. Like she needs his reminder to stay quiet.

Her eyes lock on his mouth, and she tells herself it's easier to read lips that way. Lush, full lips softer than she imagined until he skimmed them on her knuckles. What would they feel like on her—

Give me the knife.

His mouth forms the words. Scowling, she shakes her head.

Brown loafers shuffle past the desk. "She's gotta be in one of the offices." He's over by the side door, and thank God Seb had the sense to pull the chair in after them. They're hidden well under here.

Black loafers cross to the side door. "I'll bet she went outside."

"We can't let her leave. It's not about Duck Toes anymore."

"Yeah."

The guy with the brown loafers lowers his voice. "You really think she knows about Issela?"

Nic's mouth goes dry. *Issela?*

Seb studies her face. She fights to keep her breath calm, to let nothing show. She's practiced this a thousand times.

"Still can't believe Issela's alive." Brown loafers stomp around the desk. "How'd that slip through?"

"Dunno."

A grunt from the owner of the brown loafers. "Heard a rumor

she's the one who took out Duck Toes. Figured it'd bring his dad out of hiding and then—"

"Shut it!" Black loafer guy hits the desk. "This place could be bugged."

Nic's heart races. Issela? Alive? It's not possible. It can't be.

Also, Duck Toes was *her* hit. Goddammit.

Seb knocks her knee with his.

You okay?

Nodding, she drags her eyes off his mouth.

"I'm taking the side door." Brown loafers move to the entrance. "You check the other offices."

Seb puts his hand on her knee. Palm up, a pleading look in his eyes.

The knife. He mouths the words again.

Nic hesitates. Hates herself for being rattled. Hates that handing her blade to Sebastian is her best option.

Trust me.

It's the last thing she wants to do, so why is she doing it?

Palming the blade, he brushes her fingers with his. Watches her face like he expects a reaction, but she won't give it to him.

Nic grips her Glock. At least her hands aren't shaking, though the rest of her feels quivery and out of sorts.

Issela.

Seb grabs the base of the chair. Winks at her. *Winks,* for God's sake.

Biceps flex as he shoves the chair crashing across the room. A shot rings out and Seb springs like a tiger.

"Who the hell are y—"

A choke tells her the blade's been put to use. A body hits the floor as another shot zings past.

Is Seb hit?

Nic leaps to her feet. Blinks at Sebastian standing two feet away with a 9mm Smith & Wesson. It's the other man's gun, threaded with a silencer. At his feet lie the redhead and a bald goon she's never seen before.

Lifting her gaze to Seb, she licks her lips. "Thank you."

He shoves the gun in his waistband. "You need to get out of here."

"Me?" Is he kidding? "We're in this together."

"No." He's pulling a phone from his pocket, and it's not the iPhone she's seen him with before. This looks way more high-tech. "I can have a cleaner here in ten minutes. Get back to your table and tell them you tripped and fell and tore your dress and you need to leave. Tell them—"

"They'll say they're coming with me." It's the female code, leaving with the friends you came with. "I can't just—"

"Find a way." He's tapping the phone, texting someone. "Meet me in an hour at the Coquille Diner on Third. You know it?"

She nods and fights to wrap her head around what's happening. Sebastian LaDouceur, the man she's vowed to hate. The man whose charm masks something sinister.

The man who just saved her life.

"Okay." They'll sort it out later.

Seb looks up. Surprise lights his eyes, like he didn't expect her to agree. She's fought him since the first day they met. In the back of her mind, she amends that.

He doesn't remember the day you met…

Shoving the phone in his pocket, Seb clears his throat. "Go on. My contact's on his way."

Nic grips the hem of her gown, and his eyes drop to her legs. She starts to move past him, but he's so hard and big and… something happens. He catches her hand, or maybe she grabs his.

That's all it takes, and she's pressing her body to his. Seb's hands span her waist as he draws a sharp breath. Blue eyes flash in the glow of the exit light. He raises one brow as Nic goes up on tippy-toes like she's been sucked into a black hole.

"Fuck," she says, and kisses him.

Seb stiffens, then yanks her closer. His lips claim hers and *oh God*... they're really as soft as they look. His tongue dips into her mouth as she claws at his shirt and wonders how he'd feel boosting her onto the desk. What he'd do if she wrapped her legs around him and—

"Go." He pulls back and hands her the knife. "I'll meet you at the diner."

Nic swallows. *Adrenaline.* That's all this was. She steps back and shoves the sticky blade in her purse. "Be careful."

As he nods, she sees he's breathing hard. "One hour."

Touching her mouth, Nic moves to the door. Her hand finds the knob, and his voice behind her makes her blood go cold.

"A pleasure working with you, *Rogue.*"

CHAPTER 3

*S*eb sees the Volvo's headlights slash the dark. He waits
as she slips into the spot beside him and kills the
engine.

As her lights blink out, he pictures her next move. Nic
swinging one bare leg out the door. Nic striding through the
parking lot in her red dress, heels clicking the pavement. Her
hand on his car as she pops the passenger door and drops beside
him in the BMW.

But she gets out in jeans and a sweater the color of oatmeal.
Her face is scrubbed clean, and she looks wholesome and young
and not at all like he's expecting. Seb follows with his eyes as she
rounds his car to rap on the driver's side door.

He takes his time rolling down the window. "I'll have the
bacon burger with fries, hold the onion." A glance at her sneakers. "You forgot your roller skates."

"And you forgot I'm not impressed by your wise guy routine."
She hooks a thumb at the diner. "I'm hungry. Let's go."

He wasn't planning to go inside, but she's got a point. "I
suppose loitering in a dark lot under a sign for waffles isn't the

26

best way to cap off that kind of evening." He gets out and follows her across the parking lot.

There's no response from Nic, but he sees her shoulders stiffen. *That kind of evening.*

Just like that, he killed two men in cold blood. No regrets, since they came to kill Nicole. They'd have done it, too. He still can't believe she gave him her knife. It's the closest she's come to acknowledging he's not the devil incarnate.

They're on the sidewalk when the diner door swings open and a middle-aged couple rolls out. The woman's eyes brighten. "Nicole!" She pulls her in for a hug, and Nic hugs back. "You got a cheese stick craving, too?"

"You know it." Nic smiles at the husband. "Did you get your chocolate shake?"

"Vanilla this time." The man pats his middle. "I'm on a diet."

Seb stands there feeling awkward. Does Nic know everyone in town? He's still a newcomer, the guy with the billboards. They might know his face, but not the rest of him. Not the real him.

No one knows the real Sebastian.

"This is Dr. LaDouceur." She touches his arm and Seb comes alive. "He runs a dental clinic by my daycare."

"Sebastian." He shakes the guy's hand, then the woman's. "Pleasure to meet you."

"Monica and John Parkhill." Monica's eyes linger on Seb's chest. "I've seen you around."

"I've got one of those memorable faces." Great for a dental practice. Not great for his other line of work.

John threads his fingers through his wife's. "We've been looking for a new dentist."

"We'll come find you." Monica drags her eyes off his chest. "You're taking new patients?"

"Sure." Might as well. "Actually, hang on." He turns and jogs back to his car. Retrieves two toothbrushes, one red, one blue.

Returns with one in each hand. "Clinic number's on there. Website, too."

"Great." Monica pockets the toothbrush. "Lovely to meet you."

"Likewise."

Nic's silent as they watch the Parkhills walk to their car. Once they're inside, he looks at her. "Smart thinking."

"What's that?"

"Making sure we're seen mingling at a small-town diner. Clever."

She cocks her head. "Maybe I just wanted cheese sticks."

"Okay."

She turns and shoves through the door. "Or maybe I don't trust that your car's not bugged."

"Can't blame you there." Also, it is.

A sign at the door says, "seat yourself," so they do. A booth at the back, far from other tables. Nic's been here before.

She sits first and picks up the saltshaker. Turns it over and studies the bottom. "Is that where you planted it?"

"Planted what?" He drops to the bench across from her.

"Whatever listening device you used at the event." She sets down the salt and stares at him. "The way you *just happened* to know my tiger story and the gassy crab puffs?"

"Pepper." He smiles as a waitress approaches. Pretty brunette with round hips and a notepad. Sebastian scans her nametag. "Evening, Heather."

"Oh, you're the dentist!" Giggling, she drops menus in front of him. "No sweets for you."

"Harsh." He hands Nic a menu and flips his open. Closes it without looking. "I already know what I want."

Heather wiggles her brows. "I'm sure you do."

Nic snorts, but Sebastian doesn't look at her. He'll get an earful the instant Heather's out of sight. "Cheeseburger with fries and Dr. Pepper." He hands back the menu.

"One doctor for Dr. LaDouceur, coming up." She giggles and swivels to Nicole. "You know what you want, honey?"

"Double order of mozzarella sticks." Nic hands over her menu. "Can I get one of those shakes with orange sherbet and buttermilk?"

"Coming right up."

They watch her walk away. He's not sure what to say, but he's contemplating wisecracks when she speaks. "Doesn't it get old having women throw themselves at your feet?"

He looks down at his Berluti oxfords. A $2,000 splurge his first year in dental practice. Seb shrugs and meets her eyes. "I don't see you down there."

"I'm immune to your charms." She folds her hands and looks around. "My grandma used to bring me here every Saturday. Jen had 4H, and Teo had math club, so it was just Nondi and me."

The sharing stuns him too much to make a crack about Matteo and math club. He scans the diner, taking in the battered wooden bar. The flowered carpet that probably hasn't changed since Nic's childhood. The silver serving station where someone's French fries wait beneath a heat lamp. He looks back at Nic. "Seems like a nice place."

"You've never been?"

"Nope." He picks up the saltshaker. She's smart to want this conversation on neutral ground. "So. Rogue."

She doesn't blink. "And you're *The Dentist*." Delicate fingers hook air quotes around the words.

Seb sighs. "I don't know why everyone makes it scary. I really am a dentist."

"Obviously." She looks around, making sure no one's listening. "Everything went okay?" Nic lowers her voice. "Back at the—"

"Yep." The Union sent two guys in tuxedos to haul bodies out the back door.

"Not our men," one of them said to Seb as they packed up.

Sure.

They'd have said that either way, but the denial got him thinking. "You didn't recognize either of them?" he asks Nic now.

"No." She frowns and picks up the pepper shaker. Glances at the bottom, then sets it back on the table. "The redhead looked familiar, but I couldn't place him."

"Same."

She's not meeting his eyes. "You know why they want me?"

He knows why *he* wants her. A thousand reasons, starting with how cagey she's being. "The hit on Duck Toes?"

She nods once. If she's surprised, she doesn't show it. "He put his wife in intensive care twice last year. Got a slap on the wrist. Then she vanished."

Seb's heard the intel. Debbie DeCosta didn't just vanish. Debbie DeCosta now swims with the fishes.

A lightbulb blinks on in his brain. "That's your thing."

Her eyes swing to his, but she doesn't react.

"Hitting guys who hit women." He watches her face, hoping she'll appreciate how he squeezed dual meaning from the verb. "You take out guys who get away with it."

She doesn't respond. Just picks up the pepper again. When she speaks, her voice goes soft. "The law lets men get away with hurting women all the time."

"But you don't."

Her eyes shift to his. "Correct."

God, she's good. Way too good for him. "I looked you up," he says. "While I waited in the parking lot. You've got quite a reputation."

"My record's clean."

"Wasn't talking about police record."

She nods and doesn't argue. "Same with you."

"Me?"

Her shoulders lift beneath the chunky sweater. "From Special Forces to black ops to The Union. Dental school as a cover."

"Maybe I like teeth."

"Maybe you do."

Nic did her homework. He's not surprised, but he's impressed. "I like to stay busy." Makes it easier to outrun his demons.

Drawing a breath, Nic meets his eye again. "Thank you."

Seb stares. "For what?"

"For what you did back there." Her eyes drop to her hands. "I work alone. I'm not used to counting on anyone else."

Maybe she doesn't know how much she just revealed. "My pleasure." It really was. Seeing her in action. Working beside her. "Can I ask you some ques—"

"You knew there was a hit on me."

It's not a question, but he nods. "Yes."

Her eyes lock with his. "From your contacts at The Union?"

"It's complicated." It isn't, but why should he share if she won't? "Who's Issela?"

Nic doesn't flinch. Doesn't smile or frown or even blink. He's watching for all of that. "Issela?"

"Those men in the office—they said the name *Issela.* Thought you might know who she is."

"I don't."

She's lying. He wouldn't know if he hadn't spent months studying her. Counting the freckles beside her right eye—four of them—or the dimple in her left cheek that shows like the sun when she smiles.

Nic's not smiling now. She's also not telling him something. Who is Issela? Another operator, but how does Nic know her?

He wants to ask more questions. How long she's been Rogue and what sent her down this path. Which weapons she loves and how it feels to hide this from family. He opens his mouth, but none of that comes out.

"Why do you hate me?"

Her eyes flash. Of all he might've asked, that's not what she expected.

"I don't hate you."

"Liar."

Her lips twitch. "I don't trust you. There's a difference."

"Why?"

She's considering her answer. Green eyes search his like she's looking for something. Recognition? A reason to trust him?

"Here you go, hon!" Heather bustles to the table with a plate in each hand. She sets a burger in front of him, smiling with freshly painted lips. "I got you extra fries."

"Thanks." He looks at Nicole. Her face goes blank, and that's that.

Seb sighs and picks up his burger.

* * *

It's barely sunrise when he phones Matteo. Too early to call, but Teo picks up on the first ring.

"What?"

Seb clears his throat. "Do you know anyone named Issela?"

"Jesus Christ."

"What?" This must be big.

"You're seriously calling me about some woman you want to shag?"

"What? No." Okay, he could have started better. Foreplay's not just for sex. "Not a woman. Okay, probably a woman, but not one I plan to bang." Maybe. He hasn't met her, so he can't rule it out. "It's just a name that came up on a job I did. *Didn't* do. Got asked to do, but—"

"Does this story have a point?"

Seb's not sure anymore. "Tell me about Nicole."

"No."

"I'm serious."

"Since when?"

"Huh?"

Matteo clears his throat. "In all the years I've known you, you've never been serious." There's a long, pregnant pause. "Which is why you're not getting near my sister."

Ouch. As insults go, he's not wrong. "Pretty sure she wants me."

It's such bullshit that Teo doesn't dignify it with an answer.

"Anyway, I can be serious." Sometimes. "In a relationship—"

"No." Matteo sighs. "You're not her type, Seb."

Maybe that's why he wants her. He'd like to be the sort of guy who's her type. Someone stable and trustworthy and decent and—

"I'm still invited to dinner next Friday, right?"

"Yeah." Matteo grunts. "Is Terri coming?"

It's nice they include his grandma. "She's sitting it out. Bunko night."

"Jen said you can skip bringing salad this time. Her garden's overflowing."

"Okay." He'll bring flowers instead.

There's something else on his mind, but Seb hesitates. "What do you know about Danny 'Duck Toes' DeCosta?"

"Not much." Matteo sounds thoughtful. "You know who he is, right?"

"Was." Does Teo know he's dead? Maybe not that Nic killed him, but—

"That hit didn't leave many people brokenhearted, if you catch my drift." Matteo pauses. "You've done work for the Dovlanese government. You're familiar with the DeCosta family?"

A light blinks on in Seb's brain. "*Those* DeCostas?"

"Yeah." Matteo sounds growly. "Big crime family. Always thought they had something to do with my parents' murder, but I couldn't prove it. Nondi wouldn't talk about it, so... dead end."

In a manner of speaking. "You think the hit on DeCosta has ties to your family?" He's toying with fire, but for Nic's sake, he'd like to know. "There's a connection?"

"Unlikely." Another pause from Teo. "Duck Toes was estranged from his family for years. Tried to get some sort of crime syndicate going in the Pacific Northwest, but he wasn't very good at it."

So Seb's heard. "You're saying Duck Toes lived here, but the family's back in Dovlano?"

"Dunno. The parents vanished a few years back. Don Julio and Tammy DeCosta?" Matteo sighs. "Some folks think Duck Toes knocked 'em off. Got tired of being the family fuckup."

This conversation's depressing. It's also not getting Seb any closer to finding out how Nic stirred up a hornet's nest.

He won't betray her. He'd die before telling Teo what he knows.

Still. "You still keep tabs on your sisters, yeah?"

Matteo growls. "Dante keeps Jen safe."

"From what I've seen, *Jen* keeps Jen safe."

Another growl from Teo. "It's teamwork. And no, before you ask, you can't form a team with Nicole."

Like it's up to her brother. "Kind of a dick move, getting between me and my future wife."

When Teo sighs this time, it's heavier than the growl. "Why are you so hung up on my sister?"

"Nicole?"

"Yes, Nicole. If it were Jen, Dante would have snapped your neck by now."

Not untrue. "Have you *met* Nicole?" He knows he doesn't deserve a woman like that, but his idiot heart hasn't gotten the message. "Your sister's amazing."

"Unquestionably. But you've had a different woman in your bed every night for as long as I've known you. Why Nic?"

A good question. One he's not sure he can answer. "Maybe because she hates me?"

"So, what—you make her fall in love with you and then lose interest?"

It sounded good until that last part. "Why would I lose interest?"

"Because you always do."

"Harsh."

"Maybe, but it's true." Teo's growl smooths out. "Give it up, Seb. You're a good guy, but Nic needs someone serious. A guy without a bunch of skeletons in his closet."

"Yeah, fine." He rubs his jaw and wills himself to listen.

"So, we'll see you next Friday?"

"Yep." Sebastian spins his keychain on a finger, the brass-tipped bullet glinting in lamplight. "Text if you need something." He hesitates. "Or if you get the urge to dig up more intel on the DeCosta hit."

"Will do."

As he hangs up, he hears Teo's words again.

A guy without a bunch of skeletons in his closet.

A guy who deserves someone like Nic Bello. That'll never be him.

Snatching his keys, Sebastian stalks to his BMW. Puts on his sunglasses and cranks up the music.

Drives to the 24-hour shooting range to blast the shit out of some memories.

CHAPTER 4

"**Y**ou're sure you don't want to come with us?" Jen has a hand on the door of her farmhouse. "I'll let you ride the horsey."

Dante says something in her ear, and Jen turns a lovely shade of pink. Nic rolls her eyes, but the truth? She loves seeing her sister happy.

Nic sets down her eReader and props her feet on Jen's coffee table. "I'm going to pretend he just whispered his cornbread recipe." She rests a hand on the arm of the couch. "I'd rather believe my baby sister doesn't do dirty talk about riding horsies."

Jen giggles. *Giggles,* for God's sake. She's so sweet Nic can't stand it. "So that's a no?" Jen jiggles the doorknob. "Edgar Allen Pony wants to see you."

"I've met your new horse already." Nicole crosses her sock feet. They're fuzzy and printed with puppies. "Remember? I took that video of AJ riding him."

"Yeah, but this time Matteo's riding Spongebob Horsepants, and Renee's riding Maple Stirrup, and AJ gets Pony Soprano, and it's this whole family thing."

"I'm not sure my heart could handle that much cute." It's true, even if she's hiding it with sarcasm. "Seriously though, I'm waiting for a call."

"New daycare client?"

"Maybe."

It's not that, but Nic isn't lying. If her hacker pal lands in an abusive marriage, Nic will gladly tend the woman's future kids. See? Daycare connection. "Take pictures for me, okay?"

"Okay." Jen bites her lip. "Sebastian's coming."

"Coming *here?*" Why is her heart racing? *Stupid, stupid, stu—*

"I guess Teo invited him to dinner." Jen shrugs. "Which is fine because we're all sort of family. Just—be nice, okay?" She slams the door before Nic can argue.

"I'm always nice." Nic's muttering to an empty room as she picks up her eReader.

She reads the same paragraph three times without catching any words. It's a good book, too. A romance, though she won't hold that against it. Nic believes in happy endings. Not for her, but it's great for her sister. For Matteo, too, which is crazy.

Two out of three Bello kids isn't bad.

Tired of trying to read, Nic gets up and pads to the fireplace. Bends to grab the photo album in a basket by the logs. She flips through slowly, pausing on a picture of Nondi at the beach. Nic's grandma has an arm around teenage Teo, which makes Jen about six and Nicole ten. In cutoff shorts, Nic scowls at the camera, clutching her sister's hand as the waves flap fiercely at the sand.

She flips back a few pages. Touches a picture of her parents at the hospital, the day they brought Jen home. "I wish I remembered you." She has flashes of memory, sure. They died before her sixth birthday, so yeah... the memories are there.

But they're fuzzier than she'd like them to be. "Jen's marrying a good guy," she tells her mom as she flips to a spot near the back of the book. "And Matteo's fiancée is amazing."

The new page she's flipped to shows her teenage life. Nic doing Jen's hair for prom. Jen on a horse for 4H. Teo scowling up from his computer as Nondi gives him a noogie. Nic with a pack of girlfriends on a senior trip to Seattle.

She touches a photo, finger grazing the face she'd know anywhere. "You can't be alive." She squeezes her eyes shut. "That wouldn't make sense."

Ding-dong!

The doorbell scoops her from the dark thoughts. Shoving the album in the basket, she strides for the door. Catches herself walking fast and slows because of course it's Sebastian. Why race to see him?

Because he's Jen's dinner guest?

Because he saved your life?

Because seeing him makes you feel like you swallowed warm Pop Rocks?

She's scowling as she throws open the door. "Hey."

"M'lady." He dips in a bow and holds out a bouquet. Snapdragons. Her favorite. "These are for you."

She hesitates. "Not for the hostess?"

He whips a second bouquet from behind his back. Daisies, this time. "For your sister."

"That's... thank you." She takes both bouquets, but doesn't move to let him in. Breathing deeply, she lets herself sniff the snapdragons.

Clearly, she's stalling. Trying not to look at him. To forget the kiss and anything else that happened. "Look, I think it goes without saying that my family doesn't know about my career." Nic stares him down. "My *other* career."

Seb cocks his head. "Should we tell them over the salad course or wait for apple pie?"

"Seriously, Sebastian. If it got out that—"

"Hey, Nic?" He doesn't wait for an answer. "Before I broke out a Beretta at a party, did you know about my side job?"

She hesitates. "Yes."

Both brows lift. "Really?"

He really doesn't remember. Nic's not about to tip her hand. "Matteo said you're some sort of military guy?"

"Ex." Blue eyes go stormy. "Army. Special Forces before I—" He clamps his mouth shut. "Long story."

"I've got time."

"I don't."

He's gone tight-lipped, like her brother. That's saying something. Nic knows not to push. "But you're an operator."

"Sometimes." He doesn't break eye contact. "So I think it's safe to say I can keep my mouth shut."

"Okay." She needs to stop looking at his mouth. "Thank you."

"Sure."

Awkward silence stretches like Silly Putty. She should invite him inside.

"Almost forgot." Reaching behind him, Seb whips out a stuffed tiger. "This is for you."

Nicole blinks. "Did you have that in your pants?"

That makes him snort. "There's a punchline in there about wedging wild animals in one's butt crack, but no." He holds out the tiger, and she takes it. "Saw that when I was shopping for stuff to give kids who get scared at the dentist. It made me think of you."

"Thanks." She holds it gingerly, smoothing rumpled fur where he must've had it hooked on his belt. "I love it."

"You said you wanted a tiger."

Her eyes lift to his. "Which you learned from eavesdropping illegally on my conversation."

"Minor detail."

There's no point being pissed. It's a nice tiger, and the flowers smell like heaven. She sticks her nose in the bouquet again. "I appreciate it." She steps aside so he can pass. "Welcome to my sister's humble abode." Like he hasn't been here a hundred times.

He ambles through the kitchen, looking strong and suave and

out of place between the crockpot and a KitchenAid mixer. "This was your grandma's house, right?"

She stiffens, glad he's not looking at her. "Nondi had lots of properties. Jen got the farm, Teo got the beach house, and I got—"

"The daycare." He turns and leans against the counter. "Grandma was a real estate baron?"

"Something like that." She sets the flowers on the counter. Sets the tiger beside it, then turns to fix a photo on the wall. It's Jen and Dante, laughing in a field. Their engagement photo, proof her sister's grown up.

"Got a vase I can put these in?" She turns to see Seb pointing at the flowers. "I've got mad skills at floral arranging."

"I'm sure you do." Striding to the sink, she bends to open the cupboard beneath. Feels Sebastian's eyes on her butt as she digs around for a sturdy, square vase of cut crystal. Another made from pink glass. She carries them to Jen's butcher block and sets them on a cutting board. Seb's eyes follow as she drags a knife from the drawer.

"That looks good on you."

She looks up. "My Miss Gigglewinks T-shirt?" She had them made special for her daycare.

"Yes, but no." He points to the knife. "The blade. The way you handle it."

It's easy to pretend she doesn't catch his meaning. "Gotta trim the bottom off the stems so they can soak up water."

"And here I thought you were beheading them."

She hacks at the snapdragons, then grabs the other bouquet. "Which ones did you say were for Jen?"

"Why?"

"Because hers go in the pink vase." It was Nondi's favorite. One she brought from Italy.

She doubts The Dentist cares who gets which flowers, but he surprises her. "The daisies are Jen's. Snapdragons are for you."

She watches his face for the quirk of a lip. It's tough to tell if he's joking. "Is there a reason?"

Thick forearms flex as he leans on the counter. "Daisies are dependable and classic. Sweet and pretty in a wholesome sorta way." He grins. "Exactly why Dante loves your sister."

Nic looks at the snapdragons. "And these?"

The heaviness of his gaze makes her glance away to arrange the blooms. Even with her eyes on the flowers, she feels the weight of his stare.

"Aptly named," he says. "When you press the sides of a snapdragon bloom together, the shape looks like a dragon's mouth."

Is that an insult or a compliment? "And that made you think of me."

"A little." He shrugs when she looks at him. "They're said to symbolize graciousness, but also deception." Leaning back, he kicks long legs in front of him. It's weird how he looks both lazy and lethal.

"There's this old wives' tale," he continues, "about concealing a snapdragon somewhere on your body to make you irresistible to others." His dentist grin goes cocky. "Maybe that's your secret."

Nic's knife halts mid-cut on the daisies' stems. "You're suggesting I stuffed a snapdragon in my cleavage?"

Laughing, he holds up both hands. Big palms, big fingers, big wrists. How does he fit those in patients' mouths?

"Hey, no judgement." He's still chuckling. "But if you'd like to let me frisk you—"

"I'll pass." Goosebumps trail her arms, and she hopes he doesn't notice. "Where did you learn all this about flowers?"

"My grandma's a florist."

"Yeah?" So he has a living grandma. "Is her shop here in town?"

"Nah, she sold it." A light flickers out in his eyes. "Terri helped raise me, along with my dad. When he passed, I brought Terri

41

here to live with me. Didn't like the thought of her being all alone."

"Your grandmother lives with you?"

"Works with me, too. She's my receptionist a few days a week."

"*That's* your grandma?" Nic knows who he's talking about now. "The badass older lady with purple-streaked hair."

"You've met?"

"We've crossed paths in the parking lot." Her first surprise from Sebastian. She'd pegged him as a guy with a busty bimbo tending his front desk. "That's sweet of you."

"I'm a sweet guy." The wicked grin comes back and it's definitely not sweet.

Nic clears her throat. "Tell me more about flowers. About their meanings."

It's a random ask, but Seb doesn't blink. "You want what the book says or my personal take?"

"By the book. I don't care what you think." That's a lie. "Okay, both."

"Sure thing." He's grinning as a stem stub goes flying. Seb catches it in one hand. "Name a flower. Any flower."

"Roses."

"What color?"

She starts to say red, but that's too easy. "Coral."

"Traditionally, coral roses represent modesty, friendship, or sympathy."

Nic knows she should find this weird. So why is she charmed? "What's Sebastian LaDouceur's take?"

"Coral roses mean 'I want you to know I think you're different from other women.'" His grin goes wider. "Also, I hope you'll let me feel you up."

"Really." She looks at the snapdragons. Better not ask his take on these. "How about lilies?"

"Stargazer or calla?"

She doesn't know the difference. "Calla."

"Traditionally, they mean life, fertility, and beauty."

"And your take?"

His grin goes wicked again. "'I've been thinking a lot about vaginas. Yours, in particular.'"

Nic blinks. "What?"

"That's my take on them." He shrugs. "Wasn't speaking to you specifically."

"Of course." Heat floods her face, which is dumb. She's not a blusher. "Hyacinth."

"Dedicated to the Greek sun god, Apollo—he's also known for archery. You give someone hyacinths for luck before a sporting event."

"That's very specific."

"You want my personal spin?"

Very much. "Might as well."

"Hyacinths mean 'I've done something very wrong, and I hope you never know about it because I'd like to touch your butt.'"

She snorts and tucks her snapdragons in their vase. "Orchids."

"Refinement, charm, beauty, love."

"And your take?" She's suddenly thirsty. Jen keeps glasses in the cupboard behind him, so she stretches up to grab one.

Mistake.

His body heat seeps through her pores as the hem of her shirt rides up. He doesn't answer, and when she looks at him, he's studying that swath of skin.

"Desire." It's a low growl, and he clears his throat. "They mean 'I want you to think I'm charming and rich and sophisticated, so you'll let me bend you over the kitchen counter and fuck you silly.'"

Nic swallows hard. There's heat in her face and her belly and between her legs. She should slap him or step back or run like hell from this kitchen.

She holds his gaze instead. "Is that so?"

"Yep." Keeping both hands planted on the counter, he watches her face. "Anything else you want to know?"

Why I kissed you the other night.

Why I want to kiss you again.

Why I'm stepping toward you right now—

"Hey." He breathes the word with heat in his eyes.

"Hey." Why is she grabbing his biceps? "Um."

He laughs and slides his palms to her waist. "You're in my personal space." His grip keeps her there.

"Is that a problem?" He smells like bay leaves and clove. Like sex and desire.

"Depends." His throat rolls as he swallows. "You planning to knife me in the back?"

"Not at the moment."

"Then we don't have a problem."

Nic licks her lips. "Stop talking and kiss me."

He pulls her hard against him. It catches her by surprise, and she lands on his chest with a gasp. Then his mouth claims hers, hot and fierce.

Their first kiss caught him by surprise, but Seb has the upper hand now. He's walking her back, pressing her against the counter as his big, hard body grinds into her.

Nic groans and nips his bottom lip. Why does he have to be this good at everything? She wants to punch him, claw him, drag her nails down his back as he drives into her and—

"Nic?" He draws back with pupils flaring. "You want me to stop?"

"Depends." She drops her eyes to the front of his jeans. "Is that a pocket pistol in your pants?"

"Not this time."

Heat floods more than her face. It's not just his biceps that feel big. Faking boldness, she slides a hand between them. Squeezes that thick length through his jeans, and now it's his turn to groan.

His words bounce in her brain.

Let me bend you over the kitchen counter and fuck you silly.

She's a fool for wanting that. For wanting *him*, this man who reminds her of the worst parts of herself. The worst choices she's made. There's a dark side to Seb's kind of charm. She knows this better than anyone.

So why is she kissing him?

"Sebastian." She moans against his mouth. "Upstairs. The guest room. I need you."

"Really?"

His shock knocks her off-guard, and she tries to move away. "If you don't want—"

"No." He grips her waist. Drags his teeth down her neck, then up to nip her earlobe. "You have no idea how much I want."

She might have some idea.

It's a bad one, but that's not stopping her. "Please. Let's—"

"Sorry!" The door bangs open and Jen tumbles through. She's looking at Dante, not Nic and Seb as they spring apart. "That took a little longer than we thought." Jen flings her sunglasses on the counter. "Oh, flowers—those are pretty."

"They're yours." Nic steps back and drags a hand over her mouth. "Seb brought the daisies for you."

Renee rolls in, holding three-year-old AJ. Matteo brings up the rear, scowling at Sebastian. His eyes dart to Nic. Then back to the dentist. "You're unbelievable."

"Thanks." Sebastian shoves his hands in his pockets.

"It wasn't a compliment." Matteo keeps glaring, but Sebastian's unflappable.

Nic puts a few feet of distance between them. "How's the new horse?"

"Great." Teo looks at Nicole. "You okay?"

"I'm excellent." She's far from excellent, and her whole family knows she nearly banged the dentist on Jen's kitchen counter. Even AJ's eyeing her with suspicion.

"Your shirt's funny, Miss Nicole."

"What?" She looks down and *whoops*. The tail of her tee is tucked in her bra. She tugs it down fast. What's wrong with her? "Want to help me set the table, buddy?"

"Yeah!" The boy scrambles to get down as Nic grabs plates from a cupboard. Forks, too. She drags a drawer open so hard it nearly flies off its rails.

Seb's eyes track her as she grabs a stack of Jen's gingham napkins. Tucking forks inside, she sets the stack on the table. "Remember our lesson in 'Table Talk' about washing your hands first?"

AJ nods. "With soap!"

He scurries off as Nic sets a plate at the head of the table. As she thunks down another, she remembers she hasn't scrubbed her own hands. Hands that slid up the dentist's shirt, trailing washboard abs and—

"Don't forget to scrub under your fingernails," she yells to AJ in the downstairs bath.

"Okay, Miss Nicole."

Face flaming, she doesn't look at Seb. Doesn't turn as she stomps around the table, shoving gingham cloth through Jen's cast iron napkin rings. If she looked over her shoulder, she'd see Seb's eyes on her. She knows this in her bones.

But Nic doesn't look back. Not ever.

* * *

"You really don't have to do my dishes."

Jen stands toweling the skillet Nic just washed.

"You made dinner and fed seven people." Nicole swipes suds off Nondi's stoneware baking dish. "I'm doing *our* dishes, not *yours*."

"Same thing." Jen grabs the baking dish and rubs it with a red towel. "Besides, Dante made most of dinner. And Renee picked lettuce and tossed the salad, so I really didn't do much."

"Hosting's a pain in the ass. It's why I never do it." Among other reasons. Chief among them, her apartment, two blocks from the daycare, doubles as her own private arsenal. It's all secured in gun safes, but still. Nic doesn't like letting anyone in. "Anyway, we're almost done."

Jen watches as she shuts off the water and starts wiping down the sink. "You okay?"

"Of course. Why?"

"You seem quiet." Jen bites her lip. "Next week's the anniversary of when Nondi died. Thought maybe you're feeling emotional."

"Maybe a little." Maybe *a lot*. Not just because their grandma died. "You ever think about what you'd say to her?"

"Nondi?" Jen frowns. "Like if she didn't die?"

"I guess." Nic stays focused on the rag, not meeting her sister's eyes. "What would you want to talk to her about?"

It's playing with fire, asking stuff like this. But Jen doesn't know that. "I'd want her to meet Dante," Jen says. "To know how I saved the vineyard and fought back when—"

"Yeah." She doesn't want to hear the rest of that. How her sister almost died at the hands of a lunatic. She'll never forgive herself for not figuring it out sooner. Not helping Jen when she needed her.

Or maybe Nic's missing the point. "Standing up for yourself is important." She looks at Jen. "Nondi believed that completely."

Jen's biting her lip again as she hangs the skillet on the rack above the stove. "She made sure you knew how. After what happened with Clint, she taught you all those martial arts skills. Took you target practicing and everything." Jen makes a face. "I'm the dummy who sat back like some silly pacifist instead of learning to fight when—"

"Don't." She grabs Jen's arm, forcing her to look. "What happened to you wasn't your fault. It's never the victim's fault."

Her sister flinches at the word *victim*, but nods. "I know." Once edge of Jen's mouth quirks. "I hope you remember that, too."

"I do." They're tiptoeing into tough territory, so she'd better change the subject.

But Jen's a kid sister, so of course she keeps pushing. "Ever wonder what happened to him? Clint, I mean."

Nic knows what happened. "Not really."

"I sometimes worry he's out there hitting other women. Or worse—"

"He isn't."

Jen looks startled. "You've checked?"

"Yeah." Clint is no longer treating women as his personal punching bag. Nic needs this chat to be over. "Tell me about the rehearsal dinner. Did you pick a caterer?"

"Yes! I totally forgot." Jens's face brightens as she hooks the dish towel on its hanger. "My friend Michelle—the one who fosters dogs?"

"We're having dog meat for dinner?"

Jen whaps her in the arm. "I don't care about dinner. I'll get sandwich trays from Costco or something. But Michelle, she's got three litters of puppies—*three*! And she's bringing them all so we can help socialize them. Isn't that the best thing ever?"

"For your rehearsal dinner?" It's Jen, so… yeah. "It's perfect."

"Thanks." Jen smiles. "I thought so, too. It's my dream wedding event, really. All these cute, roly-poly little puppies running around while we practice vows or whatever the hell you're supposed to do at a rehearsal dinner."

"What *are* you supposed to do at a rehearsal dinner?" Nic's never wondered before.

"Beats me." Neither has Jen, apparently. "Pet puppies. Eat sandwiches. Make sure you can pick your betrothed out of a lineup of friends and strangers."

"Sounds good." It does, actually. She's closed down her daycare the week of the wedding so she can help with whatever Jen needs. "I'm happy for you, hon."

"I'm happy for me, too. And for Teo." Jen's grin gets impish. "And for you, judging by what I walked in on with you and Sebastian."

Not this. "I kinda hoped you didn't see that."

Jen grins bigger. "Either he wants you even worse than he's let on, or he came to dinner with a banana in his pocket."

"Ugh, stop. You're my baby sister." She flicks Jen with a dish towel. "You shouldn't know about bananas."

Jen rolls her eyes. "I'm marrying a six-five studmuffin. I know all about bananas."

Matteo ambles in looking pained. He's got a child's sneaker in one hand and a scowl on his face. "I'm pretending you two are having a thoughtful conversation about fruit."

"Nope, dicks." Nicole grabs him in a bear hug, pleased with the distraction of making her brother squirm. "Can we keep going, or is the owner of that shoe right behind you?"

Teo sets the sneaker on the counter and grabs a glass from the cupboard. "It's AJ's new thing. He'll hide a sneaker so we have to spend time looking for it instead of going home and going to bed. Renee's upstairs with Dante helping him look."

"Our nephew's a smart boy." Nic nudges Jen. "Like the rest of clan Bello."

Jen frowns as she watches their brother fill his glass at the tap. "We were talking about Nondi earlier. How it's almost the anniversary of her death."

He frowns and sips his water. "I was just thinking about her. How it happened in October, and I couldn't fucking be here."

Nic will never forgive the asshole cop who locked Teo up. If Reggie Dowling weren't behind bars, she'd shove one up his ass and twist. "I hate October."

"That's when Mom and Dad died, too." Jen looks at her hands. "Kinda why I wanted to get married this month. Break the bad luck curse, you know?"

"You already have." Dante's the best thing that happened to

Jen. Also a safer subject than their parents' murder. "He's good for you," Nic adds. "Dante's a great guy."

"Yeah." Teo gives her an odd look. "I always wondered if it bothered Nondi. Taking in her dead daughter's children like she did."

Jen gives a shaky laugh. "We were such a handful."

"You were a handful." Matteo drains his water glass. "I was a mature, responsible young adult stuck with two bratty sisters."

"Ain't that the truth." Nic checks her watch. "I should go. There's some new curriculum I have to review for class."

Translation: She needs to call her hacker friend, Erin. To find out what she's learned about the DeCosta job. About who might've targeted her and whether there's intel on Issela.

"I'll walk you out." Matteo heads for the door. "See if AJ stuck the shoe under his car seat or something."

Nic spends a minute grabbing her things and kissing everyone goodbye. Tucks the tiger in her purse and tries not to think about Seb.

Once they're outside, Teo drops the cheerful dad act. "What the hell was that with you and Sebastian?"

Ignoring him, she taps the unlock button on her Volvo key. "I'll take 'what is none of your business' for a thousand, Alex."

"Come on, Nic." He scowls. "I love him like a brother, but Seb's not relationship material."

"Perfect." Her brother knows damn well she doesn't do relationships. "I'm looking for a cheap lay. Think he's into that?"

"Nicole—"

"No, Matteo, listen." She turns and puts her back to her car. "I love you like a brother because you *are* my brother, which means I see your faults the way you see Seb's. You might've had your record wiped after prison, but don't think I don't have my sources. Don't think I don't know there's plenty of stuff that would've landed you in the slammer, anyway."

Her brother frowns. "That's… not comforting." The frown deepens. "I thought we didn't talk about this stuff."

"We don't. We also don't talk about my sex life." Or lack thereof.

Matteo's grimace is reward enough for her. "Fine."

Folding her arms, she leans back on her car. "My point is that we both have secrets. You and me, we're more alike than you want to admit."

"Also not reassuring."

"Just trust me, okay? I know what I'm doing with The Dentist."

Her brother's eyes search hers. "All right." A muscle ticks in his jaw. "I just don't want to see you hurt again."

Nicole lifts a brow. "You think Sebastian would hurt me?"

"Not that way." He scowls. "Not like Clint."

A shudder chatters down her spine, but she doesn't let him see. "Goodnight, Teo. I hope you find your kid's shoe."

"Goodnight, Nicole." He pulls her in for a hug. "I hope you find whatever the fuck you're looking for."

So does she. "Thanks."

She gets in her car and watches him walk to the house. No stopping at the car, no searching for sneakers. Figures. He knew damn well AJ didn't stash it out there. He wanted to badger her. Annoying, if it wasn't also touching.

Speaking of touching… what was that with Seb?

All through dinner, she felt him watching her. Felt his hands at her waist as she relived the steel press of his cock against her. As she begged him to take her upstairs and—

Well. That's done. She can't take back her silly little slip, but she can make sure she doesn't slip again.

Checking her phone, she sees a text from her hacker. Erin Adele, code name EZ for reasons Nic's never known. They keep details to a minimum.

. . .

CALL me when you get this.

NIC LOOKS BACK at the farmhouse. She should wait 'til she gets home, but it's late, and she's already dialing the number—

"Rogue?"

Nicole licks her lips. "What did you find?"

"You're right about the contract. The Union called in the hit on you."

Nothing she hadn't guessed already. "Retaliation for Duck Toes?"

"Yeah, but get this." There's some tapping like Erin's doing a Google search. From her time working with the tech geek, Nic knows it's more complicated. The woman's hacker skills rival Matteo's. "The Union didn't hire both goons. One was a freelancer."

Freelancer? Like Sebastian. "Who did he work for?"

"Still trying to find out. Goon number one—code name Red— took the job from The Union. But the other guy, Blake—he took a different contract."

"For me?"

"Looks like it. His had more specific instructions—dead or alive, but a bonus for bringing you in alive. Seems you're the key to helping them find another operative who's gone rogue."

Rogue.

The name Nondi gave her the day she found Nic sobbing into a newspaper article. Her grandma dried Nic's tears, then touched her hand.

"The woman who died." Nondi touched the paper. "He's responsible, yeah?"

Nic didn't need to ask who she meant. "Clint." Nic squeezed her eyes shut and tried to make it all go away. "Yes."

Nondi went silent a long time. When she spoke again, her voice pitched low. "You think it makes you weak. Getting hit?

Like it's a sign you weren't strong enough. Let me tell you something, girl—they target the strong ones."

Nic blinked at her grandma, eyeballs stinging. "What?"

"They try to break you down. To prove they can do it." Nondi clenched her jaw and looked deep in Nic's eyes. "But the thing about the strong ones? We fight back. Maybe not right away. But we always get even."

Nic swiped Kleenex shreds off her lashes. "What do you mean?"

Nondi looked out the window where Jen and Teo's cars would be if they were home. "I know people," Nondi said slowly. "People who track men who slip through cracks. Abusers who slide on technicalities." Nondi looked her dead in the eye. "There's a way to fight back."

"Nic?" Erin's voice brings her back to the present. "You still there?"

"Yeah."

"There's one other thing. The Duck Toes job?"

"What about it?" She's taking a risk, talking this long with Erin.

The hacker clicks some keys. "The jobs I send through to you? They're normally random. Just—your number comes up, and it gets assigned. You follow?"

"I think so." Nic chews her nail. "Was something different about this one?"

"Yeah. Uh—looks like someone requested you specifically. Your name's in the file. It's highlighted in yellow, which means it's something big. A high-priority job."

That's... odd. "Does it say why?"

"No." Erin taps more keys. "There's an alarming lack of detail on this one, actually. But the job was handpicked for you."

"Huh." She's not sure what to make of that.

"Look, I won't tell you to watch your back." Erin sighs. "You're smart enough to know that. But friend to friend, I've gotta tell you this is bigger than your normal job."

"Yeah." She holds the phone tighter, breathing in and out. She darts a glance at the house. Matteo lumbers out with AJ in his arms, Renee's hand in his back pocket. AJ's asleep with both shoes on his feet. Crickets buzz outside as Dante joins them on the porch. He puts an arm around Jen as she steps outside and frowns at Nic's car. They're wondering why she hasn't left yet. Nic wonders the same thing.

"I'll watch my back," she says to Erin.

"Yeah, okay." The hacker sounds worried. "Stay safe out there, okay?"

"Good night, EZ."

She hangs up and slips the phone in her purse. Waves to her scowling brother, to her befuddled sister on the porch. Then she shoves her key in the ignition and cranks the engine. Hits her headlights and aims down the drive, out on the highway past Taco Bell and Sebastian's cheerful face on the billboard.

Put your smile in safe hands.

Shivering, she turns down a road she's never been before. Not officially, though she's cased the joint. Six times in the last week, she's driven past this nondescript bungalow.

Killing the engine, she looks at the flowers. Jen made her take them, vase and all. From the Volvo's cupholder, the snapdragons bob in cheerful pink and red.

Nic grabs her purse and slides the Glock inside. She's not taking any chances.

On shaky legs, she makes her way to the porch. Inhales deeply and taps the door. When it opens, she draws another breath.

"Hey." Seb stands shirtless in the doorway. Muscles lit by moonlight flow beneath the band of low-slung jeans.

Nic feels her jaw unhinge and her heart speed up.

Hears her voice blurt the words bubbling through her brain.

"I need you."

CHAPTER 5

I need you.

He's dreamed for months of Nic Bello on his doorstep, her sweet voice whispering those words. He dreamed her gaze would trail his chest, his abs, the ink on his left pec. That she'd like what she sees.

As her eyes drag back to his, she draws a breath. "Are you going to make me beg?"

He'd like that very much. "Depends on what you need."

Nicole licks her lips. Also part of his dream. "I need—"

"Who's at the door?" His grandma shuffles out in a red robe. She's clutching a jar of peanut butter and has curlers in her hair. "Oh, hello. I'm Terri. Sebby's grandmama."

That's not how the dream went.

With a smile, Nic extends a hand. "Nicole Bello." She shakes his grandma's hand. "I own the daycare across from the clinic."

"That's right!" Terri's face brightens. "I thought you looked familiar. You have the cutest little cardigans."

"Thank you." Nic flicks a glance at him, then back to Terri. "I'm sorry to show up late. I needed a word with your grandson and didn't think."

"That's all right, honey. Have you eaten yet?" Terri waves her spoon, and Seb's sure he's about to watch his grandma hand his dream girl a jar of Skippy. "I've got crunchy or creamy."

"I'm fine, thank you." Nicole slides a look at him. "I can come back later. Or tomorrow—maybe you're free for lunch?"

I need you.

Seb grabs her hand to stop her from stepping off his porch. "Now's good."

"You're sure?" She doesn't look at Terri, but his grandma gets the hint.

"I can see you two have some catching up to do. I'll leave you to it." Jamming the spoon in her jar, Terri steps back. "Nice finally meeting you, Nicole."

"Great meeting you." Smiling, Nic gestures to her hair in curlers. "I love your purple."

"Thanks." Terri lifts a hand to her head. "It makes patients smile, and I like surprising people."

She wanders off before Seb can say surprise isn't a plus for most dental patients. She's right that the hair makes people smile. So does Terri's sunny disposition. It's one reason he hired her.

As Terri disappears, Seb looks at Nic. "Want to come in?"

Nicole hesitates. "Maybe I shouldn't have come."

But she doesn't leave. He holds the door wider, like he's coaxing a feral cat. "I've got a soundproof bedroom."

One brow lifts. "If that's your idea of foreplay, it needs work."

"I'll keep that in mind." He shoves a hand in his pocket. "I'll even let you sweep for bugs." Stepping aside, he gestures up the stairway. "Come on. I don't bite."

As Nicole shuffles past, she mutters something that sounds like "too bad."

But that can't be right. She hates his guts. Or does she? That scene in Jen's kitchen has him confused. Confused and aroused and completely off his game. Not the best way to be as he admires her butt moving up the stairs.

"Stop staring at my ass, Minty Fresh."

He snorts. "You've got eyes in the back of your head?"

"Nope." She looks over her shoulder. "Just a brain inside it."

Fair enough. "First door on the right. Bug sweeper's on the nightstand. Help yourself."

He wants her to feel safe. Tough as she seems, Nic Bello has a soft underbelly. It's another thing drawing him to her.

"Thanks." She heads straight for the nightstand and grabs the sweeper. "My mentor trained me on this same model."

Most guys he knows wouldn't use the sweeper. Would insist they believe him without some macho display of trust.

Nic grips the device as she turns to face him. "You knew I was coming?"

"Nope." He plucks a mini flashlight off the dresser and fidgets with it. "If I had, don't you think I'd have set condoms on my nightstand instead of surveillance equipment?"

"Dream on." She starts a slow sweep of his bedroom. He watches, wondering what she sees. What she makes of his green and white bedspread or the cheerful fern on his windowsill. The collection of comic books on his bookshelf by the door. The keychain in his candy dish with its bullet poking over the rim.

He sneaks another look at her ass. Naturally, that's when she turns. "That's not fair."

"Your ass?"

Nicole blinks. "What the hell is wrong with you?"

"Many things." He sets down the flashlight and sinks to the bed. "What's not fair?"

"What I just said. *Dream on?*" She bites her lip. "I'm a grown-ass woman. I can't blame you for the condom crack. I practically jumped you on my sister's kitchen counter."

This feels like a trap. "Doesn't give me the right to presume." Or to admit the condoms are inside the nightstand, not on it. Baby steps.

Nicole huffs a breath and slides the sweeper over his lamp.

She handles it like a pro, and he adds that to his list of things he loves about her. "It's also not fair of me to show up here asking for your help without telling you all the details." She turns and meets his eye. "But that's what I need to do."

"Okay." As demands go, he's heard worse. "Would it help if I tell you some things I don't tell most people?"

Another blink from Nic. "What do you mean?"

Sebastian leans back on his hands. Sees her gaze skate over his pecs. "You have things you can't share. I have things I can't share." *Won't* is more like it, but why split hairs? "Figured if you're feeling vulnerable about sharing private things, I'd join you."

"I'm not feeling vulnerable." Her eyes slide from his pecs to his… private things.

That's hot.

Seb clears his throat. "I used to wet the bed."

That's… not hot.

But Nicole bursts out laughing. "Tell me this wasn't in the last few years?"

"You laugh, but it's serious. Nocturnal enuresis can make a kid feel pretty awful."

That sobers her up. "Sorry, I wasn't laughing at you. You just surprised me."

"My dad's the one who figured out the problem. Minor kidney infection. Antibiotics cleared it up right away."

"Your dad?"

He didn't mean to share that. "A dentist, like me." Didn't mean to share that, either. "Dead." Why is he telling her this?

Sympathy shimmers in her eyes. "I'm sorry."

"Thanks." He scratches his shoulder, making his pecs ripple. Not on purpose, but he keeps going when her eyes caress his chest.

"Tell me about the tattoo." She points at his chest and… okay, yeah. Maybe she wasn't checking out his muscles. "'Patients first?'"

"Would you believe I take dentistry very seriously?"

"No."

"Didn't think so." He grins. "For the record, I do." Seb clears his throat. "I'm ADHD. Have been all my life, but it had drawbacks in my military career."

"Drawbacks?"

"A good sniper needs a steady hand." He shrugs, and her eyes shift to his shoulders. "A cool head. Lots and lots of patience."

"Ah." Nic gives a knowing nod. "Spelling's not your forte?"

"Funny." He actually won his statewide high school spelling bee, but no need to go there. "*Impatience* to get a tattoo made me pick a parlor with less-than-stellar spelling skills."

Nic laughs. "You mean it really was supposed to say 'patience'? I was kidding."

"Yep." Another shrug. "I left it alone because it's a good reminder. Added the word 'first' after 'patients' when I finished my dental degree, plus the insignia for dentistry."

Nic bends forward, peering at the ink. "A snake wrapped around an arrow?"

"A staff." Sebastian's staff responds to the tickle of her breath against his chest. "A physician's staff with a snake representing healing and rejuvenation, since they shed their skin." He puts a hand on his lap and prays she moves back before the blood all leaves his brain. "The foliage has thirty-two leaves representing the number of permanent adult teeth, and twenty berries for—"

"Baby teeth?" She draws back, and Seb thanks his lucky stars. "I've seen the symbol, but never knew what it meant."

"Now you do." And now he can think without a hard-on sucking up his blood supply. "My dad got one like it, so we'd match."

Why the fuck did he bring up his dad again?

"Anyway," he says quickly, "that's the story of the tattoo."

Seb lets his fingers trail the edge of the ink. Nic's nod shifts from sympathy to hunger as he flexes his pecs.

Problem solved.

She drags her gaze back to his face. "I lost my dad, too."

"And your mom." He nods at her surprise. "One of a tiny handful of details Teo shared about your childhood. I'm sorry."

"Thanks." She sets the bug sweeper on his nightstand. Jumps back fast when her arm brushes his. "I hardly remember my parents. I was little when they got gunned down."

So many questions. Ones Teo never answered. "Where did it happen?"

"Dovlano." She pronounces it like Matteo does, a Dovlanese accent tipping up at the end. "It happened at my grandma's house. She'd moved to America by then, but she had homes in Italy and Dovlano. Mom and Dad looked after both places."

It's more than Teo's shared in all the years they've known each other. He's transfixed. Afraid to breathe for fear she'll stop sharing.

"Do you know who killed them?" He stops touching the tattoo and sets his hands down. Nic's eyes jerk to his. "Your parents, I mean."

She draws a sharp breath. "I'm sorry, could you please put on a shirt?"

Seb blinks. "Is there a problem?"

"The problem is that you're too damn hot for your own good." Nic folds her arms. "You know this, smug bastard. Stop flaunting."

The grin spreads before he can stop it. "You're sexy when you do your mad teacher act."

"Not an act." She watches him walk to the bureau as he takes his time finding his favorite Looney Tunes T-shirt. "I'm human. I can find you attractive without wanting to jump your bones."

Her words from the kitchen ring in his ears. *"Upstairs. The guest room. I need you."*

"Stop thinking about my sister's kitchen," she says. "I had a moment of weakness. We all do."

He's well aware. "Fine." He tugs the shirt over his head and returns to his spot on the bed. Hesitates. Then pats the mattress beside him. "Come on. I'm clothed now. Have a seat."

"I'll stand."

Sebastian sighs. "At least grab a chair. You're making me nervous hovering like that."

They're magic words, since she drops to his desk chair. It's then he decides that's key. Admitting weakness—nerves or fear or desire—gets Nic Bello to let down her guard.

"Thank you." He bumps her shin with his bare toe. "You want me to keep going with the secrets, or are you ready to spill yours?"

"Not ready." She bites her lip. "How'd you end up doing what you do?"

He knows what she means but plays dumb. "Dentistry? My father's a dentist." His heart hitches when he hears his mistake. "*Was.* He died two years ago."

"Recent." She looks startled. "I'm sorry."

He nods and looks away. Prays she can't read minds. "Thanks."

"Was he an operator like you?"

That throws him. So does the fact that he brought up his dad a second time. He never does that. "No. My dad was the sweetest, kindest, most earnest man who ever lived."

"So what happened?"

It's his own damn fault they're talking about this.

Not the only thing that's your fault...

Seb clears his throat. "Pop fell in with the wrong crowd."

"Same with my parents. I mean, I've heard." Nic looks at her hands. "Teo never told me much, but I asked Nondi about them. *Crimtinaffa,* she said."

"Mafia." He absorbs her surprise. "I've done jobs for the Dovlanese government. I know a few words. Know about the big crime families, too."

"That's how you know my brother."

He's not sure what Teo's told her, and he won't betray a friend. "How about you? How'd you end up... working?"

"As a daycare owner?" Her turn to skirt the question. "Got my degree in early childhood education. I always wanted to work with kids."

"And moms who've been abused?"

There's no flinch. No indication he's touched a sore spot. Maybe he hasn't. "Dads, too," she continues. "I take in kids from all kinds of parents getting out of bad situations."

It's how Renee came to put AJ in her daycare. How she wound up tucking Teo's son in a school run by AJ's own auntie. Talk about wild odds.

"Tell me about your grandma." Her question throws him off guard. "You're close?"

"Very. My mom was... not in my life." Again, they're treading touchy territory. "My dad mostly raised me, but Terri helped."

"And now you're taking care of her." She nods with something close to admiration. "Did she serve?"

Seb blinks again. "Serve what?"

"In the military?" Nicole rolls her eyes. "The anchor on her right arm. Navy?"

He cocks his head. "The flower tattoo?"

"They're wrapped around an anchor. I noticed last week when we crossed paths at the dumpster. Before I knew she was your grandma."

"Huh." He never thought to ask. Just thought it seemed cool that his florist grandma took her job to that level. "She used to let me draw on it as a kid."

"Her tattoo?"

"Yeah." Nostalgia seeps between his ribs and into his chest cavity. "I'd take my felt pens and draw more flowers. Red ones, purple ones, yellow." So many flowers he'd fill her whole upper arm. "She grew up in Florida. Her dad was a boat builder."

Seb never met him but assumed that's why she got the anchor. Lost in his own thoughts, he nearly misses the smirk in Nic's eye. "What?"

"What *what*?" She's back to being guarded.

"You didn't answer my question. About how you came to open the kind of daycare you run," he adds quickly before she can play dumb.

Nic looks at him for a long time. "You want me to tell you I got hit, right? That's what you're expecting?"

It is, but he'd rather not hear it. Wants more than anything to be wrong about this. "Who was he?"

She holds his gaze like it's a game of chicken. Like she knows already she'll win. "Ex-boyfriend. Clint. And yes, I let him get away with it."

Oh, God. "I doubt very much anything was your fault. If a man hits a woman—"

"Please don't mansplain domestic abuse." She stands and starts pacing. "I meant I packed my bags and walked away within hours of the first strike. No way was I sticking around to let the son of a bitch do it again."

"Then what—"

"He did it again." She whirls to face him, and the fury in her eyes sucks his lungs empty. "Not to me, but to his next girlfriend. And the one after that, until he landed the next one in the ICU. She died two days later, and the prick skated on a technicality. She had a heart condition, they said. Would have died anyway, they said." She's spitting words like shrapnel, a good indication what she thinks of this *they*.

"I'm sorry."

"So was he." Her jaw tightens. "I made sure of it."

It explains a lot. "How did you—"

"I thought this was a free exchange of information." Nic folds her arms. "Tit for tat?"

The setup's too good. "We already covered tat. Grandma's anchor. My tattoo. If you'd like to move on to *tit*—"

"God, you're a pig." Nicole huffs. "It's the charm that's your weapon, isn't it? Draw the enemy close with charisma and then you move in for the kill."

"Harsh."

Nic starts to pace. It's almost like she doesn't see him anymore. "No one suspects the goofy guy with the jokes and the sparkling dentist smile and the stupid, perfect pecs—"

"Hey now." None of that sounds like a compliment. "I didn't kill *you*, did I?"

Fury fades from her eyes as she stops pacing. "Thanks. I guess."

"You're welcome." A pause. "My pecs are perfect?"

She's scowling, but the twitch of her lips gives her away. "I said stupid."

"And perfect."

"And stupid."

"And—"

"Sebastian."

He loves how she says his name. "What?"

Green eyes lock with his. She's not smiling anymore. When she draws a breath, perfect breasts press the front of her T-shirt. *Miss Gigglewinks.* God, he wants her.

Nicole shuts her eyes like she can't say what's next with him in her line of sight. "I forget why I even came here but I can't stop looking at you like I'm some stupid, horny teenager, and I hate that, but that doesn't stop me from wanting to fuck your brains out, and I hate myself for it, but that still doesn't make it go away, and I hate that even more."

Wow.

For a woman who said "hate" three times, there's an awful lot of "want" in those words. She doesn't open her eyes.

"Nicole."

64

"What?" She keeps one eye shut but peeks through the other. "You're going to make some stupid joke now, aren't you?"

"Define stupid."

She laughs. Laughs and points to her chest. "I rest my case."

It's not her case that interests him. It's the perfect breasts rounding the front of her sweet daycare shirt. It's the curve of her waist. The hollow of her throat he kissed just hours ago. "What should we do about this?"

He doesn't expect an answer. Definitely doesn't expect the long, slow sigh. "Get it out of our systems, I suppose." Nic folds her arms and parks her butt on the edge of his desk. "Got a problem with that?"

He doesn't. Does he? "You're suggesting a grudge fuck?"

"Sure. Makes sense."

Seb can't believe he's about to say this, but—

"No." Now he's the stupid one. "Nic, wait." She's standing again, so he stands, too. "Believe me, I want nothing more than to throw you back on this bed and strip off your panties with my teeth before spreading your legs and—" Okay, this isn't helping.

Nic turns to face him. There's challenge in her eyes. Challenge and... lust? "Go on."

He shouldn't. "When we do finally fuck—and make no mistake, we will—" He stops because he's lost his train of thought. Also, half his brain cells. "It'll be because we both want each other one hundred percent. None of this fifty-fifty lust and hate thing."

"Cocky bastard." Her lips quirk again. "You're underestimating current hate levels."

"Sixty-forty?" He steps closer, craving her heat. "Fifty-five-point-eight and forty-four-point-two?"

"Still off." So is her voice, high and tight and quaky.

Seb steps closer. "Can I kiss you?"

"Can you stop at just a kiss?"

Doubtful, but he'll try. Tasting her again, it's all he can think about. Slowly, Seb slides a hand around her waist. Her flesh feels warm through thin cotton, and she tilts her head back to meet him. Her lips part, and he brushes them with his. As his tongue grazes hers, she gives a soft moan.

Seb's a goner. He's going under, drowning in her heat, kissing her with a hunger that stuns him. Every molecule in his body hums a song he's never heard before.

This one. This one. This one.

Nic matches him, clawing his shirt. Her teeth clamp his bottom lip as she wraps her arms around him. He's grabbing her ass, hoisting her up as she grips his hips with her thighs.

It's Seb who breaks first, tearing his mouth off hers as he turns toward the bed. "I never was good with boundaries."

"Wha—*oh.*" Her breath whooshes out as he throws her on the bed and drops between her legs. Heat seeps through her jeans, and he's sure she feels every inch of his hard-on. She's grinding against it like the Lord put it there for her use.

Maybe He did.

"Sebastian." There it is again, the breathless way she says those syllables. Her legs clench around him as she draws him to her core. "Don't stop."

Like he could. He's tugging her shirt, one hand tunneling to find her breast. It's soft and lush and fits perfectly in his hand. If he could just unhook her bra—

"Wait."

Seb blinks, fingers frozen on her bra clasp. "Okay." He blinks a few more times, bringing himself back from the edge. Scanning her eyes, he can't read what's got her pumping the brakes. "Something wrong?"

"Yes." She licks her lips, and he tries not to stare at her mouth. "We've met before."

There's not much blood in his brain, so maybe he's missing something. "Yes. At your sister's vineyard. At my clinic. At your daycare. At the gala for—"

66

"Not what I meant." She shuts her eyes, and he wonders if etiquette requires he let go of her bra clasp.

"Nic?"

"Yeah?" She's still not looking at him.

He settles for cupping his hand around the bra hook. "You've lost me here."

Nic opens her eyes. "Three years ago, we met. Longer, actually." The rise of her breath shoves her breasts against his chest, and he tries not to lose the train of thought. "At the Spirata Hotel in Washington," she continues. "I didn't know you then, but now I do, and I can't unhear what you said in that room and—"

"Annie." Memory floods in a warm rush. "You're the room service girl."

Holy shit.

On some level, he must've known, but no. Seb was a clueless asshole, like always.

"You remember." She licks her lips again. "Also, the window washer."

It all makes sense now. "You took out our target."

Something goes hard in her green eyes. "I didn't know it was you. I didn't even *know* you. Just that another enforcer had a room below the penthouse." Her expression eases. "If it makes you feel better, I also drugged the occupants of the rooms above and below yours."

That doesn't make him feel better. Her bra clasp in his palm barely does. "So why—"

"Why do I despise you?"

Present tense. Seb makes a note of it. "That would be nice to know."

Nic huffs out a breath. "You came to the door all rippling muscles and dazzling smile. You had the charm dialed up to eighty. You made me laugh and made me reconsider eliminating you." Her jaw clenches. "I almost botched the job because of you."

"Thanks?" Definitely doesn't sound like a compliment. He

fumbles back through his brain to recall that day. "We didn't drink the drugged milkshakes. I tested for roofies and tossed them."

"Smart." The hardness stays in her eyes. "You remember what you yelled? To someone else in the room—your girlfriend, presumably."

"Not my girlfriend." He won't give Dante away, but he can give her this. "And I wasn't yelling at him. I was reciting the last words of some dickhead terrorist we took out years before."

"Huh?"

Good God. This explains so much. "I was repeating someone else's words. I'd never say shit like that for real."

Nic's jaw clenches. *"Forget the petty shit you think you know."* She speaks slowly, reciting the awful words he quoted to Dante. Words she couldn't have known weren't Seb's. *"And get your ass back in the bathroom, ho."*

Good memory. "That's right." Seb searches her eyes. "You have to know I'd never say that to a woman. To anyone. *Jesus.*"

She's searching his eyes right back. "I don't know that, actually."

"Trust me."

There's the jaw clench again. "Trust gets earned."

Message received. "Should I take my hand out of your shirt?"

"I don't have to trust you to fuck you." She watches his face, relishing the shock he can't seem to keep off his face. "Just know that I've made it my life's goal to eliminate men who dial up the charm to get away with hurting women."

Is that who she thinks he is? "I don't hurt women."

One pale brow lifts. "The Countess Wioletta job?"

Nic's done her homework. "I make an exception when someone kills four kids." And the family dog, which got Dante involved. Seb's getting off track here. "I'd never hit a woman."

Nic nods once. "Be that as it may, I target men like that. Narcissists, abusers, serial charmers with a sadistic streak." Nic searches his eyes to see which he is. "I destroy men who hurt women."

"Good." Sebastian draws his hand from her shirt. Slides it to the small of her back. "Because I'm not one."

Nic doesn't answer. Doesn't look convinced, either. "So." She huffs out a breath. "Are we going to do this or what?"

"Now whose foreplay sucks?"

"You're complaining?"

"No." She could have his balls in a pair of pliers and he'd still want her. "All right."

One edge of her mouth quirks. "You can unhook my bra now." Her gaze darts to the nightstand. "Do you have condoms in there, or should I grab my purse?"

Oh. So this is happening? He's half afraid to breathe for fear of screwing this up. "I—"

Bam!

BamBamBamBam!

"Is that gunfire?" Nicole sits up and shoves him off her. "I *knew* you were lying about the soundproof bedroom."

That's the least of his concerns. "Someone's shooting." He's up in an instant as his hard-on goes down. Thumb on the gun safe, he waits for it to read his print. "Are you armed?"

"Purse." She grabs it off the floor, and there's the Glock again. "Where's Terri?"

God, his grandma. If she's hurt, he'll never forgive himself.

You'll never forgive yourself, anyway.

"Stay behind me." It's a dick thing to say, and he expects her to argue as he shoves his feet in loafers.

But Nic doesn't fight him. "I've got your back."

He knows it. It's another thing he loves about her as he creeps down the stairs, weapon at ready. "Terri?"

Nothing.

"Terri?" Seb's heart clogs his throat. "Are you okay?"

"Sebastian Orel LaDouceur." His grandma appears at the

bottom of the stairs. She's gripping a bolt-action Ruger rifle he's never seen in his life. "How many times do I need to tell you it's disrespectful to call your grandma by her first name?"

He never thought she'd shoot him for it. He's honestly too stunned for words.

Lucky for him, Nic steps forward. "Ms. LaDouceur, are you hurt?"

"No, but whoever's shooting up the neighborhood should be." Terri blows a purple curl off her face and points the gun at the window. "Rotten kids."

There's no way it's kids, but Seb sees no reason to scare her. "I'll check it out."

Glancing behind him, he sees Nic frown. *"We'll* check it out."

If Terri's alarmed they're both armed, she doesn't say so. She knows he's ex-Army. Knows his dad took him target practicing for fifteen years. But Nicole—

"I have a concealed carry license." She keeps the gun ready as she looks out the window. "Some of the kids at my daycare come from difficult situations. I need to be able to protect them."

"Of course." It's explanation enough for Terri. "Don't you kids go rushing out there. The police are on their way."

Great. He glances at Nic. "You good?"

She knows what he's asking. "Licensed and registered."

She means the gun, but the subtext is there. Seb saw for himself her record's scrubbed clean, but still. If there's a warrant for her arrest, he needs to know now.

Nic shakes her head. "I'm good."

Red and blue lights bathe the driveway. "We should put these away." He looks at Nic. "No sense getting shot by accident."

"Here." She opens her purse, and there's room in there for both guns.

Seb hesitates. He never surrenders his weapon. *Never.*

But his own words ring in his ears.

Give me the knife.

His brain paints the image of Nic's eyes as she handed him the blade. He'll never forget it. Fear mixed with trust mixed with resignation mixed with determination. Seb still can't believe it.

Gritting his teeth, he sets the Beretta inside.

Terri turns away. "I'll put this back in my gun safe."

"You have a gun safe?" He's talking to air since she's already gone. How did he not know this?

"She's your grandma." Nic looks at him with pity. "You see a fragile old lady and not a badass."

So Nic's not the only one with a sweet alter ego. Another cop car comes up the drive, and Sebastian grabs the doorknob. "Ready?"

She nods, and they step outside together. Shoving hands in his pockets, Seb pastes on his best aw-shucks smile. "Evening, officers. Thanks for coming."

"You heard the shots." The tall one circles Nic's car, frowning.

That's when Seb sees it. The cracked windshield. Casings on the pavement.

And on the driver's side door, painted between bullet holes, a message:

Next time, *Granny gets it.*

CHAPTER 6

"**K**ids." Sebastian shakes his head and gives a sad but pleasant smile.

It's the first time Nic's grateful he's got more charm than sense.

But that's not fair. She's thinking snarky thoughts while he throws the cops off their trail. He's being smart, not smarmy. It isn't his fault he's got a gigolo brain, a stripper body, and a Boy Scout smile.

"I hate all the crime we're seeing in this town." Nic hugs herself and steps close to Seb. For solidarity, not because she wants him. "Just last week, someone tagged my daycare with graffiti."

The short cop with a mustache looks up. "You've got kids?"

"I run a childcare facility." Nic draws her arms back so he can read her Miss Gigglewinks shirt. Both cops' gazes linger too long on her chest. Not for the first time, she's grateful for the D-cup distractions. "I grew up here. It's awful how crime's impacting our neighborhoods."

The cops exchange a look. "You'd be surprised," says the tall cop with eyes the color of bread crusts she cuts off picky students' sandwiches. "We've even got organized crime."

"Organized crime?" Nic blinks, the picture of innocence. "You mean like The Godfather?"

"Something like that." Mini Mustache straightens, eager to enlighten the sweet young teacher. "Had a big hit go down real recently. Mob boss, Danny 'Duck Toes' DeCosta. Out of our jurisdiction, or we'd have been all over that one like—"

"It's under investigation." Bread Crust shoots a look that makes his mustachioed comrade shrink. "Anyway, we need you to step aside while we process the crime scene. Either of you see what happened?"

"We just heard the shots." Sebastian shrugs. "We weren't even sure that's what it was. Thought it might be fireworks."

Mini Mustache chuckles as he circles the Volvo. "Definitely not fireworks." He whistles low. "They sure did a number on your car. Any idea what the message means?"

Nic bites her lip.

Next time, Granny gets it.

As her gut twists in a tight knot, she looks at Sebastian. "Your grandma doesn't have any enemies, does she? Someone who's threatened by her or maybe—"

"Terri?" He makes a sound between a laugh and a choke. "My flower-arranging, churchgoing grandma, *Terri*? The one who's inside right now baking cookies in her robe?"

Even the cops look doubtful.

They're not wrong. Nic knows damn well the message on her car isn't meant for Seb.

But it's not because Terri's too old or too sweet or whatever bullshit their patriarchal brains keep telling them. That makes Nic's blood boil.

Besides. She can't say what she suspects. Not yet.

"Sebastian." Her voice goes kitten soft as she rests a hand on his arm. "Is there a chance you're underestimating your grandma?"

She looks deep into his eyes, imploring him to bite. To relive the shock of seeing Terri in her robe with a gun gripped in steady hands.

Besides, Nic's doing him a favor. If that weapon's not registered, Terri's in trouble. He'll think that through before letting the cops talk to her. It's an act of benevolence, leading Seb down this path.

Keep telling yourself that.

Sebastian's throat rolls. "I—shit." He drags a hand over his head. "I don't think so, but my dad—" His voice breaks, and so does Nic's heart. His eyes darken as they swing back to the cops. "My father was killed three years ago. He got in over his head with gambling and—" He breaks off again and shakes his head. "He died owing a lot of people money."

Oh, shit.

Nic bangs her head on the wall in her mind. This isn't what she meant to do.

Bread Crust is frowning now. "This situation with your dad. Was it here in Oregon?"

"Florida." Seb's arm tenses beneath her fingers. "I went down to help, but I was too late. I tried to pay off his debts, but wound up making funeral plans instead and—anyway." He looks at Nic. "I thought I made sure the bookies wouldn't come after me. After Terri."

Nic knows what he's telling her. She sees it in the pools of his eyes. Sebastian got revenge. He made sure every last mobster paid for killing his father.

And now, Nic's got Seb questioning himself. The self-loathing in his eyes splits her heart in half. This wasn't her plan. She needs to fix this.

Mini Mustache clears his throat. "Think we could have a word with your grandma?"

"What for?" Seb frowns at the cops. "Terri wasn't there. She's still mourning her son. Still fragile. If you—"

"Sebastian?" Terri's voice rings from the steps. "Don't you go mollycoddling me. If these officers need to ask me something, we should let them do their jobs."

"Ma'am." Bread Crust doffs his hat. "We won't be long. Just a few questions, and we'll be on our way."

"Come on inside." She holds open the door. "You should know I've got a registered rifle that belonged to my late husband. It's locked in the gun safe, and I've got peanut butter cookies in the oven."

Bread Crust heads for the door. "Thank you for being honest, ma'am." His quickened steps say he's more thankful for the cookies.

Terri ushers him through the door, a portrait of matronly wholesomeness. Sebastian starts to follow. "I'll join you."

Mini Mustache puts a hand out. "Sorry, son. We prefer to question folks separately. Keeps things clear and unfiltered. You understand."

"I—" Seb rubs his jaw. His helpless expression nearly undoes Nic.

As her heart twists, she touches Seb's arm. Turns back to Mini Mustache. "Do you need to ask us any questions?"

He shrugs. "Pretty much did already. You can hang out here while Officer Meisner has a word with your grandma and I process the crime scene."

Nic looks at his name badge. *Blake*, it reads, and Meisner must be Bread Crust. "Are we free to go?"

The cop shakes his head. "I might have a few more questions in a sec, so don't go anywhere."

She fakes a shiver. "Would you mind if we went inside and grabbed jackets? Or we could wait in Sebastian's car."

Mustache looks between them, then shrugs again. "I'd rather you stay close by. Car's fine."

Terri calls out from the porch. "Sweetheart, catch."

Seb turns to snag the keys she's tossing him. He looks at Nicole. "Come on."

Leading her to his black BMW, he keys it open. Nic hesitates, then gets in the passenger side. Shuts the door hard, then looks at him.

"Disarm it."

Sebastian blinks. "Disarm what?"

"Whatever listening device you've got in here." Nicole folds her arms so he can't see her hands shaking. "I need to speak freely."

She watches his eyes as he processes that. Nodding once, he reaches in the glovebox and draws out a recording device. Holds it so she can watch as he switches it off.

Nic meets his eyes. "Is that everything?"

"Yes." Hesitation. "Fine." With a sigh, he reaches for her boobs. A big palm folds over her left one as she gasps and—

"Got it." He plucks a bug off the seatbelt and hands it to her. "Satisfied?"

"No." Her voice sounds way too breathy. "I mean, yes."

"What?"

"Nothing." Nic clears her throat. "That's all of it?"

"Yeah."

This time, she believes him. A glance out the window finds Mustache moving around her Volvo, paying no mind to them.

She tests him to be safe. "Officer Blake, I'd like to confess to being a sex addict."

Nothing. The cop doesn't turn. She looks at Seb, who's staring at her. "Call me nuts," he says, "but I don't think the police can help with that."

"I need to know he can't hear." She knocks on the window, confirming it's bulletproof glass. "Had a feeling, but I wanted to be sure."

Blue eyes hold hers, and he nods. "Is there something you wanted to say?"

Nic darts a glance at the cop. He's facing away, so even if he reads lips, he can't see her. "I'm going to tell you something." She locks her eyes on Seb, searching for signs she can trust him.

She has to. There's no choice now.

"Okay." His voice pitches low, waiting for the trap. "Go on."

"No joking around this time. I need you to swear you won't tell a soul. Not your grandma. Not Matteo. Not your buddies at The Union."

"All right." He's all business now, not even playing coy about the Union thing. "Is a promise enough? You need me to sign in blood or something?"

"Tempting, but no." She draws a breath. "Consider this, first: It would be easy right now to lead you down the trail of thinking this has something to do with Terri. That's your Achilles heel, Sebastian. Another woman might take advantage of that."

"I—" He stops and stares at her. "I don't know what to do with that."

"You're already worried there's a connection to your father and what happened and—" She stops when pain sears his eyes. "I don't want that." She lays a hand on his arm. "What I'm about to tell you is a form of mercy. Remember that, please."

"Okay." Confusion clashes with the pain in his eyes. "Spit it out, Nic. Whatever it is—"

"I think my grandma's alive."

Seb blinks. "Come again?"

Nicole draws a breath. "Matteo told you she died of cancer, right?"

"Matteo never told me anything. Matteo is... Matteo."

"Right." God, where does she start? "A few months after Teo went to prison, Nondi sat Jen and me down and told us she had stage four ovarian cancer. Incurable. She wasn't willing to try chemo, which, if you knew Nondi—" Nic sighs. "It wasn't strange. Neither was her goal to go out on her own terms. To not let anyone be there at the end."

Sebastian's brows furrow. "You're saying you didn't see her die."

"Correct." She pulls more air into her lungs. There's not enough of it in this small space. "But you have to understand that wasn't weird. Not to us. The people who knew her. But I knew her better than my brother and sister did."

"What do you mean?"

She squeezes her eyes shut. This part's hard. "Nondi trained me." Nic opens her eyes. "After Clint hit me, I moved home for a little while. Didn't talk to anyone about what happened, but Nondi knew." Nondi always knew. "When the story came out about Clint killing his girlfriend, she took me under her wing."

Sebastian stares. "What are you saying?"

"My grandma was an operator." Nic grits her teeth. "Might still be."

"Holy shit." Sebastian shakes his head slowly. "How—why—"

"She worked as an enforcer in Dovlano." She draws a breath, not sure how much she should share. "This was after she came to America. She mostly took jobs overseas, so she traveled a lot."

"Jesus." Seb's fingers find his keyring. He rolls the bullet between his fingers. "When Teo said your grandma was gone all the time, that's not what I thought he meant."

"Teo never knew." This part's even trickier. "He never knew why she got into it, either."

"Why did she?"

Nic looks into his eyes. The darkness there tells her he's guessed already. "She got hit, too."

"God."

"My grandpa." She presses her lips together. "It went on for years, I guess. I never met him. Eventually, he died. Nondi always kicked herself that she didn't do something sooner, but—" Her voice breaks off, and she takes a few breaths to get it together. "She helped me understand it wasn't my fault."

Seb's jaw clenches. "I guess it beats therapy."

She laughs because why not? His words make her feel better, and they both could use that now. "Nondi didn't specialize like I did. She took other jobs. Avenging unsolved murders was her specialty."

"Revenge." He nods and looks out the window. "Powerful motivator."

"Yeah." Nic takes a shaky breath. "Anyway, that's how I got into it. My grandma taught me."

Seb stifles a laugh. "And here I thought Terri taught me something edgy when she showed me how to spit off a bridge."

She wants to laugh but can't. This is too important. "The name those guys said at the event—Issela?"

"You said you didn't know who that was."

"I lied." She does that sometimes.

"No shit."

"Like you've never done it, Minty Fresh? Please."

"Point taken." He rubs his palms on his thighs. "Go on."

"Issela is Nondi's code name—it's her name, backwards."

Sebastian tilts his head. "Alessi?"

"It's Italian. A unisex name, and yeah, I know—seems silly to have a code name so close to her own, but that's the point."

"What's the point?"

"Hiding in plain sight. No one expects some sweet old lady to be a coldhearted killer." Nic draws a breath and sees the spark in Nondi's eye. The look she'd get when she'd pulled off some sleight of hand. "You should have seen some of the stuff she got away with. Boarding a plane with a live grenade because no one checks an old lady's knitting yarn. Waltzing into a target's living room posing as a housekeeper because, obviously, some gray-haired little grandma is harmless. That's what you think, right?"

She's speaking in general, but Seb frowns. "I know anyone can be a killer, but this doesn't add up." He shakes his head. "Why would she fake her own death? It doesn't make sense. She'd know how much it would hurt you."

That's true, and it does hurt. "Maybe she had something to take care of, but she meant to return."

She hears how crazy it sounds. Sees doubt in Seb's eyes and doesn't blame him. "Never mind." Nic grabs the door handle. "Forget I said anything, okay?"

"Nicole, wait." His hand closes around her arm, and she hates how her skin lights up. "I'm not saying I don't believe you, okay? You're not the only one here with trust issues."

"What do you mean?"

"I mean, the first time we met, you served me a poisoned milkshake. Call me suspicious, but I need to digest this."

Pun intended? She decides not to ask. "Keep in mind, you didn't even remember meeting me before. I could have taken that information to my grave."

"That's... not as comforting as you think it is."

"Sebastian." It's a fight to keep the panic from her voice. "I need your help."

Seb drags his hands down his face. "Look, I want to believe you. To buy this version of the story you're spinning. My other choice is thinking someone's after Terri."

"Doesn't feel good, does it?" She hopes she's not overplaying her hand. "Thinking someone might want to hurt your grandma."

His throat rolls as he swallows. "She put Band-Aids on my boo-boos and baked me snickerdoodles."

"Nondi did that, too." Technically, chocolate chip, but why wreck their bonding? "She also taught me to use a garrote and how much nerve agent it takes to incapacitate a two-hundred-pound man."

Seb winces. "I didn't need to know that."

"You did." She puts a hand on his arm. "I'm laying my cards on the table here. I want you to know I'm being straight with you."

He stares at the hand that's touching him. So long she starts to draw it back. His words stop her. "What do you want from me?" His eyes meet hers, and there's a lost little boy in there. "My dick. You made that clear. Or was that a ploy to get my help?"

She yanks her palm off him and grabs the door handle. "Fuck you, Sebastian."

"That's what I thought." Seb's face goes stony. Blue eyes search hers. For the first time, there's no trace of mirth. "You say I use charm as a weapon, and you're right. The Boy Scout act gets me further than other operators get being menacing or cunning."

She absorbs his words. Dante's menacing, and her brother's cunning. She doesn't need a decoder ring to catch that. "We all use the tools we're given."

"That we do." He drags a hand down his face. "And you want to use me."

That stings. "Your contacts. With the Union."

She waits for him to deny it. When he doesn't, she presses. "I have sources for intel, same as you do. It's how I knew you'd staked out that hotel three years ago."

"But your intel has holes," he says slowly. "Correct?"

She hesitates. What will she lose by admitting it? "Correct." Nic bites her lip. "No matter how hard I dig, I can't break the Union's system. But I think they know something about Nondi."

"You're asking me to snoop." His voice sounds tired, and he's not looking at her now. Just watching the cop pacing slowly around the Volvo. "You want me to put my neck on the line, knowing damn well that could get me killed."

"No." Nic drops her hand from the door.

He's right. That's exactly what she's asking.

Or what she would have asked if he hadn't put it that way. "Look, I'd never ask you to use Union resources to save me."

"I already did."

She flinches. There's iron in his voice she's never heard. "I know that, and I'm grateful, but I didn't ask." She touches his arm again.

Muscles, taut and twitching, bunch beneath her palm. He still won't look at her. "But for my grandma—for Matteo's grandma—"

"I'll see what I can do." His jaw tightens. "One more thing."

"Yes?"

She's braced for a come-on. For some sex joke to defuse the tension. As his eyes swing to hers, she sucks in a breath. His eyes are icy blue in the beam of the porch light, and she knows what the question will be. Her answer, too.

Yes, I'll sleep with you. A hundred times if you like.

"If you tell anyone my middle name," he says, "I'll kill you."

Nic bursts out laughing. "Oral? I wasn't going to say anything, but—"

"*Orel*," he corrects. "My mother has roots in the Czech Republic. It means 'eagle.'"

"I'm sure it does." Fighting a smile, she gives a serious nod. "Very noble."

And noteworthy he used present tense for Mom. Another slip of the tongue like with his father? Or is Sebastian's mother still alive? Now's not the time to ask.

"I promise not to tell." She forces herself to sound solemn. "Your secret's safe with me, Minty Fresh."

"And yours with me."

Nic shivers, not nearly as reassured as she'd like to be.

* * *

NICOLE WAITS DAYS TO hear from him. Not the first time she's busied herself with blankies and crayons while watching her back in the parking lot. Each time the phone rings, she's sure it's Nondi. Or Sebastian with news about—

"Hello?" she answers when she sees Seb's name on the readout.

So much for not sounding eager.

"You alone?"

Nic looks around her classroom. There's a blue shelf piled with stuffed animals leering through glass eyes. Student drawings line the walls, a riot of red and blue Crayola. "Yes." She moves a bin of Legos off her chair and sits down. "Any news?"

"The Seahawks won by three points last night," he says. "A dairy cow got loose on the Amity-Dayton highway and stopped traffic for an hour."

Is he being a smart-ass or hinting it's not safe to talk? Tough to tell with Seb. "Do you want to come in?"

"Where are you?"

"You mean you don't have eyes on me at all times?"

She's joking, but also not surprised when the daycare door swings open. "Am I allowed?"

God, he looks good.

"Not normally." She speaks into the phone, though he's ten feet away. It's tough not to smile, especially with his big frame filling her doorway. His jeans fit like they're custom made, while his dark blue scrub top looks like it's sewn to his body. There's a medical mask pulled down below his chin, and his biceps give her the urge to book a dental cleaning.

Nic licks her lips. "There's a strict rule with families," she continues. "Don't stop by without an appointment. That way, no one crosses paths. Also saves them from running into my personal guests."

"Are you inviting me to be your guest?"

She'd invite him into her panties right now if he asked.

But no, that's not why he's here. "Come in." She's still speaking into the phone, and she doesn't want to drop it. This feels safer somehow.

"Thanks for the warm welcome." Seb's eyes trail her body. As he steps through the door, he doesn't drop his phone, either. "Nice sweater."

"Thank you." She tugs it around her, conscious of the knitted row of elephants parading across her breasts.

Seb sees them, too. "What did the elephant say to the naked man?"

"I have no idea."

"How can you drink through something so small?"

Her mouth feels dry, but she's determined not to be charmed. "Elephants don't drink through their trunks. They use them like a tool to transport water into their mouths."

"I know. But thanks for womansplaining elephants to me."

"That's not a thing." She hates how much she wants him.

"Huh." He grins as he circles her classroom, surveying the space. The phone's still pressed to his ear as he ambles past the art supplies. "Elephants also use their trunks like a snorkel to breathe when they swim, which leads me to my next bad joke."

"Wonderful." It's a struggle not to smile. Not to watch his ass as he prowls the perimeter of her classroom. She shifts the phone to her other ear. "Feel free to keep that joke to yourself." She should definitely hang up.

"What's the fun in that?" He's got his back to her now, and she wonders what it would feel like to sink her nails in bare muscle. "What's the worst way to flirt with a woman in a hot tub?"

Her traitorous brain spools pics of Seb wet and shirtless. "I'm confident you know this."

As he turns, his grin sends her heart spinning into her throat. "Announce 'up, periscope' as you slowly float your boner to the surface."

"Nice, Minty Fresh. That's the first time someone's made a hard-on joke in my daycare." It's totally not. She made one last week when Jen stopped by after hours. "I'm hanging up now." She pulls the phone from her ear and taps it off. Sets it on her desk and folds her hands like a good little teacher.

Sebastian gives a straight-faced head shake as he tucks his

own phone in his pocket. "I'd give up the job forever if I had a nickel for every time a woman hangs up on me."

She doubts that's even a little true. "Maybe women find you repulsive?"

Stepping close, he quirks an un-repulsive eyebrow. "Do you?"

"Absolutely." She shivers as he hovers over her. The scent of his aftershave makes her girl parts sit up and beg. "I just threw up a little in my mouth."

He laughs and grabs one of her tiny plastic chairs. Flips it around to straddle it. "I can tell by how your nipples perked up."

Jerking her cardigan closed, she decides to kill him. "I'm wearing a padded bra."

"Not a denial."

There's no point denying what's true. "Maybe you're in the habit of discussing your private parts in your workplace, but I'll pass." How long can she keep up this prim and proper act before she launches herself into his lap?

Sebastian grins like he's read her thoughts. "You might not discuss it, but don't think I didn't notice you looking at my dick just now."

Busted. Nic clears her throat. "Do you have news that doesn't involve sports teams or livestock?"

"Depends." He surveys the room, frowning at the life-sized cutout of Big Bird behind her. "Is that bugged?"

"Is that a bird mite joke?" It's tough to tell with Seb. She gets up and peels the poster off the wall. Turns it around so he can see both sides. "Not bugged."

"How about the playhouse in the corner?"

"Of course not." Nic looks at the red and white plastic structure. "That's where I keep my guns."

"You know, I almost believe you."

Slipping a hand in her desk drawer, she pulls out a bug sweeper. "Have at it, Minty Fresh."

"Don't mind if I do." He takes his time sweeping the room.

Nic tries not to watch as he waves the wand over bookshelves and building blocks, paint sets and cubby holes. When his back is turned, she hardly stares at his ass at all.

"Want me to flex?" He looks over one shoulder and winks. "My butt's famous, you know."

"Please." If that's a joke, she doesn't get it.

If it's not, she believes it. It's truly a work of art.

"Not joking." He turns to watch her face. "Check out the credits on the last Cooper Judson flick." He lopes over and sets the sweeper on her desk. "Right there at the end—body double, Sebastian LaDouceur."

"You're lying." She's not sure he is.

With a shrug, he picks up a pair of plastic safety scissors. "That's the only one where I got that label. In all the others, I'm 'stunt double.' Guess my ass gets different billing?"

Nothing in his expression says if he's pulling her leg. "You want me to believe you've stood in for Hollywood legend Cooper Judson and never mentioned it 'til now?"

Grinning, he flips open the scissors. "I'm a man of many talents."

She doesn't doubt it. Also doesn't know how to stop herself from staring at his hands. She's seen them swathed in latex gloves at his clinic. On the grip of a gun at the charity event.

But her body recalls the weight of them on her waist, his palm on her breast, his breath against her—

"Sebastian, focus." She folds her hands again. "Is there something you're able to share with me?"

"Many things." He flips the scissors shut. "But as far as The Union goes, no."

Her heart sinks with a sad splash. "You mean you won't tell me."

"I mean the info's locked down tight." Another scissor flip. His expression's inscrutable. "If there's buzz about your grandma, I'm not seeing it." Another flip. "Doesn't mean it's not there."

"I see." She's struggling to keep it together. "So that's it."

"Nope." He gives her a long look. "There's a way into the back end of the system. It's doubtful your hacker could do it. I know someone who could."

"Oh?" The hope in her voice makes her eyes sting.

Seb gives her a long look. His fingers grip the scissors. "Your brother."

"No."

One brow lifts. "You don't trust Teo?"

"It's not that." Nic weighs her words. "If I'm wrong about Nondi," she says slowly, "it'll break his heart all over again."

His eyes hold hers like he's searching for truth. Maybe he finds it because he nods. "Understood." A pause. "Not to mention blowing your cover."

"There's that."

Seb nods again. "So we're stuck."

"There's really nothing you can share?"

Another long pause. She watches the wheels behind blue eyes so bright, it hurts to look at them. "There was one piece of intel. Might be nothing, but—"

"Tell me." Nic grips her desk. "Please."

One edge of his mouth quirks. "You're cute when you're eager."

"Fuck off." She says it in her sweet teacher voice to take the sting out. "Sebastian, pl—"

"I hacked the files on *you*."

Nic blinks. "There's a file on me?" She shouldn't be surprised. "I mean—"

"The job that was taken by our friends, Brown Oxfords and Black Oxfords. Shall I continue?"

"Please." Her voice squeaks a little.

"The file's not especially long, but it did contain one line I couldn't decipher."

It's her first time wanting to kiss a guy tapped to kill her. "What was the line?"

"It read, 'the dressmaker was dirty.'"

Nic lets go of the desk. "What does that even mean?"

"Not sure. Thought you could tell me."

"I—have no idea." She really doesn't. Drags her brain, just in case. "I'm coming up empty."

Sebastian's eyes narrow. "Where'd you get the dress you wore the other night?"

"The red Badgley Mishka?"

"Yeah." He draws out the word like he's tasting it. "Very hot, by the way."

"Very shredded, thanks to Brown Oxfords and Black Oxfords." She laces her fingers together. "I got it at a consignment shop in Portland for twenty bucks. A steal for a designer gown. I had a local seamstress make some tweaks."

Seb looks suspicious. "What sort of tweaks?"

Nic tips her chin up. "If you must know, she let the bust out and took the hem up three inches."

Blue eyes flash with interest. "Let's talk some more about your bust."

She grits her teeth. "Do you work hard to be a pig, or does it come naturally?"

"Naturally." He's entirely too cheerful about it. "Any chance the seamstress is bent?"

"She's seventy-three, and she's been altering my clothes since I was sixteen."

"And your grandma's got a secret life as an assassin."

Touché. "Thank you." Nic swallows.

He frowns. "For what?"

"For calling me on the double standard." As she draws a breath, her heart keeps pinching in itself. "But mostly for using present tense."

"You're sure she's alive?"

Nicole hesitates. "I want to believe it."

"Then I want to help you." He sets the scissors on the desk and gets to his feet. "Starting with those damn bullet holes in the wall. How long have these been there?"

"Bullet holes?" She stands and follows, laughing as he points to the wall behind her reading corner. "Those are nail holes, Minty Fresh. I used to hang student art there."

"And now?"

She shrugs. "I've been meaning to repaint."

Stooping down, he peers at the wall. "Stay here."

He's stalking off before she asks where she'd go. It's her damn daycare. If she wants to stay, she'll stay. If she wants to walk out in the parking lot and stare at his ass while he—

She'll wait.

Nic paces the room until he marches back in with determination on his too-handsome face. He's wearing blue surgical gloves and holding—

"Is that toothpaste?" She frowns at the tubes, and yep—definitely toothpaste.

"In my experience, most paint schemes fit one of two color palettes." He twists the cap off one tube. "Crest white or Colgate blue." Squeezing the end, he smears some paste on his finger. "This is a job for Crest."

She steps close to watch him dab it in the hole. "You're not seriously putting toothpaste on my wall."

"You're not seriously complaining that I already made it look a hundred times better." He squeezes more paste on his finger and fills the next hole.

"Huh." He's got a point. "Smells better than caulk."

"Since I'm a gentleman, I won't even make a caulk/cock joke." He doesn't turn to see her biting back a smile. "There." He straightens and swings a hand to show off his handiwork. "Much better, eh?"

"I'll be damned." She surveys the wall. "I'm impressed."

"If I'd known toothpaste impresses you, we'd have had a much different start." Spinning around, he moves to the space behind her desk. A violent swirl of red crayon mars one wall where Misty Holmes expressed her budding art skills this morning.

Seb stoops to study it. "How old is the kid who drew this?"

"Five." She bites her lip. There's a new baby in Misty's family. Her mom thought it might help to read *How Babies Are Made*. "It's anatomically correct," Nic adds.

"I see that." Seb pulls a toothbrush from his pocket. "Helpfully labeled, too. You want to wipe out the drawing and leave the word 'penis,' or clear off the whole thing?"

"The whole thing, please."

"Kind of a shame." He spreads some Crest on the bristles. "Gotta use a non-gel paste for this trick."

"Noted." It's official. She's a loser who gets turned on by dental products. There's probably porn about this.

Knowing that doesn't stop her from watching him work the brush against the wall, his long fingers flexing on the toothbrush shaft. God, he's got great hands. Even in those stupid blue gloves with tartar control paste smeared on his knuckles. What the hell is wrong with her?

Flashing a grin, he moves to the next drawing. "Will you call me a pig if I tell you I'll need to rub extra hard to get off the vulva?"

"I'll call you a pig no matter what." She can't watch. It's too much. "But you're right that the student used a little thicker crayon stroke there."

"No judgement." He goes to work on the word "vagina" and Nic takes a step back. "Whatever does the job."

Nic licks her lips. "Do we need to let the toothpaste sit, or do we wipe it off?"

"The paste takes crayon off pretty quick." He straightens and yep—all gone. "But unless you like your walls smelling like spearmint, you may want to wipe them down."

"I'll grab paper towels."

Her face feels hot as she rushes to the sink to wet a wad of Bounty. It's the dumbest thing ever, getting turned on by this. By a man who wields charm as handily as he holds a toothbrush.

Only one of those is deadly, a sharp, shiny blade meant to cut out her heart. Nic's brain knows better, even if her body doesn't.

Dabbing her face with the wet towels, she steals a look to be sure he's not watching. He's bent at the waist, working a spot near her baseboards. His glutes flex as he stoops to scrub harder.

"It's right around the twelve-minute mark," he calls.

"What's right around the twelve-minute mark?" Dropping her hands, she wets the paper towels again.

"The scene in *Survivor Six*. The one where I play Cooper Judson's butt."

Nic grits her teeth. "I don't care about your butt."

"Coulda fooled me, the way you're staring." He straightens and spins with a flourish. "Good as new."

"Thank you." Nic hurries over to wipe the wall. "I appreciate the help." Might be the first time she's ever uttered those words. "I could have done it myself, but—"

"You wouldn't have gotten to ogle me then." He tugs the towel wad from her hands. "I've got it."

She tries to grab it back. "Sebastian—"

"I made the mess," he says, holding the drippy blob overhead so she can't reach. "It's important to clean up your own messes."

"Tell that to the demon child who made the marks." Nic grits her teeth. "Thank you, Sebastian."

"You're welcome." He's smiling as he goes to work wiping down the walls. "You're good at your job."

Something warms at the center of her chest. "That's the first time you've complimented something besides my tits or my firepower."

"I'm a pig, remember?" His shoulders tense as he keeps scrubbing. "Really, though—you never use students' names. You're careful with security. That's smart."

He's called her smart and good at her job in the same breath. He must want something.

But he's scrubbing her walls and not staring at her tits, so she'll be damned if she knows what it is.

Keep your friends close and your enemies closer.

Nondi's words float through her mind, and Nic tells herself that's why she's watching him. It's got nothing to do with the ripple of muscle in his back.

Seb stands and wipes his hands on the paper towel. "Another reason you're good at your job," he continues. "I read about that time you shot an abusive dickwad who tried to kidnap a kid. Had a hunch then you weren't an ordinary daycare lady."

"Right." She tried like hell to keep that one out of the press. "I worried someone might notice. Might guess it wasn't just dumb luck."

"Your secret's safe with me."

She's starting to trust that's true. Starting to trust *him*. "What are you doing next Friday?"

"Friday?" He cocks his head. "Attending Dante's rehearsal dinner."

"My *sister's* rehearsal dinner." It's tough not to sound snappish. "Come with me."

He tosses the towel at the trash bin without looking. It drops straight in the center. "As your date or your partner in crime?"

"Yes." She bites her lip. "We're both going. Might as well go together, right?"

"I suppose." It's her fault he sounds suspicious. "What does the date thing entail?"

"We stick together. Scan for threats. Watch each other's backs and be ready for attack."

Seb quirks an eyebrow. "That's your idea of a date?"

"What's yours?"

He shrugs. "Same." Heat fills his eyes. "Maybe with a chance of getting naked."

"I can't promise naked," she says. "I'm supposed to stay with Jen that night." She pauses, pretty sure her joke's about to fall flat. Pretty sure it's not a joke. "But if you play your cards right, I'll let you touch my boobs."

"Deal." Seb grins. "It's a date."

"Deal." She sticks out her hand, and he shakes it. Swoops of energy pulse up her arm, and she fights like hell not to like it. "Here's to working together."

"To mixing business with pleasure," he adds as another current shoots through her.

For the oddest instant, she thinks he might kiss her hand. But no, he gives a firm shake and lets go like a gentleman. Like a business associate and not a guy she's picturing with his shirt off.

Seb drops his hand and steps back, shooting her his same cocky grin. "We can touch base later about the date. Stay safe out there."

"I always do." She starts to stack student worksheets, giving her hands something to do as she watches him walk from the room. As soon as he's gone, she drops into her chair.

What was she thinking, inviting him to Jen's rehearsal dinner?

True, he was already going. Also true, she needs to keep him close since he's got access to intel she can't get on her own. For all his faults, Seb's got a strong sense of justice. Probably more motivating than her boobs when it comes to getting his help.

With a sigh, Nic gets to her feet and crams worksheets in her organizer. Wriggles into her flak vest and pulls on her cardigan to hide the Glock's holster. At the door, she hesitates. Listens for threats—The idling of a car? The snick of a shotgun?—then sets the alarm, locks the door, and steps into the dimming dusk.

Goosebumps dust her arms as she crosses twenty feet of asphalt to reach her car. The windshield's been fixed, the graffiti buffed out, but she still feels a chill as she keys her car open.

She was careful on the Duck Toes job. So careful, just like always. But somehow they tracked him to her. Somehow, she messed up. That's not like her.

Or maybe this job wasn't like the others. What did EZ mean about someone handpicking her to take out Duck Toes? Who would do that, and why?

Shivering, she commands herself to stay present. Maybe she's paranoid, but it feels like someone's watching her. She scans the nearby rooftops, searching for a sniper's scope.

Nothing.

Seb's car is gone, so he's already left the shared parking lot. That's fine. Nic doesn't need a guy protecting her. She protects her own damn self. Herself and anyone cowed by someone they used to trust. Someone they loved who betrayed them in the worst way possible.

Shivering again, she throws her bag on the passenger seat and slings herself behind the wheel. Pulls the door shut and flicks the locks, scanning the hedges for threats. Behind bulletproof glass, she's safe to study closer. To peer between branches and buildings and—

There!

What is that?

Nic squints at a boxwood hedge, frowning at the flash of metal. A hint of bright fabric. Whoever's in there needs lessons on camouflage.

Touching her Glock, Nic draws a breath. Remembers Nondi's words from years ago.

"The trick to beating fear is to run toward the threat instead of away." One edge of her mouth twitched as she handed Nic a rifle. *"Helps if you're armed."*

It does indeed.

Drawing her weapon, Nic rehearses what she'll say if a neighborhood cop sees her stalking through the parking lot. She's got her concealed carry license and the trust of local law enforcement. They know about Miss Gigglewinks. About Nic protecting students at all costs.

They just don't know who else she defends.

Edging toward the shrubs, Nic squints at the flash of metal. Not a weapon like she thought. It's a metallic streamer like the kind they used in last week's craft project. And orange construction paper ringed in green fringe. Probably Tina Payne's homework. She's always dropping things on the way out to her mom's car.

As Nic gets closer, she sees it's not Tina's work. It's a typewritten page glued to paper she swears came from her own craft drawer. With a hand that's none too steady, she snatches the page off the branch.

Be wary of men with killer smiles and cute butts.

Nic whips around, scanning for faces in the shrubs. For the source of the threat.

But no one's nearby. Even the café on the corner is closed up tight. Nic's alone.

Shivering in the breeze, she sprints back to her car. Locks the doors tight and drives straight to her sister's house.

Jen throws open her door before Nic even knocks. "Are you okay?" Her sister's brow furrows. "You look like you've seen a ghost."

"I'm good." Nic hugs her sister hard, hoping Jen doesn't see she's shaking. She's normally so steady. "Is Dante here?"

"He's bowling with Matteo."

The doubt in Jen's voice makes Nicole draw back. "You don't think he's lying, do you?"

"About bowling?" Jen snorts and leads them to the kitchen. "Definitely."

Nic grabs a carrot off a cutting board. Starts slicing it in coins like the ones sputtering in a pot on Jen's stove. "You don't sound very worried he's being untruthful."

Jen moves beside her, green eyes guarded. "He's not with another woman, if that's what you mean."

"It isn't."

Her sister hesitates. "He'd never hurt me, Nic. If that's what you're worried about—"

"It's not." Nic squeezes her eyes shut. Why is she being like this? "Dante's amazing. He treats you like a queen, and I'm so fucking happy you met him."

"Nicole?"

She opens her eyes and sees pity in her kid sister's face. "There are good men out there, you know." Jen bites her lip. "They're not all like Clint."

"That's the problem." She draws a shaky breath. "I didn't know *Clint* was like Clint." He was so handsome, so charming, so—

So much like Sebastian.

Nic grips the carrot harder. "He seemed like such a good guy."

"Which makes it not your fault he turned out to be an abusive asshole."

Nic flinches. "I know that."

Jen takes the knife from her hand. It's only then Nic notices she's holding it in a fist.

"I know it's hard to trust," Jen says. "It sucks so much the way you learned that, and I wish I could take it all away. But eventually, you'll find someone worthy of your big heart." Jen pauses, searching her eyes. "Maybe you have already."

Nic shuts her eyes again. She hates feeling weak. Hates not knowing whom to trust. Is Sebastian the man she wants him to be?

Or just another charmer sent to break her down?

Drawing a breath, she opens her eyes. Pastes on a smile for her sister. "Come on."

"Where are we going?"

"Living room." She wipes her hands on her jeans. "I've got the sudden urge to watch an action flick."

"Yeah?" Jen grins. "I'm up for that."

"With popcorn. And wine. Maybe Milk Duds."

"Count me in." Jen scrapes the carrots into her stew and gives it a stir. "I've got Netflix and Hulu. What did you have in mind?"

"Oh, I don't know." She tries to sound casual, but she's kidding herself. Her sister knows her too well. "Maybe a Cooper Judson flick. *Survivor Six?*"

Jen laughs and slings an arm around her. "The one that shows his butt?"

"Exactly," Nic says, and lets her sister lead her to the living room.

CHAPTER 7

"*I* honestly can't tell who's a cop, who's an operator, or who's just a regular person." Sebastian scans the crowd around the barn. "Teachers or veterinarians or whatever."

"Or dentists?" Matteo sips a cup of sparkling water. "It's an event filled with Dante's friends. Everyone's got another identity."

Point taken. Sebastian keeps scanning, knowing damn well he's not watching strangers. He's watching for her, for Nicole. His date.

Don't dates arrive together?

"Stop it."

Seb looks at Teo. "Stop what?"

"Looking for my sister."

"What makes you think I'm looking for your sister?"

Matteo stares.

"So what?" He sounds defensive. "She's my date. I'm supposed to keep an eye out."

"I'm still not buying it." Matteo grips his cup tighter. "Nic hates your guts. Why would she agree to be your date?"

"Maybe she plans to poison me?"

"Hmm." Teo looks thoughtful. Not for the first time, Sebastian wonders what he knows about his sister. "She's been on edge lately."

"Nicole?"

"Yes, Nicole." Matteo glares. "Contrary to what you think, women have feelings and personal experiences. Not just tits and ass."

"Hey, now."

The man speaks from experience. Not the stuff about emotions, though Seb knows that's true. But it's also true he's let his buddies think he's a cad. A good-time guy, a ladies' man. Not a guy who loves or hurts or has emotions deeper than a kiddie pool.

Seb clears his throat. "What are we supposed to do at a rehearsal dinner, anyway?"

"Rehearse something?" Matteo scowls at the crowd. "I should know this. Renee's been talking about scheduling ours."

"Right, but what are you rehearsing? Is it like target practice or something?"

Matteo looks unsure for the first time since... well, ever. "I'll look it up," Teo decides. "Or we can ask." He nods toward the farmhouse, and Seb looks to see Jen and Renee and Nicole stepping out onto the porch.

Dante's on their heels, a squirming puppy crooked in each enormous arm. The man scans Jen with adoration, and Seb knows for sure he's never seen his pal this happy.

Lucky bastard.

Lifting a hand, Seb waves them over. "Hey, guys. Over here." Time to play it cool with Nic, who's stunning in a body-hugging peach dress.

"Renee." Matteo says his fiancée's name like a religious rite, syllables sliding out in reverence. "Great dress."

"You like it?" Renee smooths a hand down the front. The two

of them trade a look Sebastian can't read as his gaze shifts to Nic's.

She's watching her brother with a knowing smile. "It's a Badgley Mischka ruffle floral print dress with an empire waist that Renee's totally rockin'." Nic reports this with a wink as she slides a look at Seb. "We got it at my favorite boutique in Portland."

If that's a clue, it's lost on him. Or rather, he's lost in Nic's eyes, green and glinting with sunlight as the breeze catches her dress hem and it flutters against his leg. She brushes it back, pink-tipped fingers catching the hem.

"Badgley Mischka?" He draws a breath and wonders what perfume she's wearing. Something flowery and mysterious. "That's a dressmaker or a style of dress?"

"Badgley Mischka is the designer, and empire waist is the style." Her eyes hold his, and he forgets about trying to decode her clues. There might not even be a clue. He's looking for something that's not there.

Dante sets the wriggling puppies on the grass. "Badgley and Mishka are good names for these guys. We've got fourteen more to name."

"Hey, buddy." Sebastian squats as a fuzzy black puppy chews his shoelace. "Probably not great for your teeth, you know."

"How cute are they?" Nic drops beside him in the grass as the rest of her family disappears, discussing dogs and dresses and whatever else they're talking about. Seb stops listening.

"Hi." Nicole's cheeks flush a little. "I didn't know you were already here."

"Got here twenty minutes ago." He tries to play it cool as he pets the other puppy, a white one with brown spots. "I feel like we've already screwed up this date. Was I supposed to pick you up or something?"

"We already discussed this, remember?" She rubs the black pup's belly as it flops by her knee. "I'm staying here to help Jen with wedding stuff. It wouldn't make sense for you to pick me up."

"Then how am I supposed to bust out my best moves in the backseat of my car later?"

"Charming." Nic rolls her eyes. "For the record, you'd have to do a lot better than sweaty sex in a BMW."

"For the record, I'm up to the task." He does his best not to notice her shiver. "Point me to the nearest horizontal surface, and I'll rock your world." He considers that. "Or vertical. I'm flexible."

"You're also a pig." She doesn't sound bothered by that. "Speaking of pigs, how perfect is it that Dante's pig is their flower girl?"

Seb follows her gaze and yep—there's Zsa Zsa trotting by the big man's side. Dante squats and sets another armload of puppies on the grass. The pig snuffles them as the pups roll and tumble in the grass. One gives a yip, and the puppy next to Seb perks up.

"Is that your friend over there?" He scratches its brown and white backside. "Should we say hi?"

"Now you've done it." Nic laughs as the new pups scamper toward them, plowing through too-tall grass. "It's a puppy stampede."

"With pigs and horses and chickens as an audience." Seb sits cross-legged to make more lap room. For Nic or for puppies, he's not particular. "I can already see this is Dante's dream wedding."

"Jen's, too."

Seb smiles. "No wonder they're perfect together."

He sounds like a damn Hallmark movie, but Nic's distracted by dogs. She opens her arms as the puppies fling their furry bodies at them. "Hey, guys!"

The pups skip her and leap for Seb, scrambling up his legs and into his lap. He laughs and throws a hand out so he doesn't fall backward. "Jeez. That's a lot of tongue for a first date." He sputters as a puppy licks his ear. "You can't buy me a drink first?"

Nic's watching with a look he can't read. Bemusement or wariness or something almost sweet. Freeing his face from tongues, he checks to make sure no one's listening. Just the puppies, none of whom look to be bugged.

"What were you hinting about back there?" he asks.

"Hinting?" She looks truly perplexed.

"Something about Renee's dress?"

He's mulled for days on the encrypted words from The Union. *"The dressmaker was dirty."*

He still can't figure it out.

"Oh. It wasn't about that." Nic laughs and shakes her head. "Don't tell me you haven't noticed."

"Noticed what?" Color him clueless.

"Renee and Teo? How she only had water with dinner last Friday. Or the way she keeps touching her belly. Or how Matteo's sticking to her like creepy cling wrap?"

"Matteo's always like that." Seb puts the puzzle pieces together. "She's pregnant?"

"Beats me." Nic pets the black and white puppy licking Seb's ear. "But that's my guess. Figured you'd seen the same things I had."

"Huh." It hadn't crossed his mind. "You catch a lot of clues I miss."

"Only when it involves women." She studies him like she's just piecing it together. "That's your weakness."

"No shit."

He didn't mean to say that. Concentrates hard on scratching a puppy's ear so he won't have to address it. "What I lack in perception, I make up for in charm."

"No shit." It sounds way less cheerful from Nic. "You've got that in spades, Minty Fresh."

"Charm?" Three puppies climb his abs like a ladder, scrambling to get to his face. "Why do I think that's not a compliment?"

"Oh, hey!" Nic grins as the fourth puppy chews the toe of his shoe. "Maybe you're perceptive with women after all."

"Still not thinking that's a compliment."

She rubs the shoe chewer's ears and looks away. As Nic scans the crowd, Seb gets the sense her heart's not really in their sparring. Nic sighs. "She should be here."

Not much perception needed to know who she means. "Your grandma?"

"Yeah." Nic's gaze swings back to his. "She didn't care much about marriage. Not for herself, anyway. But she always wanted better for us. For Jen and Matty and—" She stops, frowning. "Anyway, she would have loved this. Jen getting hitched here at the farm?"

He's missing something, isn't he? Something more obvious than the way Renee touches her belly and smiles at Matteo by the barn. Guests stroll the pasture, no one in a hurry to rehearse anything. A crowd near the barn snacks from big bowls of kettle corn. Three guys with guitars strum near a row of vines. A fall breeze shifts with the cinnamon smell of leaves and ripe grapes. It's a perfect, bucolic scene.

Still, something makes his arms prickle. He shifts closer to Nic, swinging his gaze back to hers.

"Are we supposed to be doing something here?" He should maybe admit he's not sure how rehearsal dinners work.

"Hell if I know." Nic shrugs. "Jen told us to go enjoy ourselves. Said she wasn't even sure she planned to rehearse anything except maybe wearing the dress."

"She wants to practice wearing the dress?" He didn't know that was a thing. "I thought it was bad luck for the groom to see the bride before the wedding."

Nic tucks a shock of blond hair behind her ear. "You don't strike me as superstitious, Minty Fresh."

"I'm not."

"Neither is Jen." Nic shrugs. "Jen doesn't get glammed up

much. I guess she wants us all to play with puppies for a while, and then she'll put on the dress. Maybe we'll eat sandwiches or something."

"That's a rehearsal, huh?"

"For the Bello family?" Another shrug. "Yep."

"Huh." The puppy chewing Seb's shoe takes a break, and Nic rubs the rounded egg belly with her pink-painted fingertips.

He'd kill to have her touch him like that. He'd also kill not to be a loser, getting jealous of a dog.

Nic looks up like she's read his thoughts. "Uh-oh."

"What?"

She points at his shirt. "Your charm might win you all the puppies, but it also gets you piddled on."

Sebastian looks down and— "Damn." Warm wetness seeps through the cotton. He frowns and tugs on his shirt. "Shit."

"Technically, just pee." Nic laughs. "Still gross. I'm sorry."

Seb tugs on his shirt again. "I'd let someone pee on me any day of the week if I knew it made you smile like that."

"Your charm knows no bounds. It's a wonder I'm not naked already."

"Lucky for you, you're my date." He grins and watches her flush.

"Regretting it by the minute. Come on."

She gets to her feet and offers a hand up, but Seb waves her off. "Where are we headed?"

"You've got a spare shirt in Jen's laundry room."

"I do?" He's not in the habit of shedding clothes at friends' houses. "I think I'd remember stripping at your sister's place."

"Clearly not." She starts for the farmhouse, and Seb trails her like a puppy.

Real puppies follow, nipping his heels as they all cross the pasture. "Wait—that time AJ knocked his grape juice on me?"

"Bingo. You stripped down to your T-shirt so Jen could use the stain stick. Never came back to get your shirt."

"Guess I forgot." Is it a sign that she remembers him stripping?

"You're a dumbass." Dante comes around a corner of the barn with two more puppies in his arms. "Got yourself peed on?"

Seb looks at his shirt. "I don't know why everyone's making it sound like I asked for it."

"Maybe you did." Nic looks at Dante. "Are you and my sister rehearsing something at some point?"

"Dunno." Dante sets the puppies down and pauses to scratch his pig's ears. Zsa Zsa grunts at the newest batch of wriggling canines. "I'm in charge of puppies. Not sure about anything else."

Sebastian scans the field until he finds Jen. She's in cutoff shorts and cowboy boots, leading a thoroughbred through a field. AJ and another kid cling to the saddle, laughing as Renee runs along taking photos.

Seb looks back at Dante. "If this is your idea of a rehearsal dinner, the wedding's gonna kick ass."

"That's the plan." Dante lumbers back to wherever he keeps getting puppies. There must be a pen of them somewhere, or maybe they're spurting like stardust from some puppy black hole.

"Must be nice," Seb murmurs. "Knowing exactly what you want."

Nic looks startled, and he knows he's spoken out loud. Her lips part, and he aches to kiss her again. "What do *you* want, Minty Fresh?"

So many things. Redemption. Forgiveness. *Her.*

"I want," he says slowly, "to change out of this wet shirt."

She pats his abs beside the pee stain. "Good plan."

He follows her to the door as Nic calls out to Dante where they'll be. "Tell Jen to text if she needs help rehearsing anything."

"Yeah." Dante sets another pair of puppies in the grass. "The schedule's real important."

Nicole grabs Seb's arm and pulls him through the door,

throwing him a smile that makes his heart drum harder. "I don't think they're in a big hurry to practice getting married."

He tugs the wet cotton off his abs. "More time to practice for the honeymoon."

"That's my kid sister." She's trying to sound scandalized, but the smile in her voice says otherwise.

"Newsflash," Seb says. "Your baby sister's getting banged by Dante every chance she gets."

"And loving every minute of it, I'm sure." Nic rolls her eyes. "Can we be done discussing my sister's sex life?"

"You started it." Or did she? He's not sure anymore.

Seb follows her down the hall, not even sure where she's going. He'd follow her to the landfill if she kept smiling like that.

"I'm glad she found someone," Nic's saying. "After that asshat she dated before—"

"Johnny?"

"Yeah, Johnny." Surprise fills her eyes as she turns in a doorway to face him. "I forget sometimes how long you've been hanging around."

"You make me sound like a puppy."

Her mouth twitches. "That explains my urge to whack you with a rolled-up newspaper."

"And my urge to hump your leg?"

Nic shakes her head. "You're a pig."

"Oink." Seb tugs his shirt as she leads him through a room he's never seen. A sewing table fills one corner, mounded with piles of bright fabric and an old Singer machine like Terri has.

An ancient washing machine lines the opposite wall, with an equally ancient dryer beside it. There's a rack on one wall with a big white wedding gown blooming below.

Seb turns in a circle to take it in. "What is this place?"

"Nondi's sewing room," Nic says. "Jen's sewing room now, though Dante does more sewing than she does." She points to a hook beside the door. "He even irons."

"Dante ironed my shirt?" He touches the sleeve and yep—that's definitely his. The same man who dug shrapnel out of his arm is now ironing his apparel.

Nic shrugs like it's not that weird. "That's their agreement—Jen washes, Dante irons."

"Huh." There are aspects to his friend's domesticity that he never imagined. "One day you're snapping the neck of the Duke's attempted assassin, the next you're measuring starch."

That's hopefully not a secret since it made headlines in Dovlano. Nic doesn't look surprised. "Strip, so we can get that soaking."

"Anytime, babe." Sebastian unbuttons his shirt.

Nic tries to roll her eyes, but they snag on his abs. "Good Lord, Minty Fresh—do you do sit-ups in between patients?"

He combs his brain for a smooth line. "You can touch, but I'm covered in pee."

That wasn't a smooth line.

She laughs anyway and points to a utility sink. "Soak your shirt in here. I'll grab a rag."

As she disappears, he strips off the shirt and drops it in the sink. Scrubs and splashes and gets his hands good and sudsy. Feeling her behind him, he looks over his shoulder. "Anyone tell you that you shouldn't sneak up on people like that?"

"Yes." She hands him a soapy washcloth. "Right before I put a bullet between their eyes."

He didn't need to know that.

And yet... he kinda did.

"What was your first job?" He goes back to scrubbing, surprised he hasn't asked this yet. "Your first target. Clint?"

"No." Her voice sounds stony as her eyes spear his back. "I couldn't find him right away. Settled for taking out a doctor."

"A doctor?"

"Surgeon." She steps to the side, boosting herself up on the washer. Her heels drum the door with a hollow clang. "A hand surgeon who liked backhanding the women he dated."

"Shit." Seb doesn't like the story, but he likes having Nic where he can see her. Still scrubbing, he keeps her in his periphery. "How'd you know this doctor?"

"One of the women he dated was a friend of mine from college. Agatha." As she draws a breath, he sees her breasts move. "He turned the cops against her. Convinced them Aggie's the one hitting *him*. The guy's got money and power and status, and who's going to believe some underpaid social worker over a surgeon? Didn't take much to convince them all she's crazy. Stressed, volatile, overly emotional—you know the drill."

He wishes he didn't. "What happened?"

"I wanted to make sure." Nic folds her arms. "I'm all for trusting women—especially Aggie—but I needed proof. I wired a hidden camera to catch the next time he hit her. It happened, obviously. Because it always happens."

"Then what?" Part of him already knows.

"The asshole skated." Her voice goes hard and pointy. "Apparently, it's illegal to tape someone without their knowledge in the great state of California. Did you know that?" The sharpness in her voice tells him not to answer. "She was still struggling to make a case when he hit her again. Harder this time. Knocked out half her teeth. She had to eat through a straw for a month. And if that wasn't bad enough, she learned he had another girlfriend. Want to know how she found out?"

"No." He definitely doesn't.

But he needs to hear it. Nic needs to tell it.

"They met in the hospital." Nic chokes out a laugh that's not a laugh at all. "How's that for irony? She met the other woman at physical therapy and started swapping pics on their phone. Turns out they had the same boyfriend. The same reason for being in the hospital."

"Jesus."

"And the same reason they couldn't win against him. Too much money. Too much power. And they both used to sleep with him, so—" She shrugs, eyes going glassy. "There's the *love* thing to contend with."

She says *love* like it's a bad word. He can't blame her.

"Anyway, I took him out. Heart attack. Fitting, don't you think?"

He's not sure what to think. "How?"

"Nondi knew a lot about poison." Nic bangs her heels against the washing machine. "Like Grandma used to say—no need to make a mess with guns when arsenic does a cleaner job."

Jesus. "And Terri taught me how to get stains out of whites." He stops scrubbing his shirt and looks at it. "I think I'm done here."

"Good." Reaching between her legs, she swings open the door of the washing machine. "Toss it in the machine and we'll finish it off."

"Thanks." He shifts to the space between her thighs. Swear to God, he doesn't mean to brush her breasts with his shoulders. It's not on purpose.

Neither is Nic's sharp inhale. "Nice boob graze, Minty Fresh."

"Sorry." He *is* sorry. That's if she wants him to be. Something in her eyes says she might not. "I can move."

"Don't." She grabs him by a belt loop and jerks him close. "Tell me *your* most memorable job."

Seb's jaw tightens. "No."

"No?" Nic lifts a brow. "Why not?"

"Because I don't like remembering that stuff." Some jobs more than others. "I don't like sharing."

She tilts her head. "I shared with you."

"You didn't have to.

"Fair enough." Her eyes sweep his. "I thought we were opening up."

She thought wrong. Seb doesn't open. About childhood

bedwetting, sure. But nothing that matters. Not in a way that lets her see who he really is. What he's done.

He pulls a shaky breath and starts to draw back. Nic hooks her ankles behind his butt. "Hey. Was it something I said?"

Sebastian's heart hurts. He thinks it's his heart, anyway. It's been a while since he looked for it. "What will it take to make you drop this?"

Nic's lips part. "What are my choices?"

Is he imagining the invitation in her eyes? It's a risk he's willing to take. "Let's make a bet."

Challenge makes her eyes flash. "What kind of bet?"

He shifts between her thighs, and her eyes flash again. Maybe it's not the challenge. "Let me get you off."

"Doesn't sound like a bet to me." Her voice goes breathy. "Need a refresher on how gambling works?"

"I'm good." The word *gambling* chills his core, but the heat in her eyes thaws it out. Hot, cold, love, hate, desire, regret... it's almost too much to process.

Don't think about Pop.

Don't think about Pop.

Nic must read something in his eyes because she grabs another belt loop. "Hey. I'm teasing, okay?"

He nods until he finds his voice. "I can get you off without laying a hand on you."

Nic blinks. "What?"

"Five minutes or less," he says. "I'll make you come without lifting a finger."

One blond brow lifts. "Magical as your cock may be, penetration alone doesn't do it for most women."

Something tells him she's not most women. Not the point, though. "No penetration, either."

Both brows go up this time. "What, like some magic phallic voodoo? Abra-ca-dickra? Presto-chimbo?"

Sebastian frowns. "*Chimbo?*"

"It's penis slang in Colombia. Weirdly enough, it means 'fake' in Paraguay and 'worn out' in Venezuela." Nic gives him a sweet smile. "All phallic words, if you think about it."

They're getting off track here. "So that's the bet. Five minutes or less, I make you come. No hands."

Now she's intrigued. "What are we betting?"

This part he hasn't thought through. Seb's good at improvising, though. "If I get you off, I win."

"What do you win?"

"My mouth on you." He grins as her thighs clench his hips. "If I lose, you can write 'Seb's a lousy lover' in lipstick on my bare chest and make me walk across the pasture."

"Sounds distracting at a rehearsal dinner." A flush runs from her chest to her throat, so Seb knows he's getting to her.

"I won't lose." He's damn sure of it. "And we both know the closest they'll get to rehearsing anything is target practice."

He's got her there. Nic licks her lips. "I don't even like you."

That's a lie. "Yet you're considering it."

She doesn't deny it. Just holds his gaze with hers. "You're a pig."

"And still you're considering it."

Her breasts move as she draws a breath. "If I agree to this—"

Seb drops to his knees before the words leave her mouth. Shoulders her thighs apart as his fingers hook the waistband of her panties. He's careful not to touch her, to pinch the fabric with his fingers. A deal is a deal.

"Hey." She says it in that same breathy voice. A voice that's muffled, thanks to her thighs pressing his ears. "Don't you want to hear my conditions?"

He drags her panties down her thighs, groaning to see she's slick with need. He hasn't misjudged. Not this, anyway. "Do any of your conditions preclude me from putting my mouth on you?"

"No." Nic spreads her thighs and frees his ears. "But I'm not returning the favor. And you're not getting inside me, Minty Fresh."

She means more than penetration. That much he knows. "Understood."

"Why?" She breathes it on a squeak as he tastes the creamy softness of her thigh. "What's in it for you?"

"This." He slides his tongue along her seam, and Nic groans. She's sweeter than he imagined, honey on his tongue.

Nic opens her legs, fingers threading through his hair. "Jesus, Seb. You don't waste any time."

Time. He doesn't have much of it. "You're watching the clock?"

"I—yes." The word squeaks out as he sucks her clit between his lips. God, she's wet. He aches to slip a finger inside, but a bet's a bet.

"How am I doing?"

He means the time, but Nic moans. "Not bad."

A laugh slips out as he slides his tongue through her folds. "Mmm, I could stop."

"No!" Her thighs grip his head, and her voice goes muffled again. "Annanessuwantu."

The translator in his brain hears "not unless you want to," so he keeps going. He wants this more than anything. More than cake or cars or self-steering bullets.

Don't think about that. Think of what you're doing.

What he's doing is driving Nic Bello to the edge. He feels it in the quiver of her thighs. Hears it in her hushed cries. Tastes it in the rush of her arousal.

The tip of his tongue swirls her clit, and she arches up to meet him. "Jesus fucking Christ."

His thoughts exactly. This moment, these breathless seconds with his mouth on her is the closest he's come to feeling holy. Feeling worthy and good, like he's not some fake-charm fuckup.

He's going down on Nic Bello. How bad can he be?

"God, you're great at that."

See? She's gripping his hair, panting as she arches up again. "Don't stop."

He wouldn't dream of it. If she'd let him, he'd do this all night, all week, all year, hell, a whole lifetime of just—

"Oh, God!" Her scream tears through the earmuffs of her thighs as she tilts against his tongue. His hands ache to grip her thighs, to pull her close so he can do this right.

No touching, he reminds himself, and wonders what's wrong with him.

"Fuck, fuck, fuck, *fuck!*"

So, he's doing okay without hands. Teasing her clit, he brings her down gently. Nic goes slack against his tongue. Her thighs relax, and Seb knows it's over. His moment of glory, gone as her breath goes back to normal.

"Holy shit." She groans the words as she sits up on the washer. "Not a word, you smug bastard."

As pillow talk goes, it's not bad. "How long?"

Nic grits her teeth. Blows a shock of tousled hair off her face so she can see the clock. "Three minutes and sixteen seconds."

"Excellent." He gets to his feet and adjusts the front of his pants. "I win."

"What did I say about being smug?" She stretches so her breasts strain the buttons on her peach dress. "Fine. Go ahead and gloat." Nic yawns. "It'll take me a minute to muster up the energy to get mad."

"Get mad I got you off? You've got some fucked up anger issues, Rogue."

She blinks and he backtracks. "Sorry. Didn't mean to use your—"

"No, it's fine." She shakes her head, looking dazed as he hands off her panties. "I just—Not many people call me that. Not since Nondi. Not to my face, anyway."

Great. He gets her off, then reminds her of her grandma. "Can we forget I said that?"

"Why?" She hops off the washer and mops up with a tissue. That shouldn't be sexy. "It's something we have in common, Seb. We're both operators. Both good at separating emotion from action."

"Yeah." She's wrong on all counts. He's not like her at all. She's bright and kind and good hearted, while he's a phony asshole hiding behind fake charm.

He's not even with her on the platonic thing.

Seb makes a show of licking his lips. "That beat the hell out of the Costco sandwich trays." He waits for her to call him a pig. Needs to hear it, more than anything.

But Nic just laughs and pulls her panties up over her hips. "Thanks, Seb. That—you really are good at that."

"No problem." Breathing through the ache in his chest, he leans against the dryer and waits for his hard-on to fade. "Should we get back out there?"

Nic sighs. "Probably." She shoots a pointed look at his crotch. "I might be regretting my decision."

He tenses. "About me going down on you?"

"About penetration." She pats the front of his pants. "You're clearly packing more than a pocket pistol."

He laughs because it's easier than begging her to keep touching him. "Just say the word."

"Hocus-penis?" She stretches to grab a TidePod from a shelf. "Shazanaconda? Alakazamboner? Let me know when I say the right word."

How is it possible to want someone this much? A good sign he shouldn't have her.

Seb steps back again. "Dante's probably wondering what's taking so long."

"Dante knows damn well what's taking so long." She flips a

switch on the washer. "Remind me to slip back in here in an hour to toss your shirt in the dryer."

"Okay." He turns away because he can't do this part. The benign banter. The meaningless chatter. A hundred times, a thousand, he's ended sex that way. Like it meant nothing at all.

But what happened here means everything. It's never been like this before, so he keeps backing up until he hits the window. Turns to draw the curtain so he can scan the pasture.

"Doesn't look like anyone's rehearsing anything."

"Are you surprised?" Nic puts a hand on his back. "Hey."

"Hey." He doesn't turn to look at her.

"You okay?"

"Yeah, why?"

A pause. "You got kinda quiet there. Did I do something wrong?"

Seb shuts his eyes. Lets the curtain drop from his hands, but he doesn't turn around. "You came on my face and then complimented my cock." Gluing on a grin, he faces her. "I'd say you ticked all the boxes for doing everything right."

"Pig." She slugs him in the arm, and Seb lets out a breath.

He's still got it. He can hold it together just fine when his dream girl tunnels too deep into his brain.

Nic moves away, fingers trailing the sleeve of the wedding dress hanging against the wall. "This was our mother's dress. Nondi brought it all the way from Dovlano."

"It's nice." That's what he's supposed to say about a wedding dress, right? "Jen's wearing it for the wedding?"

"Yeah. It fits her perfectly." Nic bites her lip. "Nondi felt bad there's just the dress now."

"Just the dress?"

She shrugs and straightens the hem. "There's a ring. One passed down through Nondi's line to the women in the family." Her voice quivers. "It went missing when our mom was murdered."

Shit. "Nic." He touches her arm. "I'm sorry."

"About a ring?" She shrugs and steps back. "I'm not big on jewelry, anyway."

It doesn't take a genius to see she's dodging the subject. They're alike in that way.

Sensing she'd rather not talk, Seb studies the dress like he's mesmerized by seed pearls and lace. He peers at the neckline shaped in a satin vee with— "What does that tag say?" He squints to read it.

"Huh?" Nic moves close enough to touch him. Does her best to sound out the words. "'Orgistla sra morello tu pa calla dopiste' and then a weird, wavy logo." She frowns. "I don't know what any of that means."

He looks at her. "You know three regional definitions of a Spanish word for boner and you don't speak Dovlanese?"

"I speak some, but my reading's not great." Her chin tips up. "You read Dovlanese?"

He nods and touches the tag, straightening it to be sure of what he's reading. "I did a tour of duty in Dovlano. It's where I met—friends." He won't mention Teo and Dante. "I've always had a knack for language. Picked it up real quick, since Dovlanese has a lot in common with Italian."

"And you also speak Italian." She doesn't sound surprised. "What does the tag say?"

"It says 'proudly custom made for you by the house of DeCosta.'" He touches the logo. "I mean, I'm ninety-nine percent sure that's the DeCosta family crest."

Nic blinks. "DeCosta?"

Seb watches the blood drain from her face. "Shit."

"It's a common name." She backs up like the dress burned her. "Right?"

Seb just shakes his head. "What are the odds it's a coincidence?"

"Not high." She looks at the gown. "*'The dressmaker was dirty.'*"

Holy shit. "It wasn't about your red dress at all."

"Maybe not." She bites her lip. "That doesn't make sense. What would the DeCosta family have to do with my mother's dress?"

Wheels roll in his head. He's missing parts of the story, since Teo hasn't told him much. "What do you know about how your parents died?"

Nic hesitates. He sees in her face she's ready to lie to him.

"My dad fucked around."

Sebastian blinks. "I'm sorry?"

"Do *not* tell my sister." Nic starts to pace. "Or Matteo. It would kill them. I'm not even supposed to know."

"How did you—" Maybe that's not the right question. "What does infidelity have to do with a dress?"

"It's just a hunch, okay?" Nic lets out a long breath. "Nondi let it slip once. She said my dad made poor choices."

"Worse than getting involved with the Dovlanese mob?"

Nic levels him with a look. "She said this in the context of explaining why you can't trust everyone." Something in her eyes tells him to read between the lines. "Said my mother had a friend —a fashion designer, I guess. That my father got too close, and my mom issued an ultimatum."

Seb looks at the dress. He's still not sure he sees the connection. "The House of DeCosta. You think that's your mom's friend?"

"It would make sense, wouldn't it? If there's some connection between the person who made this dress and the reason my parents got gunned down? And if it's all tied up somehow with this big Dovlanese crime family."

It would make sense. Maybe that's why he's suspicious. "Your mother—she was Nondi's daughter?"

Nic nods, eyes darting to the dress. "Are you thinking Nondi set out to avenge her death?"

It's a leap. A big one. But Seb's landed bigger jumps than that. "Would that be something she'd do?"

"Revenge?" Nic chokes out a laugh. "Oh, yeah. Revenge is Nondi's specialty. She didn't like to talk about my parents, but I know she felt responsible. That she left instead of staying in Dovlano to get them out." She shakes her head. "My mother was her only child. Her baby. Nondi never got over that."

Wheels turn in Seb's head. "You're sure they're dead?"

She squeezes her eyes shut. "Yes. Jen watched it happen. She was three years old, so thank God she doesn't remember much. Then Matty came and found them and—" She trails off, eyes still closed. "There's no doubt they're gone."

"Same with my dad." He's not sure why he's volunteering this. Maybe he feels like he owes her. "Okay, so we're sure your parents really passed."

"Yes." Opening her eyes, she meets his and nods. "So now what? We track down the dress designer, find the connection, and then—what?"

He opens his mouth to say something. To offer comfort or kisses or whatever she needs.

Boom!

The explosion rocks him back. Grabbing Nic, he drops to the ground. Shields her with his body as the house shakes and his heart bangs a fist against his ribs.

CHAPTER 8

*N*ic's half a step ahead of Seb as she sprints onto Jen's front porch with her Glock unholstered. "Who's hurt?"

"No one." Renee runs for the house with AJ in her arms, mommy smile pasted in place. "The wedding fireworks feel a little scary, so we're going in for lemonade."

"Good idea." Seb hides his gun as Renee slips past with a curly-haired brunette behind her.

"Lovely to meet you." The woman shifts a toddler on her hip and gives a mom smile of her own. "Bree Bracelyn-Dugan. My husband's the guy with the service revolver."

Seb scans the crowd. "That… might not narrow it down."

Hiding her weapon, Nic steps closer to Seb. Police Chief Dugan—Dante's pal from Ponderosa Resort—is not the only armed guest. A guy she recognizes as the husband of Lady Isabella Blankenship moves with military precision, ushering guests through a smoke-filled pasture. Dante introduced Bradley Parker as an Army sharpshooter who's also a doctor, the latter tacked on like a lesser credential.

"Jen!" Spotting her sister, Nic sighs with relief. "You're okay."

"All the animals are safe." Jen's got a puppy in each arm and a third one strapped in a baby carrier on her chest. "Don't ask," she says when she sees Nic eyeing it. "Could someone see if Dante needs help in the barn?"

"You go," Nic says when Seb looks at her. "I'll help Jen."

With a nod, he starts toward the barn. Pauses like he wants to kiss her, but the moment's gone. It's the least of her worries now.

"Ask if he needs help with the horses," Jen shouts as Sebastian walks away. "No shooting anyone."

That Jen needs to say this at her wedding rehearsal gives Nic a kick of sadness. "What happened?" She scoops up a pair of puppies yapping at Jen's heels. "No one's hurt?"

"There was an explosion in that old storage shed on the east edge of the property." Jen jogs up the steps, and Nicole follows to the spare room. It's a makeshift puppy nursery, complete with pens and chew toys and a pee corner. "Only thing we had out there was the International truck." Jen unhooks the baby carrier and takes out a puppy. Puts it in the pen before she turns to Nic. "That truck could withstand a nuclear blast."

Or a plummet down a hillside with its brakes cut. Nic's guts squeeze as she recalls how her sister knows this firsthand. "You're sure you're okay?"

"I'm fine. Dr. Parker checked the two people standing near the barn at the time. They're both fine." Jen holds out her arms. "Puppies, please?"

She hands one over, and Jen takes her time inspecting him. Nic does the same with her sister, noting a rip in Jen's shirt. "Is that from the explosion?"

"What?" Jen looks down and rolls her eyes. "Puppy teeth. Will you relax?"

Like that's an option. She's itching to get outside, to chase down whoever did this.

"Don't bother." Jen's reading her mind.

"What?" She does her best to look innocent, but Jen's not

buying it.

"If someone did this on purpose, they're long gone," Jen says. "Matty ran straight into the explosion, because *of course he did.*"

"He's okay?"

"Of course. Went in with guns blazing; came out pissed he didn't find anyone." Jen sighs. "Was it too much to ask for a wedding rehearsal where nothing exploded?"

"In this family?"

"Right." Jen sets down the puppy and hands Nic the baby carrier. "Could you give this back to Renee on your way out?"

Because of course Nic's heading back out. "Renee brought a baby carrier?" It's way too small for AJ.

"Bree Bracelyn brought it for Renee 'just in case.'"

Nic grins. "Like it's not totally obvious by now she's knocked up."

Jen gives her a pointed look. "Guess we all have reasons for keeping secrets."

"Guess so." Seems like the wrong time to admit getting frisky with Seb in the sewing room. Or finding clues in Jen's wedding dress. "I should get back out there."

She really should. But how can she leave her baby sister? "What do you think happened?"

"I'm hardly the explosives expert in the family," Jen says dryly. "But that's where the fertilizer's stored. *Was* stored."

"Yikes."

"Could be an accident." Another look from Jen. "But Teo didn't seem to think so. You don't either."

It's not a question, so Nic doesn't argue. "The timing seems odd."

Jen lets out a long breath. "I'm calling off brunch tomorrow."

"What? Jen, no—"

"I didn't want to do it, anyway." She tucks some hair behind her ear. "I just want to get married, okay? Screw all the rehearsals and brunches and showers and whatever the hell else people say we're supposed to do. I just want a goddamn wedding to the man I love."

A fist grips Nic's heart. "You sounded like Nondi just then."

"Yeah?" Jen smiles. "I wish she could be here."

"Same."

Or maybe she *is* here. Maybe that's what the explosion is about. There's no way to know until Nic gets back out there.

"Come on." Jen grabs her arm and starts back through the house. "I need to check animals, and you need to run around outside with Teo trying to figure out what happened instead of babysitting me."

Nic goes with her, stopping to set the baby carrier outside the door where Renee and Bree sing toddler songs to the kids inside. Her inner childcare provider aches to assist, but her skills are better used elsewhere.

When she joins Jen on the porch, they survey the sooty crowd. "It really was a nice rehearsal," Nic offers.

"Thanks." Jen's smile turns wistful. "Nondi would have loved it."

Nic nods. "She would have."

"I'm going to the sheep barn." Jen grabs her in a hug, squeezing so tight Nic wheezes. "Bye!"

"Be careful," Nic calls, and Jen flips her the bird over one shoulder.

Well. Can't blame a big sister for trying. Nic studies the crowd, alert for injuries, for guilty looks, for anyone fleeing the scene with a detonator in one hand.

Nothing.

Of course, if *she* wired a bomb at a wedding rehearsal, the last thing she'd do is run. A slow leisurely stroll from the scene once the drama dies down. That's key to looking inconspicuous. To blending with the crowd and—

She scowls at the far pasture. A lone figure, bland and unrecognizable, moves slowly down the tree-shaded trail. A neighbor on a nature walk? Could be. It's the edge of the property where forest gobbles up green fields, a piney thicket splitting Jen's land from the next farm. As Nic watches, the figure in tan pants and an off-white top slips through the trees.

Something in the posture pings her memory. A whisper of nostalgia, a flicker of recognition.

Nondi?

"You okay?" Dante stops on the steps with a lamb in his arms.

"Fine." Nic stares at the trees. "Has anyone checked the grapevines to the north?"

"Huh?" Dante scowls. "You're thinking vineyard sabotage?"

"Could be." It's hardly her theory but sounds as good as any. "I'll go look for anything suspicious."

"Careful." Dante looks at her. "I don't need to tell you that, do I?"

"Nope. But thanks anyway."

"Yeah." A long pause from Dante. "He's a good guy, you know."

She's already taken one step off the porch when she stops. "Who?"

"Sebastian."

"Why are you saying that?"

Dante's icy eyes scan hers. "I see how he looks at you. How you look at him."

"I don't—"

"Don't let Matteo scare you off from what you want."

She has no idea what she wants. "Okay."

Her soon-to-be-brother-in-law takes a step back. "Take care." Turning away, Dante walks off with his lamb.

Well, that was... weird. And kinda sweet.

No time for that now.

Nic takes off at a run, zig-zagging up the hill in case anyone takes a pot shot. She's a sitting duck in the open like this, but she has to know if Nondi's out here. Besides, if someone wants her dead, they've had their chances.

"Disla." She calls the word for "grandma," keeping her voice low in case the bad guys know Dovlanese.

But the word means "mentor," too, and she'll fall back on that if she has to. "Hello?"

The crack of a twig whips her focus to a tree up ahead. She creeps closer, tiptoeing through old oaks and underbrush. Thank God she had the good sense to wear flats. A woman never knows when she'll need to chase bad guys through the woods.

Or good guys. Who is she after, anyway?

Goosebumps spray the back of her neck, and she spins with the Glock in her grip.

"Just me." Seb steps out from behind a tree and puts his hands up. There's a Walther PPS M2 in the right one. "Saw you head up here and thought you might need someone guarding your six."

"Thanks." He's lucky she's not the sort to shoot first and ask questions later. "Did you see anyone moving this way?"

"Besides you? No."

Dammit. Maybe her eyes played tricks on her. Showed her what she wants to see instead of what's real. "Any word on what blew up?"

"Radio-controlled explosive device." His voice sounds grim. "Someone who knows what they're doing. If they wanted to kill everyone, they could have."

A warning shot, then. "The guests are all okay?"

"Yeah." A pause. "Thought I heard you calling someone just now."

It's clear from the question in his eyes that he heard her call her grandma. "I might've been mistaken." Nic curls her fingers into her palm. "Wishful thinking."

"I know how that goes." His expression softens. "Maybe you weren't mistaken."

She scans the trees again. Whoever's out here won't be found. Not with a head start and a plan on their side. Leaning toward Seb, she keeps her voice low. "It doesn't make sense," she whispers. "Nondi wouldn't sabotage Jen's wedding. I doubt she'd risk attending."

"Maybe whoever did this knows that." He frowns. "Or maybe they took a chance, thinking she'd risk the rehearsal and not the wedding."

"Or maybe it's a warning shot." It could be anything, honestly.

Recalling the figure in tan pants, Nic shivers. "I might've seen her."

"Nondi?"

"Yeah." But she's long gone now, and they're sitting ducks in the woods like this. Nic sighs. "Maybe it's a lost cause. If Nondi doesn't want to be found—"

"She doesn't want to be found by the bad guys." Seb looks her in the eye. "Maybe she wants *you* to find her?"

A warm slosh of feeling fills her belly. What if he's right?

Or what if Nic's delusional? If her grandma's not alive at all.

"Nondi," she calls. "If you're out here, give me a sign. Tell me what you want from me."

Seb threads his fingers through hers. Cups his other hand around his mouth to join the shouting. "Let us help."

It's futile, yelling through the trees at a phantom. But at least Nic's not alone. Since when is that a good thing?

Sebastian turns to face her. "Let me talk to Teo. Maybe he can dig something up."

"No." Dread pools in her gut. "If I'm wrong about Nondi being alive, it'll kill him."

"I won't say a word about your grandma." He puts up his palms. "Swear to God—I'll just gather intel on DeCosta. See if there's some connection we're missing."

Nic bites her lip. "Be discreet," she says. "Please."

"I will."

"I'll talk with my tech person, too. Maybe there's something she can shake loose."

"It's a plan." He puts out a palm. "Should we shake on it?"

The snap of a twig whips them both around.

"Are you idiots coming?" Jen's at the bottom of the hill beside a row of Pinot vines. She's changed into her wedding dress and stands holding a rifle. "Let's get this started before something else blows up."

Nic looks at Seb, who's trying hard not to laugh.

"I think your sister's okay." He slips an arm around her, and Nic allows it. Because she's nuts. Also because her legs are shaking.

"Okay," she says as they start down the hill. "Let's go rehearse something."

* * *

"JULIET?" Seb's whisper-hiss beneath her bedroom window jerks Nic's gaze off her laptop.

"'*But soft!*'" he calls. "*What light through yonder window breaks? It is the east, and Juliet is the sun.*'" Seb clears his throat. "Probably shoulda been a red flag for ol' Romeo. Sticking your dick in something that'll burn it seems like a bad idea."

"Are you crazy?" Nic throws open the second-story window and stares through the darkness. He's in dark jeans and a black hoodie, a Boy Scout out for a midnight hike. "I'm surprised Teo didn't shoot you on sight."

They glance at where her brother's camper sits angled by the barn. Teo's not taking chances leaving his family unguarded.

"I stopped, and we chatted." Sebastian shoves his hands in his pockets. "He said he'll leave shooting me up to you."

"As long as he helps get rid of the body." Is it weird they're joking like this? Nic leans out the window. "Did you hear Jen called off tomorrow's brunch?"

"Smart." Seb's eyes drift to her chest, and Nic looks down to see her top gaping open. She's deciding what to do about it when he speaks again. "So, no obligations 'til the wedding Sunday evening?"

"I guess." She trailed Jen all evening, offering help with wedding prep.

"Stop hovering. I'm *fine*." Jen shoved her toward the stairs. "Go weave doilies or something if you need to feel useful. Otherwise, let's meet again Sunday for the damn wedding."

"So." Seb clears his throat beneath the window. "You're off the hook for bridesmaid duties for a day."

"Guess so."

He studies the drainpipe that runs to her window. "Is that your childhood bedroom?"

"You are *not* coming up to defile it."

Seb taps the pipe and smiles. "You must've climbed down this an awful lot."

"Twenty-three seconds." Pride gets the best of her. "That's my record."

"Nice." Seb grabs the pipe. "Not as impressive as three minutes and sixteen seconds, but context matters."

"You are *not* coming up here." It's possible she took the screen off so he could. Still, it's a bad idea...

"Time me." He swings himself up. In less time than Nic needs to glance at her watch, he's at the windowsill.

"Here." She grabs his hand. "God, you're a heavy beast."

"Thanks." He heaves himself over the edge and lands with a thud on her floor. "I used to be better than that."

"Sneaking in women's bedroom windows?" It shouldn't surprise her. Who knows how many women besides the bookkeeper have sneaked him into bedrooms and offices, closets and sewing rooms—

"It won't happen again."

Seb blinks and gets to his feet. "We're not talking about me scaling your drainpipe anymore, are we?" His grin goes wolfish. "More like you on my drainpipe and—"

"Control yourself, Minty Fresh." She plops down on her bed, conscious of her breasts moving behind her thin cotton sleep tank. "You and I are *not* getting distracted by sex. We've got things to discuss."

"Good point." He folds his arms and leans on the wall. "Is that what you sleep in?"

"Sebastian, focus." She sighs and pulls on a hoodie so he'll stop staring at her breasts. Never mind that she kinda wants him to. "I had my source do some digging."

"Oh?"

She winces as her heart balls up tight. "Rumor has it Don Julio DeCosta shot my parents."

"Don Julio?"

"Father of Danny 'Duck Toes' DeCosta." She watches his face as it registers. "Yeah. Pretty sure that's not a coincidence. She also confirmed my dad had an affair."

"With whom?"

"Rosie Porecca." Her heart squeezes again. "Don Julio DeCosta's sister."

"Huh." Seb scratches his chin. "You mentioned an ultimatum earlier. Something Nondi told you?"

Nic sighs and looks at her hands. "From what I've gathered, this Rosie chick wanted my dad to leave my mom. My dad refused." When she looks up, Seb's watching her. "I guess she didn't take it well."

"Let me guess—she told her mobster brother, who took things into his own hands?"

She shrugs. "That's the theory."

"I'm sorry, Nic." Seb pushes off the wall and comes closer. "You want to talk about it? The stuff with your parents, I mean."

"No." Drawing a breath, she rifles through her feelings. "Sometimes, it's like my parents were part of some other life that happened a long time ago. That they didn't even exist. Nondi was a bigger part of my childhood, so…" She trails off, not sure what she means.

Seb must understand, because he drops the subject and starts to pace. Starts fidgeting with his keychain like he does when he's thinking. "All right, that's good info. We're on a roll."

"Yeah." Doesn't feel like it, but okay.

Sebastian keeps pacing. "Let's focus on the present. Did the Fire Marshall have any leads on the explosion?"

"Nothing you and Teo didn't know already. Radio-controlled device. Anyone could have planted it." Any number of bad guys wanting any number of family members gone. There's no shortage of that around here.

Nic tugs the zipper on her hoodie, restless and itching to touch him. "You said you talked to Teo. Any new info?"

"Just that Duck Toes was estranged from his family, which we already knew." Seb turns and snaps his fingers. "Oh, and an unsubstantiated rumor about Daddy Duck Toes."

"Don Julio DeCosta." She likes Seb's version better. "What's the rumor?"

"That Daddy disappeared himself on purpose. That he's not really dead. That he followed Junior here to Oregon, where he's been hiding out for years."

"Huh." She's not sure what to make of that. "If that were true, and if Nondi got wind of it—"

"She'd want revenge." Seb studies her. "Right? I mean, I never met her, but it fits what you've told me."

"Yeah." For all his faults, Sebastian LaDouceur is a decent listener. "She'd do whatever it took to take him out."

"Fake her own death?"

Nic nods through the pain in her temples. "Yes." The urge to have him closer sucks the breath from her lungs. She watches him pace, wishing she could touch him. Knowing she shouldn't. "Sit down, Minty Fresh. You're making me nervous stalking around like that."

"Yes, ma'am." With a quick salute, he sits beside her on the bed. His arm brushes hers as he surveys the space.

She looks at it with him, seeing her childhood bedroom through his eyes. Nondi's hand-sewn curtains. The stuffed animals she saved. The desk where Nic spent her formative years studying English and math and bomb-making.

She edges closer to Seb. "Thanks." She lets out a breath, feeling calmer already.

"No problem." Seb bumps her with his arm. "You okay?"

"Yeah." She leans against him. "Did Teo track down anything else?"

"Not really. Just a detail about the syndactyl thing running in their family. I guess all the DeCosta men have webbed toes."

"That's... random." She laughs. "Not likely that'll lead us to anything useful."

"You never know." A grin grabs the edges of his mouth. "Family traits track down killers all the time. I once took out a guy who'd been hiding six years. No one could find him 'til I learned he donated sperm in college, and I hacked a DNA database to—"

"Okay, point taken." Does he have to be smart *and* hot? His hair looks rumpled from his climb up the house, or maybe from being Sebastian. It's rough work being strong and sexy and charming and—

"Which of your parents had this?" Lifting a hand, she strokes the cowlick at the crown on his head. "Mother, father, or both?"

His eyes go dark. "Dunno."

"Really?" She smooths it again and feels him flinch beneath her hand. "For a guy who says he's dying to have his hands on me, you're not big on being touched."

"It's not that." He shuts his eyes, and Nic's not sure what to do. She strokes his hair again, and this time, he relaxes.

Relaxes and starts to speak. "My mom used to touch my hair like that."

"Oh." Nic pauses. "Should I stop?"

"No." He catches her wrist but doesn't open his eyes. "Keep doing it."

So, she does. She keeps her touch gentle, wondering if he'll share more. It's fine if he doesn't, but—

"She left when I was little." The words rumble out like a low purr.

Touching him feels precarious, like she's playing with fire. That doesn't stop her. "You want to tell me about your mom?"

"No."

"Okay."

"But I should." A sigh as he opens his eyes.

She nearly wishes he hadn't. The pain in those deep blue depths sucks the breath from her lungs. "My mom was career military." He frowns. "Still is, as far as I know. Last I checked, she's an Army attack pilot. Captain Greta Hulth-LaDouceur— one of America's first female Green Berets."

"Oh." It's not what she's expecting. "You're not close?"

A ragged laugh rips out of him. "Haven't seen her since I was eight. That's the day she sat me down and explained how America needed her more than I did. That I had to be brave and be good for my dad while she went off and fought for my freedom."

"Wow." All right, this explains some things. "She didn't come home?"

"Nope. Not once." He draws a breath and shuts his eyes again. "Got postcards a few times, but those stopped. Joined the Army myself, the instant I could." A muscle ticks near his eye. "We never crossed paths."

"I'm so sorry." What a way for a boy to grow up. "Was it hard for your dad?"

He flinches again, and she soothes him with fingers in his hair.

"He did okay. A great job raising me. Him and Terri." Seb

pauses. "My dad never talked about her, so I knew talking about my mom was off-limits."

"That sounds... grim." She almost said "dysfunctional," but who is she to talk?

"It wasn't, though." His lashes lift as he looks in her eye. "My dad was a great guy. We laughed and joked and had a good relationship. Simpsons marathons. Road trips to see our favorite stand-ups—Eddie Murphy, Sarah Silverman, Jerry Seinfeld. Even George Carlin before he died. The old man loved comedians."

It's making more sense by the minute. "He sounds like a good guy."

"The best." Seb draws a shaky breath. "Anyway, I let him down in the end. Couldn't bring my mom back. Couldn't save him. Couldn't even be the kind of dentist he was. The guy everyone in town comes to see."

Nic knows he's wrong there. "I've seen your parking lot, Minty Fresh. You've got families lined up three deep to get appointments."

Blue eyes flicker. "Notice anything about those families?"

"Not really." She combs her brain, but it's pointless. Wrangling preschoolers doesn't leave time for cataloguing Sebastian's patients. "Are they all juvenile hitmen or something?"

He laughs a little sadly. "That might be better, huh? Nah, it's all the moms bringing them. Moms who drop their keys in the lobby and bend down nice and slow to get them. Moms who write their numbers on the intake forms and make a big show of telling me it's their private cell."

"So you're a sex object." She bites back an urge to say *suck it up*. Every woman she knows has a thousand tales like this. "Doesn't make it right, even if you're a guy."

Seb blinks. "You don't think I'm a whiny-ass baby?"

"I think you're a guy who's made the best of a shitty situation. That deep down, you're a good guy."

He sighs and shakes his head. "That's where you're wrong."

"The assassin thing?" Nic snorts. "I'm the last person to judge."

"Not that." Seb draws a ragged breath. "You're right about me using charm as a weapon." With a grimace, he shuts his eyes. "A weapon that gets people killed."

Silence floats like a feather between them. She's almost afraid to ask. "Something happened?" She swallows hard, wanting to spare him the words. "Something with your father or—" She's grasping at straws here. "—With your mother?"

"No." His forced laugh sounds more like a wheeze. "I'm sure some shrink would say mommy issues."

"Who?" Dread sours her stomach. "A girlfriend?"

"Sort of." Another ragged laugh. "Mobster's wife. One of my earliest jobs. A job where I first met—friends."

Nic's guessing she knows the friends. Her brother. Her almost-brother-in-law. "Go on."

"The plan was to take the guy out quick. Bullet to the head, nice and neat." A long pause. "I had another plan."

"To get her out?"

"Yeah. We'd been seeing each other for months." He lets out a breath and doesn't open his eyes. "I'm not proud. I knew she was married, and I didn't care because I'm a selfish prick."

Nic notices the present tense but doesn't comment. Doesn't point out that a real selfish prick would never see himself that way. Seb's self-awareness isn't the issue. "What happened?"

"She was supposed to hide in the bathroom when the shooting started. To go out the window and wait for me to pick her up at the meeting spot." He flinches. "She didn't show."

Nic's mind spins the worst scenarios. The girl double-crossed him?

It's worse. "They got to her first." His throat rolls as he swallows. "I found her with a bullet in her head and a note pinned to her sleeve. 'Greta says goodbye.'"

"Greta." Pain sears Nic's heart. "Same as your mom?"

"Bingo." He opens his eyes and looks deep into hers. "Big time mommy issues." A choked laugh. "In case you need proof I'm as fucked up as they come."

"Sebastian, no." Releasing his hair, she cups his face instead. "You can't believe that."

"I can because it's easy. It's easy because it's true." He turns his head to nip at her wrist. "Doesn't mean we can't have some fun while we—"

"Stop it." She forces him to face her, gripping his chin. "You've got more defense mechanisms than anyone I've ever met, and yeah—you're fucked up."

Seb lifts an eyebrow. "I'm hoping you've got better counseling skills with your preschoolers."

"You're not five." Her voice sounds hoarse and teary. "You're a grown-ass man with grown-ass baggage and every right in the world to feel a huge amount of pain for what you've been through."

"Pain doesn't interest me." His eyes hold hers. "Pleasure, on the other hand—"

"Sebastian." She squeezes his jaw tight.

"Ow." He could break her grip if he wanted. "You've got strong hands for a girl."

He's needling her with the *girl* thing.

Nic won't bite. "Putting up walls is how you cope. Humor. Snark. Cynicism. Charm."

Sebastian scowls. "I didn't tell you all that so you could psychoanalyze me."

"Then why did you tell me?"

The look on his face is pure mystery. "I have no idea."

Nic drops her hand but keeps her eyes on his. Deep in her heart, she knows.

You told me because you care.

Because you're starting to let me in.

Because being vulnerable feels scary, but it's freeing, too.

There's a reason she knows all this. Drawing a breath, she

folds her hands in her lap. "Thank you," she says. "For telling me that. For letting me in."

"Yeah." He scoffs and gives a wry grin. "Any chance it gets me laid?"

He doesn't sound like he means it this time. He's going through the motions, slapping Band-Aids on his heart.

"Dream on, Minty Fresh." She threads her fingers through his hair again. There's a new tenderness in her touch this time. "I faked it earlier. In the sewing room?"

The glint goes back in his eyes. "Liar."

She smiles. "Guess you'll never know."

"I'll always know." He brushes a kiss at her temple. "Always."

Nic shivers. "Well." She's practically coming right now. He's not even touching her, and she's ready to explode. "We're quite the pair, huh?"

"I'll say." With a sigh, Seb flops back on her bed. He lets his head hang off the mattress, so he's staring at her window. "So how are we finding Daddy Duck Toes?"

They're back to that again. "We need a plan."

"Good idea." A flicker of lust lights his eyes. "Let's say we both get naked and—"

His voice falls off as a paper airplane floats through the window. Leaping off the bed, they sprint for it together.

Seb gets there first and throws back the curtain. "Son of a—"

"It's a note." Nic drops to the floor with the paper airplane. Unfolds it carefully with trembling hands.

Releasing the curtain, Seb scowls. "Should you be touching that? What if it's covered in some kind of dermal poison?"

"Way to go dark, dude." She scans the words on the page as her heart starts to thud. The handwriting. She knows it.

"I don't see anyone outside." He's back at the window, but Nic's not watching.

Her eyes are on the page. Words swim on blue-lined paper as she blinks back tears. "It's a note from Nondi."

Seb whips around. "You're sure?"

"Yes," she says, and keeps reading.

NICKI,

SHE PAUSES to grip the page tighter. Nondi never called her that. Not since she was nine and a boy at the waterpark called her "Nicki Hickey." She thought it was a compliment. That he wanted to be friends when he stuck his hand in her swimsuit and laughed.

When Nic told Nondi, her grandma saw red. Explained about hickeys and boys who grab girls without consent. Searching her eyes, Nondi touched her face. "You okay, Nicki?"

"Don't call me that anymore." She shouldered her BB gun and went outside. Shot cardboard targets until her arms hurt more than her heart.

Drawing a breath, Nic starts reading again.

NICKI,

You need to stop. This comes from a place of love when I tell you to stop flashing your tits at some silly boy all over again. You're a tiger, Nicki. Not some bimbo chasing a bridal veil. Remember when you turned twelve and marched into my sewing room—yes, the same room where you fell right into that trap again today—and you asked me if a piece of cotton would work as a condom? Child, please. I know it hurts to hear, but you've always fallen for foolish ideas and toxic men. Do better, Nicki. Please, give this up.

Love,

Issela

. . .

SEBASTIAN'S READING over her shoulder. "Are you okay?" When she doesn't answer, he touches her thigh. "Hey. I only got through half of it, but she's got no right to talk to you like—"

"Get me a map."

"What?"

"A map." The page falls to the floor as Nic bolts off the bed. "A map of Oregon." She sprints to the closet where she kept her road atlas in high school. It's still there, tucked behind yearbooks and a box of old Barbies.

Sinking to the floor, she flips open the atlas. Her hands feel shaky and her heart thuds in her ears. Quick as she can, Nic turns the pages to Oregon.

"Nic?" He carries the note to her side, frowning as he drops beside her. "What's going on?"

She trails a finger up the map, then looks at the note.

He holds it out so she can read. "She's not wrong about me," he says. "I'm not a good guy, and I know I don't deserve you, but Nic—you're smart and kind and clever and fuck her if she thinks she can talk to you like—"

"It's a code."

Seb blinks. "Come again?"

"A code. She's telling me where to go." Nic draws a breath. Scans the map again to be sure.

Scans her heart to be sure about him.

She's trusted Seb with her body. Can she trust him with the rest?

Meeting his eyes, she decides. "Calling me Nicki, that's the first clue," she says. "So is the tits thing."

"Say what?" Clearly, Terri doesn't talk tits with Sebastian. "Keep going."

"It's a reference to a waterpark we visited when I was little. Just Nondi and me—the only time we did a trip like that. A boy harassed me and... well, anyway. It's a story. A story only Nondi would know."

"Okay." He's not looking like she's crazy, so either she's not or he is. "What's the rest of the code?"

Nic stabs a finger on the north-central part of Oregon on the map. "The water park was here. This speck of a town near—"

"Juniper Ridge." He nods. "That old cult compound the Judson family turned into a tiny town for their reality show."

"Right." She nearly forgot he knows Cooper Judson. "Back when it was still a cult, they let the public use the waterpark. Maybe to indoctrinate us or something?"

"Sure, okay." Seb's looking more curious. "What's Nondi trying to tell you?"

Nic scans the map again. She's still figuring it out. "I think she wants me to go there." But no, it's not that simple. Nic frowns, reading the note again. "She's giving clues how to get there."

Seb's brow furrows. "Wouldn't you follow Highway-22 east through Bend?"

"Normally, yes." Nic looks back at the map. "I'm guessing she thinks there's a trap. Or some other reason not to go that way."

"Okay."

Skimming the note again, she sees the word "trap" with fresh eyes. "That's it!"

"Keep going." He tilts the note for her, giving a clearer view. "What's the routing?"

"Look." She draws a fingertip along I-5. "This line in the note. 'You're a tiger.'"

Seb tilts his head. "That's about you wanting the pet tiger?"

"That's what you're supposed to think." She offers a smile of apology. "It's meant to throw you off. In case I can't trust you."

Blue eyes hold hers. "You trust me?"

"I—" Good Lord, she does. "Yeah." Nic looks at the map so she won't see his reaction. "Tigard's a town just outside Portland. She's telling me to go north first, not east."

He peers at the map. "Okay, then what?"

"This next line—'not some bimbo chasing a bridal veil.' The

town of Bridal Veil is right here along the Columbia River. She's saying to follow the Oregon/Washington border. And the reference to this conversation when I was twelve?"

"Did that really happen?"

"No." Nic rereads the words. Consults the map again. "I'm less sure on this one, but I think she's saying turn southeast on Highway-206. Because two times six is twelve?"

"It's a stretch, but okay." If he's doubting her sanity, he's kind enough not to say so. "Think she really saw us in the sewing room?"

"Yes." She winces. "I guess that's a clue she wrote it today? That it's not some outdated note delivered by a messenger."

He looks at the window. "Sorry you can't unsee that, Nondi."

"Let's focus." She drags a finger down the 206 Highway. "Look —where the highway curves off by Cottonwood Road Homestead and becomes Cottonwood Road?"

Seb's jaw unlocks. "'—and you asked me if a piece of cotton would work as a condom.'"

Nic gasps. "*Condon!* The town of Condon is less than twenty miles to Fossil. She's sending us to this remote part of Oregon and telling us how to get there safely."

As the words rush out, she hears them in her head.

Sending *us.*

Telling *us.*

Seb hears it, too. A slow smile hooks the edges of his mouth. "I'm going with you?"

"I—" Is that what she wants? Searching his eyes, she nods. "Yes. Yes, please."

As a slow smile spreads, Seb sticks out his hand. "Partners."

"Partners." Shaking his hand, she longs to touch more than his palm. To burrow into his chest and stay there all night.

But they've got a trip to take. "Come on, Minty Fresh." She gets to her feet and holds out a hand. "Time for a road trip."

CHAPTER 9

They're on I-5 headed north in Nic's Volvo. Seb lobbied for his BMW, but didn't mind losing.

"We're not taking your flashy compensation-mobile," Nic argued as she shoved her bag in the trunk. "We need to be quick and inconspicuous and back here for the wedding on Sunday."

"Compensation-mobile?" Seb felt fine about not driving, but having his manhood questioned? "Say the word and I'll demonstrate I've got nothing to compensate for."

"Keep it in your pants, Minty Fresh."

Tough to do with Nic looking fierce and fit in black jeans and a gray fitted top. She's got sunglasses on, blonde hair yanked back in a ponytail. One arm out the window, though it's windy and overcast through the Columbia River Valley.

Seb's never seen her more lovely. Not as Miss Gigglewinks, or even in disguise as a hotel delivery girl. For a woman of many faces, Nic Bello wears them all beautifully.

He's glad they're on the road. With Dante and Teo holding things together at home, he's got miles of passenger time to consider their approach. As Nic passes a slow-moving semi, Seb fiddles with his keychain. Watches the road for questionable cars.

Wonders what to do about this fresh, fragile thread of trust between them.

What was he thinking dumping all his secrets on her? The stuff about his mom. About Greta. Fidgeting with his keys, Seb knows he's not done.

"You okay?" She glances over with her brow furrowed. "You've been kinda quiet."

Seb clears his throat. "What's all that on your keychain?" He leans over and taps the wad of objects dangling from her ignition. "I recognize the multi-tool. Pocketknife, nail file, scissors, all that."

"You mean the kitty cat?"

He squints at the pink metal ears. "I guess I see it."

Flicking her eyes off the road, she gives him a look. "It's supposed to look sweet and harmless."

"Like you?"

Nic puts her eyes back on the road. "It doubles as brass knuckles." She says it matter-of-factly, like she's suggesting burgers for lunch. "I slip my fingers through the eyeholes, make a fist, and... pow."

"Pow." *Damn.* Impressive. "What's the rest of that stuff?"

Nic steers straight ahead as they pass a field of splotchy cows. "You mean the green crocheted penis or the pink lips?"

"All that and then some." Lord, it's like a thrift store hanging off her keyring. "Let's start with the penis."

"You would." Nic checks her rearview mirror and changes lanes. "It's Chapstick. The head peels back so you can uncap and apply."

"I... don't know what to do with that."

"Besides relieving dry lips, you mean?" She gives him another look. "Nondi crocheted it. She made one for Jen, too, but Jen lost hers. I don't even use the lip balm anymore. I just keep it to watch repairmen get uncomfortable when I hand off my keys."

"That might be the most Nicole thing I've ever heard you say."

"Thank you." She nods at the keys in his lap. "How about yours?"

"Not so fast. We've barely scratched the surface with you." Also, he's hoping she'll forget. "The pink lips?"

"A floatation device in case I drop my keys in water."

Makes sense. "The little silver tube?"

"The flashlight or the mace?"

He scans her key ring and yep—two silver tubes. "Better not confuse the two."

"Like I would." She sounds suitably appalled.

"The square-ish brass thing?"

"A lighter." She gives him a side-eye. "Also, a mini grenade, but you need a code and my thumbprint to deploy it."

Holy shit. "The white thing?"

"Phone charger. Nothing special there."

He's inclined to believe that. "The round thing?"

"Compass." Her expression goes sheepish. "Inside, there's five milligrams of highly lethal poison. Well-sealed, so it can't leak."

Since she's not naming it, he's guessing the poison's not easily obtainable. His regard for Nic's skills goes up six notches. "The little blue teddy bear?"

"Just something cute. A student gave it to me."

Seb waits. There's more to the story.

"All right." Nic sighs. "It's also a thumb drive. I had it built in. Makes for hasty downloads when I've hacked someone's system."

"You've got hacker skills?" He shouldn't be surprised, considering Teo. Maybe they both learned from Nondi.

"I'm no expert." She swerves to miss a rabbit crossing the road. "There's a contact I use for most jobs, but I can hack my way into most systems."

"A woman of many talents."

She looks at him like she's not sure that's a compliment. "How about you?"

"Surveillance is more my thing, but I'm good with computers. Not Teo's level of brilliant, but—"

"I meant your keychain." She nods at the hoodie pocket where he just stuffed them. "The bullet I've seen you fiddling with. Is it a military thing?"

So simple to say yes. To go with the easy explanation. "It's a .45 caliber hollow point." He runs his thumb along the casing. "Spent."

"I've seen." One brow lifts as she glances at him. "Doesn't answer the question, though."

His jaw hurts from clenching. He wonders if he brought this up on purpose. If letting her in last night felt so good, he needed another rush.

Or maybe Seb's a sucker for punishment. "It's not a military thing."

Nic waits, not pushing. Not telling him he doesn't need to answer if he doesn't want to. He knows this.

Also knows he might want to. Deep, deep down, on some level he rarely visits. "After Greta died," he says softly, "I was in a dark place. Real dark."

She nods and doesn't take her eyes off the road. It's easier that way, with Nic not looking at him. Maybe she knows that. "Understandable," she says.

"Right, so... I wasn't sure I wanted to stick around."

Holding his breath, he waits for her to react. For a gasp of astonishment. "I'm sorry," she says. "That sounds painful."

"Yeah." He drags a hand over his head, not sure why he took them down this path. "It's a culmination, I guess. Knowing I failed her. I failed to make my mother want to stay." He draws a deep breath. "Most bullet keychains are inert. Already spent, or maybe a gunsmith's disarmed it. But the one I had was still a live round."

Nic flicks him a glance. "That doesn't sound legal. Or safe."

"It wasn't." The sound squeezing out of him couldn't be called a laugh. It's too dry, too brittle. "I made it myself. Carried it just in case."

Her hands grip the wheel. Nic doesn't need to ask. "I'm sorry, Sebas—"

"After my dad died, things got worse." His fingers curl around the casing as he stares at the road without seeing it. "Seemed symbolic, you know? To have a live round in hand, ready to go. Ready to…" He stops himself, not needing to say the rest.

Nic's quiet beside him. She doesn't push. It's what he's always loved about her. What makes her great at her job. At whatever job she's doing.

Uncurling a fist, he continues. "I sat there in the woods near my house holding this old Heckler & Koch that belonged to my dad. To his dad before him. Seemed fitting, you know? To end it that way."

Tears shine in her eyes, but she doesn't speak. Doesn't look over. She must know he can't say this with her pouring pity in his lap.

He drags in another breath. "I sat there on this tree stump for six hours just looking for one damn reason not to do it. Just one."

Nic licks her lips. "You found one?"

"Yeah." He lets out a long breath. "Your brother."

"My brother?" She looks over and blinks. "How?"

Seb rakes a hand through his hair. "Teo was in prison at the time. Stuck there for something he didn't even do. And I sat there thinking, 'you selfish, egocentric fuck. Your buddy would give his left nut for freedom you take for granted, and you're throwing it away because you're a goddamn pansy-ass loser who—'"

"When do you get to the self-love part of the story?"

Seb chokes on a laugh. "I'll let you know when it happens." He takes out the keychain and looks at it. "Anyway, I didn't do it. Obviously. Fired the shot at the ground. Dug the casing out of the dirt, fitted it with a screw-eye, and ran a ring through it. Put a bullet in the cartridge case so it looks like a live round, but it's not. Not anymore." It could be, though. Wouldn't be hard to swap it out if he got to that place again.

Nic's quiet for a long time. He wonders what she's thinking. What time/space continuum he could enter to let him take back everything he just said.

"Hey." Her voice has the softness it holds when she talks to AJ. It's her sweet, soothing daycare lady voice, and Seb's heart rolls in a pill-bug ball.

"Yeah?"

"You're brave for sharing that." When she looks over, her eyes aren't wet anymore. There's no pity there. Just something like respect. "Brave for sticking around, which isn't to say any other decision would be cowardly. But it takes balls to do what you did."

Seb's jaw clenches. "Speaking of my balls—"

"Fuck off and let me finish." She glares at the road, then at him. "A guy like you—a military vet? A trained operator? I'm sure you're called *brave* all the time. But that kind of bravery has nothing on what you just did."

Now he's confused. "What did I do?"

"Opened up instead of cracking some sex joke. You let me in, even more than when you told me about Greta and your mom. That takes guts, Sebastian."

Right. "Thanks."

"Sebastian—"

"Hey, it's Juniper Ridge." He points at the brown and white sign saying they've got half a mile to go. He's never been so grateful for direction. "You're still thinking that's the starting point?"

She doesn't answer right away. Squeezes the wheel for a second, two, three.

Then lets go with a sigh. "It does seem to fit." Nic checks the rearview mirror. "Nondi's all about hiding in plain sight. What's more public than the set of a TV show?"

145

"A self-contained community." He's reading off the website from his encrypted tablet. "Think that's code for well-guarded?"

"Nondi doesn't need guarding." She hits her turn signal. "She's the one who guards."

"I've really gotta meet your grandma."

Nic bites her lip. "It's possible I'm wrong. Maybe she's not here, or not alive at all. Or if she's here, she won't want to see me or meet you or—"

"Hey, Nic?"

Her breath lets out shakily. "Yeah?"

"One thing at a time, okay?" They roll through the compound gates, smiling at the cheerful attendant.

Nic rolls down her window. "Hi. We don't have an appointment. I'm not even sure—"

"Nicole Bello?"

She blinks. "Yes?"

"You're expected." He slips her a card caked with purple sealing wax. "Go down about a quarter mile, then turn right. Follow the signs to the C-block cabins and find one that says, 'The Carvers.' Purple petunias in the window boxes. You can't miss it."

"Uh, thanks?" Nic takes the card and pulls forward.

Sebastian sees her hand shake. "The Carvers?" He takes the card and inspects it. "Sounds sketchy. Knife people or maybe torture experts or—"

"That's Nondi's seal." She pulls to the side and takes the card back. "We did craft projects as kids. Everyone had their own seal and colored wax. Mine was red. Nondi's was purple."

"Huh." Seb's still suspicious. "You okay handling that without gloves?"

Nic rolls her eyes and turns the card over in her hands. "What's with you and the toxin paranoia?"

"Says the woman who tried to poison me with a milkshake."

She scoffs and breaks the seal. "Three years ago, before we ever met. How long do you plan to hold that over my head?"

Seb considers it. "Until you sleep with me?"

"Do you ever stop thinking with your dick?"

It's an easy one to answer. "Not really."

He watches her open the card. Should he respect her privacy, or peer at the words? "'Dear Nic,' she reads aloud.

Seb sits up. "You're reading it to me?"

"We've come this far. I feel like sharing." Nic lifts a brow. "Shall I continue?"

"Yeah, I—" Seb drags a hand down his face. "Keep going."

She draws a breath. "'Remember when you were sixteen or seventeen and I left for a month on a job in Cairo? I met a nice couple. They offered a safe place if I needed one. Took me fifteen years to take 'em up on it, but here we are. I'll explain in a minute. Glad you're as smart as I thought you were. Love, Nondi.'"

Nic squeezes her eyes shut and rests the card in her lap. "It's her."

"You're sure?"

She nods and hands it over. Seb scans the words, not sure what he's looking for.

"She mentioned the couple," Nic continues. "Wildlife biologists—Patti and Colleen, I think? It's been a while, so I may have the names wrong. She only told me because they had a son my age."

"They're operators?" He hands back the card.

Nic shrugs and tucks the card in her purse. "Right now, I assume everyone's armed and dangerous." She puts the car in gear and pulls forward.

"Good thinking." He checks the Walther in his chest holster. "Need an extra blade in case the 'Carver' thing turns out to be a warning?"

"I'm good."

She follows the road past a handsome lodge and a lovely little lake with couples strolling the water's edge. A sunny blonde jogs past in bright pink workout gear, stopping to stretch by a big boulder. At the other edge, a fierce-looking brunette holds hands with a tall Black guy, diamond ring glinting as she gestures with her left hand.

No one looks armed, but Seb's not taking chances.

"There!" Nic jerks to a stop. "That's it."

"Huh." Seb scans the cutest cedar cabin he's ever seen. He'd assumed "petunias" would be code for something, but nope. "I wonder what they use for fertilizer."

Nic gives him a look. "Is that a bomb-making quip?"

"I'm serious; the flowers look great." Blame years of loving care from a florist. Seb reaches for the door. "Want to scope it out first?" Scratching his chin, he considers it. "Probably lost the element of surprise if it's an ambush. The guy at the gate could've —" He stops as the front door swings open. Tenses with a hand on the butt of his gun.

Two women step onto the sunny front porch. One's sturdy and stoic with a salt-and-pepper braid looped over one shoulder. The other has silver-blonde hair and crows' feet framing warm amber eyes. Both wear flowered aprons and the look of ladies who just baked cupcakes for the grandkids. The shorter one smiles, then waves as she says something to the one with the braid.

"They're packing heat." Seb nods at the pistol tucked behind an apron. The rifle held near the other's hip. "They look sweet, but they're no one to mess with."

"Nondi," Nic breathes. She's out of the car before Sebastian sees the third woman slip behind them. She's tall and rangy, with Nic's ocean eyes and a scowl he'd know anywhere.

It's Nicole Bello, fifty years in the future.

"Nic, wait." He's too late to stop her, so he gets out. No way she's going in alone.

But as the two women part to let the third throw her arms around Nicole, Sebastian feels sharp stabs of longing in his chest.

Family.

Safety.

Love.

It's the most beautiful thing in the world, watching Nic enveloped in all that strength and affection. The warmest, sturdiest blanket on earth.

As longing grabs his heart in clammy fingers, Seb starts for the door. Wonders if he's marching to his death, or to meet his future grandma-in-law.

CHAPTER 10

"Oh my God, *Nondi!*" Nic burrows her face in her grandma's chest, breathing the scent of gun oil and warm cookies. Shoving back from the hug, she scans Nondi's face to be sure she's real. "You are such a *bitch*."

Nondi ruffles her hair. "Love you, too, girl." She steps back and waves to the women flanking her. "Meet Patti Carver and Colleen Mumford-Carver. We go way back. Ladies—my girl, Nicole."

"A pleasure." Colleen sticks a Smith & Wesson in her apron pocket and shakes Nic's hand. "Heard a lot about you."

"Where are our manners? Please, come in." Patti props her rifle by the door and waves them through. "You too, young man. No lurking around outside like a common criminal."

Nondi scans Seb and frowns. "He *is* a criminal, right?"

Nic's not sure how to answer. She darts a glance at her grandma's friends as Seb steps forward.

"Dr. Sebastian LaDouceur, ma'am." He extends a hand and his charming dentist smile. "Pleasure to meet you." He shakes Patti's hand first, then Colleen's. When he gets to Nondi, his eyes soften. "We're glad you're alive."

"Huh." Nondi clasps his hand in one of her white-knuckled grips that makes him blanch. "Gonna need to get to know you before I say the same."

"Fair enough." He glances at Nic. "You good?"

The look he's giving her holds more questions.

Do you feel safe?

Is it a trap?

And an answer, too.

I've got your back.

"I'm good." Nic blinks back tears and hugs her grandma again. "It's a little overwhelming."

"Now, now." Nondi strokes her hair. "None of that shit, okay?"

Nic sniffles and looks at Seb. "Is it any wonder I'm emotionally stunted?"

Smiling, he leans against the couch. It's an open-concept space with a living room that flows through the breakfast nook to a sunny kitchen island. "You seem pretty stable from where I'm standing."

Recalling his words in the car, Nic fights pangs of guilt. "Guess it's all relative."

"Guess so."

"Come on." Patti moves through the living room past the big granite island with barstools wrapped in red plaid. "We've got cocoa cardamom muffins and cranberry orange. You like sweet or tart?"

"Tart," Nic calls as Seb says, "Sweet."

"One of each." Colleen smiles approvingly and leans on the island. "Sign of a good match."

"Don't mind her." Patti piles muffins on plates as Nondi watches Sebastian. "When you've been married as long as we have—"

"And with a new grandbaby." Colleen grabs a framed photo off the mantle. "That's our son, Joey, and his wife, Jessie, with little Joy and baby Josiah—"

"Ten pounds, six ounces at birth. Can you believe it?" Patti pours milk into big orange mugs and sets them on the island. "Joey's a former Navy SEAL, and Jessie—"

"Humanitarian work!" Colleen hands the frame to Nic, and she smiles obligingly. "Jessie volunteers all over the globe, and they take turns with the kids—"

"Such a beautiful, balanced approach." Patti smiles at her wife with a fondness Nic envies. "We're very lucky."

"You have a lovely family." Nicole hands the photo to Seb.

"Your son has your eyes. Same with the kids." He sets the photo next to Patti, who definitely shares DNA with the strapping Navy SEAL. "Great picture."

"Thanks." Patti hands him a plate and a mug. "Take a seat, honey."

Nondi's seated already, scowling from the living room armchair she occupies like a queen on her throne. "Men can be useful for propagating the species." She drags her eyes off Seb as Nic takes her milk and muffin and claims a chair next to her. "Needed a man to get me your mother, and I guess she got your dad to make you three. Other than that, never saw much use for 'em, myself."

Colleen snickers as Patti shushes her and hands Nondi a plate. "Oh, SiSi—quit it. You're just bitter you lost the bet."

"Bet?" Nic bites her muffin, warm and tangy and tasting of home. She bounces her gaze from one woman to the next. "What bet?"

Colleen takes a seat in a red leather armchair. "Your grandma bet the boyfriend wouldn't make it."

"Not *dead*," Patti clarifies, joining them in the living room with a plate of muffin in her hands. "She didn't think you'd *kill* him—"

"I might've thought that." Nondi sets her muffin on a side table and crosses her arms. She's watching Nic with an intensity that makes her squirm. "I figured you'd let him lick the peach a time or two, but trusting him enough to bring him here—"

"Nondi!" Nic laughs as her face gets warm. "Not polite."

"What?" Nondi scowls at Sebastian. "You prefer muff diving, young man?"

"I—hadn't given it much thought." He shoves half a muffin in his mouth and sends Nic a look of mild alarm.

She does her best not to stare at him. Leave it to Nondi to antagonize the first guy she's introduced in years.

"Smooching the cooch?" Nondi tries. "Yodeling in the canyon? Ordering the box lunch? Barking at the badger? Making the tongue sandwich? Kissing the biscuit? Slurping the—"

"Congratulations, Sebastian," Nic interrupts. "You've met the master of bad jokes meant to knock someone off their stride. She's your personal Yoda."

"Um, cool?" He tilts his head at Nondi. "Permission to speak plainly, ma'am?"

Nondi glares. "You think I want you bullshitting me?"

"Nope." Seb sets his plate down. "Figured I'd check, in case I read you wrong."

"You haven't." Her frown ebbs a bit. "Go on."

"For the record, your granddaughter's more to me than a piece of ass."

"Yeah?" She regards him with interest. "You like her titties, too?"

Seb shrugs. "Who wouldn't? But it's her spirit that rocks my world, if you want the truth."

"Truth?" Nondi snorts. "Nah, kid—I want you to lie to me. Maybe if—"

"Nondi, enough." Nic folds her arms and looks at their hostesses. "I'm sorry you had to hear all that."

Colleen grins. "It's the most fun we've had since Cooper Judson came banging on our door in his underpants because he locked himself out of his cabin."

"Coop's here?" Sebastian seems grateful for the subject change. "We go way back."

Nondi nods, assessing. "I thought I recognized that ass."

"Yeah?" Seb perks up at that. "If you want, I can give you a show."

"Jesus Christ." Nic looks at Nondi, who's regarding Seb with a certain new respect. "Please, don't encourage him."

"Why the hell not?" Nondi grins. "He's nice to look at. I'll give you that much."

Time to get this back on track. "I still can't believe you're alive." Nic draws a breath, so she doesn't shout profanity at an old lady. "And I *really* can't believe you faked your own death."

"Aw, hell." Eyes going soft, Nondi bows her head. "Wasn't meant to go down like that."

Nic grits her teeth, channeling her daycare lady energy into not strangling her grandma. "You told us you had *cancer*. You went away and sent us notice you'd *died*. What the hell was the plan there, *Grandma*?"

The moniker makes Nondi flinch, which was the point.

Nondi sighs. "I thought I could come back. Swear to God, I only meant to be gone a few months. It was gonna be a big Christmas surprise, with me coming home and Teo getting out of the clink and—well..." She sighs again and lets her words trail off. "It didn't go like I thought."

"But *why?*" She's grateful, thrilled Nondi's alive. But dammit, Nic wants answers. "Why did you disappear in the first place? The cancer, the funeral, the *lies*..." She trails off before she says something she regrets.

What kind of awful person does something like that?

Nondi snarls. "You know how long I've been chasing your parents' killer?"

The breath leaves Nic's lungs. "I was six when they died. I've got a ballpark idea."

"Yeah, well... you have no idea what it's like to strike out as long as I have. Decades, Nicki." Nondi stops, letting the barb land like *Grandma* did. "I knew Don Julio DeCosta killed them.

Witnesses put him at the scene. Rumors had him showing off my great-great-great-*great* grandmother's ring like some sort of trophy. Your birthright, Nicole."

She swallows hard as emotion swells her throat. "I'd have rather had my parents."

"So would I," Nondi snaps. "I knew Don Julio had a son. Danny," she spits like the name tastes bad. "I knew the kid came to America, but his father... Don Julio just vanished."

The pain in her grandma's eyes makes Nic's spleen hurt. She stretches a hand to cup the old woman's knee. "So you wanted to avenge their deaths."

"Wasn't doing it just for you." Nondi sniffs. "I'm a selfish bitch, remember?"

Nic flinches. "I called you a bitch, not a selfish one."

"Oh, so now you're—"

"Ladies." Patti clears her throat. "Let's stick with the story?"

The words melt the ice from Nondi's eyes. With a heavy sigh, she keeps going. "Got a tip a while back that Don Julio moved to America. Changed his name, changed his looks, went into hiding. Running from the mob in Dovlano." She scoffs. "Always was a chickenshit."

"So you went after him." Nic's struggling to understand. "And you thought faking your death would help?"

"The bastard knew I was on his tail." Nondi shrugs. "Figured he'd let his guard down if I were out of the picture."

"That's—noble." She was going to say *fucked up*, but why poke the bear?

"Very noble." Sebastian sips his milk and gives Nic an encouraging smile. "What kept you from coming back?"

Nondi's eyes narrow. "I kept getting close. So goddamn close I could taste it. I wasn't ready to give up yet." Her green eyes harden. "Then I heard another rumor. Don Julio planned to get married. He proposed with *our* family ring."

Sebastian frowns beside her. "He killed his first wife, right?"

"Danny's mother." Nondi looks at Nic. "That apple didn't fall far from the tree."

Nic gasps. "The Danny "Duck Toes"' job—you're the reason it came to me?"

"Yeah." Nondi nods once. "I knew you'd take the job. I hoped losing his kid might bring Don Julio out of hiding, but if it didn't..." She trails off, shrugging as she looks at Nic. "One less wife-beating killer on the planet."

"The notes in the file." Nic looks at Seb, not wanting to betray his sources. "The clue about the dressmaker?"

Nondi darts a look at Seb. "A test to see how he was with sharing crucial case information."

Seb lifts a brow. "Did I pass?"

"There, you did." Nondi rubs her hands up and down her thighs. "Anyway, the plan didn't work. Don Julio didn't come out of hiding when his kid kicked the bucket."

Seb tilts his head. "Haven't they been estranged for years?"

Nondi straightens. "Doesn't mean he didn't love his kids. Some parents have a shitty time being parents. Connecting or whatever. They still love their damn offspring."

Nic sees Seb flinch. She thinks of his mother, of the story he shared in the car. Of the pain he's endured with both of his parents. Stretching out a hand, Nic squeezes one of his. Seb squeezes back and gives a grateful smile.

Nondi's talking again. "I still couldn't catch a break. Couldn't track Don Julio no matter what I did." She swings her gaze to Patti and Colleen and smiles. "Until I came here."

Nic looks to the two women. She's missing something. "I don't understand."

"Colleen's one of the world's top hackers." Patti smiles proudly. "But she only uses her skills for good and not evil."

"I—wow." Nic licks her lips. "Thanks?"

"My pleasure." Colleen nods to her muffin plate. "Need another?"

"I'm good, thanks." Nic looks back at her grandma. "What did you learn?"

"That Don Julio has a compound less than an hour from here." Nondi growls. "That he changed his name to DJ Costa and became the most paranoid motherfucker on the planet. Never leaves the house. Stays locked down tight with an arsenal of bodyguards in his stupid, impenetrable fortress."

From the fervor of her voice, Nic's guessing her grandma tried to penetrate it.

Sebastian leans forward. "How'd you track him down?" He's looking at Colleen, and Nic's curious, too. "We've had some of the best minds in the business looking into this for years."

The older woman's eyes gleam. "A unique family trait turned out to be the ticket." Colleen smiles. "The DeCosta men have webbed toes. Syndactyl, it's called."

"Huh." Sebastian shoots Nic a look with *I told you so* laced through it.

She ignores it. "You tracked him by his toes?"

"Through a massage therapist who left a rather chilling trail in her clinic notes." Colleen's eyes go steely. "Apparently, DJ Costa has a taste for buxom brunettes, a sensitivity about his feet, and a temper when he's angry."

Nondi grits her teeth. "It's how I finally found him. How I know where he is right this second."

"So you're close." Nic slides to the edge of her seat. "What's the plan?"

Colleen stands. "Pardon us." She grabs Patti's hand. "We'll give you privacy while we go check things at the café."

"You know where the key is, SiSi." Patti squeezes Nondi's shoulder as they troop past. "Stay as long as you like this time. We've got you."

"I know." Nondi pats the other woman's hand, then waits for the door to close behind them. At last, she looks at Nic. "They're helpful with intel, but they steer clear when things get messy. When it comes to anything illegal, they'd rather not know."

"Understandable." Sebastian crosses his ankles. "My grandma left cookies on the counter when I'd sneak out in high school. The snickerdoodles I loved instead of her favorite peanut butter ones." He gives a sheepish shrug. "Always thought it was a sign she knew what I was up to and had my back."

"That's a good grandma for you." Nondi sounds impressed. "And you're a smart kid for not calling her on it. Some women operate best behind the scenes."

"The plan." Nic needs her grandma back on track. "What's your plan for taking out DJ Costa?"

Nondi slumps in her chair. "Me being dead didn't bring DJ out of hiding, but I thought for sure his kid's death would do it."

"Danny's funeral is Sunday, right?" Sebastian looks at Nic. "New piece of intel that came in through a mutual source."

From the look he's channeling, Nic knows it's her brother.

"Matteo's good." Nondi's smug, but her smile fades fast. "DJ's not going."

"To the funeral?" Nic frowns. "Costa is skipping his own son's funeral."

Nondi scowls. "I told you, the fucker doesn't leave his house."

"So, you're going in after him." Seb's put the pieces together quicker than Nic. "That's your plan?"

Nondi turns icy eyes on Sebastian. "You sound surprised."

Nic flinches. Whatever he says next will decide if he lives or dies. Maybe not that dramatic. Her grandma won't kill him, but she'll sure as hell respect him less if he steps in it.

"I think," Seb says slowly, "That I've always had a healthy respect for women." His eyes move to Nic's and hold for a few sweet seconds. "But I'm figuring out that as women age, they get stronger, smarter, and a lot more capable of cutting someone's throat."

Nondi throws her head back and hoots. "You got that right."

Wiping her eyes, she looks at Nic. "At a certain point, we're all sick and tired of putting up with men's bullshit."

Nic throws Seb a sympathetic look. "She's not wrong."

Nondi continues. "Some women bake cookies. Some take up arms."

Nic looks at Seb again. "So you know, I can't bake cookies to save my life."

"And I bake the best fucking snickerdoodles you've ever tasted." He looks at Nondi. "Let's talk about the plan."

Nondi sighs. "Costa's fiancée—Dana." She snarls the name. "The bitch with my grandmother's ring. Tuesday's her birthday. She plans to ask DJ for a baby."

Seb's brow furrows. "What, like—stealing one?"

"Far as I know, no." She looks at Nic. "She wants it the old-fashioned way, and since DJ gives her whatever she wants... well." Nondi clears her throat. "I can't let that happen. He already stole *my* baby. Stole countless other mamas' babies. If he thinks I'm going to sit back and let him find that kind of joy—"

"What do you plan to do?" Nic's afraid she already knows.

"I need him dead. Her, I don't care about." Nondi frowns. "I'd rather avoid the collateral damage, but I'll do what it takes to eliminate him."

Sounds simple enough. "Cut his brakes?" Nic suggests.

"The asshole doesn't drive." Nondi snorts with disgust. "I'm not kidding that he doesn't leave the house."

Sebastian leans forward. "Sniper shot?"

Nondi makes a sound like a growl. "No cover near the house. Motherfucker wears a bulletproof vest to answer the door, which he rarely does. I'm telling you, the man's next-level paranoid."

Nic might be, too, if she had a rep for murdering innocent people. "Bomb," she suggests.

"That's what I'm thinking." Nondi darts a look at Seb. "It's the only way I can see."

Nic knows her way around explosives. "I'll help."

Nondi folds her arms. "Suicide bomb."

Nic's jaw drops. "*That* I won't help with."

"Oh, come on." Nondi pounds the arms of her chair. "He knows what I look like. Knows what all my associates look like, so don't go thinking you'll get close and get away. He's already sent signals he'll come for our family."

"The explosion at Jen's rehearsal." Pain pinches Nic's chest. "That was him?"

Nondi nods. "He thought he'd flush me out. Almost worked."

"Jesus." Seb drags a hand down his face. "Do these people ever stop?"

"Not unless someone stops them." Nondi's jaw clenches. "Someone like me."

"No." Nic's shaking her head, frantic as she looks from Nondi to Seb and back again. "There has to be another way."

"Nicole, be reasonable." Nondi glares. "I'm already dead. What better way to—"

"No!" Nic bolts up and stomps to Nondi's chair. "You listen to me you selfish old bitch. I will not stand by and lose my grandmother *again* because you're too damn stubborn to think of some way to do this without collateral damage."

"No, you listen, *Nicki*." Nondi's on her feet, and Nic's having flashbacks to puberty. Her grandma jabs her chest with one sharp finger. "I've wanted Don Julio dead since you were in kindergarten. I'm too old and too tired to fuck around. You've got your whole life ahead of you, and I'm checked out. If I want the job done right—"

"You are such a fucking control freak!" Red fills Nic's vision, clouding her heart. Her head. "You taught me yourself, Nondi. Can you seriously not trust that I can pull off this job?"

"And can you seriously not see that I'd rather die than risk one of my grandbabies?" Rage or maybe love makes her eyes go glittery. "I taught you to fight, that's true. To take risks when you have to. But this is one risk you don't have to take. I'm willing and I want to and that's final."

"It is *not* final." Seething, Nic starts to pace. "If I have to, I'll hold you down and—"

"You will do no such thing." Now Nondi's raging. "I know where the house is, and you don't. I didn't have to bring you here. I could have stayed dead, you know. We got to say goodbye for good this time. But if you think you can stop me—"

"Ladies." Sebastian stands, and Nic turns to see him slip on the Boy Scout smile. "A moment, please?"

Nic glares daggers. "We're kind of in the middle of something."

Nondi glares. "Be fast."

Seb clears his throat. "I've got the utmost respect for what you're both saying. Truly."

"This doesn't concern you." Nic needs him to back off.

She might need him to hold her, too.

But no, it's the backing off she needs.

Sebastian moves closer and touches her arm. Squeezes once, softly, then steps back. "You're right, it doesn't concern me." He holds his palms up, smiling his charming Boy Scout smile. "But it could."

His eyes shift to Nic's and hold. "I know what it's like to think you're ready to check out. But I also know what it's like to get another shot. To discover there's still a lot of life left ahead."

Nic doesn't dare breathe. Nondi's going to deck him anyway, so maybe she should let her. Or maybe they can pin her grandma to the ground and—

"You think you have a plan?" Nondi looks at Nic. "Typical man, stepping in on someone else's takedown."

Nic looks at Sebastian. Remembers his words in the car, his hand on her waist. His gentle voice telling her he's got her back no matter what.

She's done fine on her own up 'til now. But trusting Sebastian, letting someone else in? It's a kind of magic she's never known until now.

Meeting Seb's eyes, she nods. "Let's hear it."

* * *

NIC STRIDES beside Sebastian on a narrow paver path. When they pass a pretty brunette in glasses, the woman frowns. "Can I please see your guest badge, sir?"

"Sorry." Seb opens his hoodie to flash the tag Patti gave them at the café. "Cooper's up here on the right, yeah?"

"You look familiar." The woman's frown deepens. "You're not one of his Hollywood friends, are you? Because Coop's clean, and if you're looking to get high—"

"Whoa, whoa, *whoa!*" Sebastian holds his palms out and smiles. "I knew Coop in Hollywood, yeah. But I've never done drugs, honest. I was his stunt double in a couple films. I called ahead, so he knows we're coming."

Relief floods the woman's face. "I'm sorry, please forgive me." She extends a hand to Nic. "I'm Mari Judson. We're all a bit protective of Cooper, but that's no excuse to be rude."

"Don't mention it." Nic smiles as Seb shakes Mari's hand. "I'm Nicole Bello, and that's Sebastian LaDouceur. I've got siblings, too, and I'd shiv anyone who messed with them."

Mari looks uneasy. "We don't condone violence as a means of problem-solving, but—" She nudges her glasses up her nose. "I'm glad you understand."

"Completely." And Nic's serious about the shivving, too. "Soo... next cabin on the right?"

"Close, but you're off by a row." Mari points north. "Down that way, hang a left. It's the second cabin on the right."

"Thank you." Sebastian smiles. "Congratulations by the way."

"What?" Mari pales. "Um—"

"The baby?" Sebastian winks. "I understand you're expecting."

"Oh, well. Thanks?" Mari looks puzzled. "We haven't announced it officially. Not on TV, anyway."

"I won't tell." Sebastian starts walking backwards. "Coop's thrilled to be an uncle again."

"Right, well." Mari looks a little more certain Sebastian's who he says he is. "Nice meeting you."

"Same." Seb grabs Nic's hand. "Shall we continue?"

Nic tugs her hand back. "Will you please tell me what we're doing paying a visit to Hollywood freakin' royalty?"

"Former royalty." Seb starts down the path again. "Okay, he's still famous. But he hasn't acted in years. He's just a handyman now, or something like that."

"Okay." Nic doesn't follow Hollywood gossip, so she'll take his word for it. "I'm on board with the plan, but I still don't get what Cooper Judson has to do with—"

"Sebastian, my man!" The legend himself ambles out of a cabin with a grin that's a dead ringer for Seb's. Same lean physique. Same rangy build. Seb's dark-haired to Cooper's sunny surfer locks, but hair color's not tough to change. Nic admires the similarities, but for her there's no contest.

Cooper Judson's handsome. Sebastian's fucking hot.

It's possible she's biased.

"Mari texted to say you got lost." Cooper shakes Sebastian's hand and turns to Nic. "You must be Nicole. Heard a lot about you."

"I—yes." She looks at Seb. "What exactly did you tell him?"

"That I'm meeting his dream girl." Cooper grins. "It makes sense now. If I weren't in love with someone else, I'd totally steal you away."

It's clear he's kidding, so Nic laughs. Hollywood charm isn't so different from Seb's. Just a little less lethal. "Nice to meet you." She looks at Seb. "I'm sorry this loser's butt took the spotlight off your otherwise flawless acting in *Survivor Six*."

Sebastian quirks an eyebrow. "I thought you hadn't seen it?"

Nic shrugs. "I might've watched since then. Can't blame a girl for inspecting the goods."

"I feel violated." Seb looks at Cooper. "Is it wrong I kinda like it?"

Coop laughs. "I like *you*," he tells Nicole. "Come on. I've got everything you need in the garage."

Intrigued, Nic follows him around the cute cedar cabin to a small garage. As he rolls up the door, she's braced to see bomb supplies. Maybe a rocket launcher or—

"Stage makeup?" She blinks as Cooper opens a case. "That's what this is about?"

"Seb says you're getting dressed up for some party." He winks at Sebastian, and Nic wonders what he knows. "Help yourself. This stuff's just going to waste here, so I don't need it back."

"Thank you." Sebastian takes the case as Coop hands Nic another box. "Lots of wigs in here. Some padding, some costumes. Even some facial prosthetics if you want to really change your look. Seb knows what to do with it all." He elbows him. "You got plenty of tips from that makeup artist who used to follow you around. What was her name?"

"Becca." Sebastian looks pained. "I didn't take her up on her… offers."

Cooper grins. "Your boyfriend was a gentleman at all times. A perfect professional."

"I'm well-acquainted with his *professionalism*." Way more than Cooper probably knows. Nic pulls out a dark wig. "These are really nice."

Seb picks up a box. "You sure you don't mind us taking all this stuff?"

"Not at all." The actor grabs another box and stacks it on the one Sebastian's holding. "Look, I'd love to stay and talk, but I've got family dinner in twenty minutes. You sure you don't want to come? Lauren's husband, Nick—he makes a mean veggie lasagna. I already called, and there's lots of extra food."

"Some other time." Seb shifts the boxes to grip his hand. "Good luck with the show, man. And with the woman—maybe I can meet her sometime?"

"Absolutely." A little light leaves Coop's eyes. "Just need her to stop thinking I'm an asshole first."

With a look of sympathy, Seb claps Coop on the shoulder. "You'll figure it out."

"Thanks." They shake hands again and say their goodbyes, loading their arms with the goods.

Once Cooper's out of earshot, Nic looks at Sebastian. "He seems nice."

"You seem surprised."

She shrugs and starts walking down the path toward the car. "I'm not into Hollywood stuff, but every red-blooded American grows up knowing who the Judsons are. I just thought they'd be more... more..."

"Snobby?"

"Something like that." Adjusting her grip on a box, Nic looks out at the lake. "I guess I ought to know better about jumping to conclusions." She bites her lip. "I haven't said I'm sorry yet."

Seb looks at her. "For what?"

"For snapping at you since the day we met." She pauses, choosing her words carefully. "For thinking you're a smarmy, phony charmer instead of a complex human being."

He snorts and shifts the boxes in his arms. "Can't say you were too far off."

"Don't do that." She steps in his way, forcing him look at her. "You're a good man, Sebastian. I'm sorry I didn't give you credit for that."

His throat moves as he swallows. "Thanks."

"You're welcome."

A spark lights his blue eyes. "Want to get naked?"

"God, you're a pig." She turns and starts walking again. Holds her box a little tighter. "Okay."

"What?"

"I said okay." She looks at him. "We can't implement our plan until tomorrow morning, anyway. We've got time to kill."

Sebastian chokes beside her. "Anyone ever tell you your foreplay needs work?"

"No."

"I don't blame them." He's befuddled as he walks beside her. "Are we getting naked in Patti and Colleen's guest room, or should I clear space in the Volvo's backseat?"

"Now whose foreplay needs work?" Butterflies flit through her belly as she keys open her trunk. "There's a hotel in town about thirty minutes from here." She tries to sound breezy, but her belly's turning somersaults. Can he tell? "I can call for a reservation."

He shoves his boxes in the trunk, then grabs hers. Nic starts to protest. "I don't need your help lifting—*oh*." Seb whips a hand around her waist and pins her to the car.

Blue eyes drill hers, hot and hungry and possessive. "In a sec."

He kisses her, mouth claiming hers as big arms bracket her body. Fingers flow into her hair, unwinding her ponytail as his free hand grips her waist.

Arching against him, Nic grinds on one hard thigh. She's kissing him back, stars blinking behind her eyelids.

Holy cow, the man can kiss.

When he breaks away, Nic catches her breath. "What was that?"

"Foreplay." He grins and holds up her car keys. "Also, grand theft auto. I'm driving. Get in."

"Pig." She wants to protest, but her legs might not be sturdy enough to drive. "Fine."

He strides around the car to open the passenger door, handing her in like a perfect gentleman. "You've got a great ass, Rogue."

"Shut up and drive."

Laughing, he shuts the car door. Comes around to the driver's side and shoves the seat back. "Hollywood stunt doubles get lots of training on driving fast as hell, but safe."

"Oh?" Her voice sounds weird and squeaky, and there's a heated buzz between her legs.

Seb puts a hand on her thigh. "Promise I'll have us to the hotel before you can say 'multiple orgasm.'"

Nic tips her chin up. "I hope you can do more than *say* it."

Grinning, he guns the engine. "Count on it."

CHAPTER 11

*H*e's got the pedal to the floor, driving faster than he has since the day he raced to the airport hoping to save his dad. Same day he met Nic, which technically means he drove *away* from her.

Now he's driving toward her. Not literally, since she's sitting beside him looking hot as hell, even in a dark wig and glasses.

He's driving toward a future with Nic in it. Nic *naked*.

He can't start thinking beyond that. Not even if she's sweet and smart and willing and—

"Sebastian, slow down." Nic puts a hand on his leg. "You want to get arrested?"

He eases off the gas. "Will I get a conjugal visit from you?"

"No." She slides her hand up his thigh. "Is that your keys?"

"My keys are in my jacket." And his dick is in her hand. He grinds his teeth and tries not to embarrass himself.

"Wait." Nic's hand tenses, making his cock twitch. "We need to call your grandma."

There's not much blood in his brain, so he must've heard wrong. "You don't need permission from Terri to touch my dick."

Or other parts of him. Watching the road, he tells himself to keep both hands on the wheel. Maybe he'll grope her with his toes?

"Sebastian, focus." Lifting her hand off his hard-on, she snaps her fingers. "Slow down and let's call Terri so we know the best way to execute the plan."

Easing off the gas, he grudgingly admits she's right. "Fine." He nods at his phone in the console. "You'll need my thumbprint."

And he'll need to slow down some more. So much for being inside Nic in the next six minutes. He holds out his thumb, and she scans it. "Speed dial two," he says. "Hit the pound sign, then the red key, and an asterisk to encrypt the call."

Nic arches a brow. "Is this some kind of black ops military-issue phone or something?"

"Or something." He nods to the holder on the console. "You can put it on speaker."

"Really?"

He shrugs. "You trusted me to be there when your grandma rose from the dead. The least I can do is let you listen in while I talk with mine about flowers."

"Thanks." Nic goes silent as the phone rings.

Terri answers right away. "Sebby, honey—I'm so glad you called. Do you know where I put that big jar of Skippy?"

"The one you got at Costco?" He looks at Nicole. "Did you try the top shelf of the pantry?"

"I would, but you got testy with me the last time I climbed on the step stool."

"Right, I'm sorry." He hates the risk of her falling when he's not home. "If you can hold out 'til tomorrow, I'll be home to get it for you."

"Wonderful." A pregnant pause says she's got something on her mind. "Everything okay, sweetheart? You haven't done anything to scare off that sweet Nicole, have you?"

Nic covers her mouth. Her shoulders shake with laughter, and

Seb looks away so he doesn't snicker. "Everything's great with Nicole. Matter of fact, I'm hoping to get busy with her real soon."

Flinging the hand off her mouth, Nic smacks him. Hard.

What? he mouths.

Like Terri knows that expression. "Busy *working*," he adds for Nic's benefit. "We're doing a project together." He clears his throat. "Anyway, T—Grandma, I have a question for you."

"Fire away, Sebby."

He guides the car around a pothole. "Just wondering about flowers." How does he ask this the right way? "Something traditional for a funeral."

"For a man or a woman?"

"Man." That's easy enough. "Nothing too frilly. And... uh, the family has Dovlanese roots. So maybe something culturally appropriate?" It'd be just his luck he'd pick chrysanthemums and find out those mean "go fuck yourself" in the Dovlano tradition.

"Okay, okay." Terri makes her thinking noise. "Are these being sent to a funeral home or delivered in person?"

Leave it to Terri to ask the right questions. "In person. Does that matter?"

"It can." There's a sound like a chair dragging across the floor, and Seb knows she's plotting to get the peanut butter. "Will there be a card with the flowers?"

"I guess?" He glances at Nic and wishes he hadn't. She's so sexy, so lush. He's having trouble remembering why he made this call. "Sure, yeah. There's a card."

"Roses," Terri announces. "White and yellow with a few pops of color thrown in—pink or even lavender. Some fresh fern fronds and a little ivy to keep it classic, and a clear, square, gender-neutral vase."

Sebastian blinks. "Really?"

"Yes." She sounds certain. "Sebby?"

"Yeah."

There's a long pause. "When women get flowers, they smell them first."

He darts a glance at Nic. "Okay?"

"Men grab the card," Terri continues. "There's rarely any smelling. But they open up that card right away."

"Ohhh-kay." If she's speaking code, he's not reading it.

In the passenger seat, Nic sits very straight. Nods a few times as she jots notes while Terri keeps talking.

"I'm just saying," his grandma continues. "If someone wanted to use flower delivery to... well... deliver something else? There's a way to do it right. To ensure the job goes well."

Holy fucking shit.

Even Nic looks stunned. No more note-taking. She eyes him with a curious look. Sebastian shakes his head, not sure what's happening.

"Have I lost you, Sebby?"

"Uh, no. I'm here."

"And this is an encrypted line?"

Jesus Christ. Seb drags a hand down his face. "Yeah. Yeah, it is."

"Don't sound so scandalized, sweetheart." His grandma chuckles. "I've been on this earth a lot longer than you, and I know when my grandson's got something on his mind. Is Nicole coming to dinner this week?"

He shakes his head again to clear it. "I, uh—haven't asked her."

"Don't be shy. And Sebby?"

"Yeah?"

"Be careful out there, okay? Call me if you have any more questions about what we discussed. I'm very discreet. Excellent at keeping secrets."

No shit. "Thank you." He hesitates. "I love you, Grandma."

"Love you, too, Sebby." A pause. "Make sure you use a condom when you get busy, sweetheart. Not that I wouldn't love a grand-baby, but—"

"Right, got it." He needs to end this call.

Terri does it for him. "Bye! See you soon, Nicole."

Nic grins. "Looking forward to it."

She taps the phone to disconnect and looks at him. "Did your grandma just tell you how to kill someone with a floral delivery?"

"I... guess so?" His mind's still reeling. "Also, how not to knock you up."

"Good skills all around."

He shakes his head, hands gripping the wheel. "Why is this more shocking than your grandma confessing her confirmed kills on our way to the coffee shop?"

"Because you have this preconceived notion of who your grandma's supposed to be. Who all old people are." She shrugs. "You thought Nondi was the outlier."

"I might've been wrong there." About a lot of things. "I should buy flowers for Terri when we get back."

Grinning, Nic puts her hand on his thigh again. "She definitely saved us time googling in dark mode. More time for other things."

He gulps as her hand slides higher. How can he go from zero to hard-on with just a skim of her palm?

"There's the hotel." He wheels into the parking lot, thanking God he had the good sense to pack fake ID and credit cards to match. This doesn't look like a place that'll take cash.

"This seems nice." She sounds surprised as she steps from the car and stretches. She chose a curly black wig and designer sunglasses, while Seb sports a blonde shag that leaves him looking like Cooper Judson in a surf flick.

Nic looks at him and laughs. "I need to get that off you as quick as possible."

"Wait here." He sprints for the lobby, half worried she'll change her mind. That hearing about key cards and checkout times will get her thinking this isn't a great idea. Maybe it's not, and he'll stop if she says to. He's a gentleman, after all.

But he hopes to God this really happens.

Pushing into the lobby, he reminds himself to stride casually to the front desk. "One room." He shoves a card and ID across the counter. "I called ahead—Terren Ketter."

"I've got it right here." The clerk with a nametag that reads *Judy* smiles as she types on her computer. "You must be in a hurry."

Seb makes himself lean casually on the counter. Even works up a yawn for good measure. "Just eager to get to bed."

"I hear ya." Judy winks and hands him two key cards. "You're on the third floor. Park anywhere on that end of the property. Elevator's just off the stairs."

"Thanks." He grabs the cards in their paper envelope and commands himself not to sprint. Not to crawl on his knuckles through the parking lot to reach Nicole because he's forgotten how his legs work.

Forget being cool. He's wanted this from the first moment he saw her. Shoving through the doors and out into fading sunlight, he skids to a stop. Where's the car?

Heart pounding, he scans the lot. She left. She actually left him alone to—

"Over here, Minty Fresh." Nic steps from behind the dumpsters. "Thought we should conceal the car."

Relief floods his chest, though he tries not to show it. "How'd you move the car if I've got your keys?"

"You don't think I'd hand over my only set?"

He catches her in five quick strides, drawing her into his arms. "Still don't trust me, huh?" He breathes the words against her throat, not caring if she trusts him.

Okay, he cares. But he maybe shouldn't show how much.

Be cool.

Don't blow this.

Don't let her see how much you want this.

How much you need her.

Nic laughs and leans back. "I don't trust anyone who might

lock my keys in the car." She kisses him quick, twirling a ring of jangling keys. "Myself included."

God, he wants her. Shoving a hand in his pocket, he comes up with both key cards. "Room 317. Up ahead at the north entrance off the—"

"Come on, man." Grinning, she sprints for the door. "You think I've got all day?"

Sebastian jogs after her, catching her as she steps through the elevator doors. He pulls her against him, Nic's back to his front as the elevator doors slide shut. "We can hurry now." Pressing the *three*, he punctuates each word with kisses at the nape of her neck. "But when we get to the room, I plan to take my time."

Shivering, Nic reaches behind and shoves a hand in his jeans pocket as the elevator starts to move. "Is that a promise or a threat?" Her fingers skim his hard-on, and Seb nearly loses it.

"Can't this thing go any faster?" He's got his hands on her waist as he scans the panel of buttons. "There's a crowbar in my bag. We could pry it open and climb the cables to—"

Ding!

The doors swoosh open and Sebastian leaps out with Nic's hand in his. Tugging her toward the hall, he skids around the corner and stops.

An elderly couple teeters side by side with matching walkers. White heads lean close together, a slow-moving barricade blocking the hall.

"And then I said to Bob," the man shouts. "Bob, did you remember to turn the furnace down when you left the house? Because we're not paying to heat an empty house. So then Bob says—"

"What was that?" The woman touches her hearing aid. "Speak up, Richard. I don't know why you're always whispering."

"Dammit, Darlene." Richard takes another shuffling step. "I said something about the house sitter. I forget."

Stifling a giggle, Nic slips a bug sweeper from her bag. Winks at Seb, then discreetly scans Darlene.

Good thinking.

The couple doesn't notice as Nic hands Seb the device. It's slow going as they march down the hall like some strange parade, Seb scanning the old man just in case.

All clear.

And no indication Darlene and Richard have even noticed anyone behind them. Richard's still shouting about the house sitter and whether he remembered to turn down the heat. Darlene's shouting over him, something about dog kibble. That's Darlene's real hair, not a wig. There's a blue tint to her scalp, so definitely not an operator in an old lady disguise.

"I swear they make these halls longer and longer every year," Richard mutters.

Nic winks at Seb. *No kidding,* she mouths.

Darlene looks at Richard. "What time did you say the happy hour special ends?"

"The Yappy Flower? Wasn't that the place we used to take Buttons for grooming? They put those damn bows on his head like he's some kind of —"

"Excuse me?" Sebastian busts out his best smile. "I'm wondering if maybe we could get past you to our room."

Darlene turns to glare. "Young people these days have no patience."

Instead of moving, she shuffles even slower. Richard's walker bangs the fire extinguisher, but he doesn't seem to notice.

"Honestly," Darlene's saying. "I don't see why they don't teach etiquette in schools anymore. Respect for your elders. In our day, we learned important things. None of this Spacebook or DicToc."

Richard chuckles and scoots his walker. "Aw, it wasn't that different for us. Remember our code?"

A faint blush rolls up Darlene's throat and fills her face. "I plum near forgot." Her laugh goes almost girlish. "You'd come calling, and my mama would chaperone. We thought we were so sneaky."

Richard's grinning now. "I'd ask you about homework and you'd ask me about chores, and then one of us would say—"

"'I think it might rain.'" Darlene's laughing now. "My stars. And you knew that meant come find me in our spot."

"Those were the days, huh?"

Seb looks at Nicole. She's listening like she shares the memory. Like she's seeing it in her mind. It's sweet, watching her like this. The story's even sweet, despite the cock-block.

"You were so naughty!" Darlene swats Richard's shoulder. Misses and hits his ear, knocking off his glasses. "You'd say what time you thought the rain might come, and that was the cue." Her blush goes from pink to crimson. "We'd touch and we'd kiss and we'd fondle and then—"

"Ah, here we are." Richard runs his walker into the door of room 315. "Where'd you put the key?"

"It must be here somewhere." Darlene unzips her purse and pulls out a ring twice the size of Nic's. "It's this one, right?" She holds up one for a Ford. "I forgot my glasses. You'll have to put it in."

Richard grabs it and jabs it at the doorknob. "Where's the damn hole?"

Nic's nearly on the floor, shoulders shaking with mirth. Seb's not sure if her inner thirteen-year-old hears "where's the hole" and "put it in," or if it's the whole conversation. There's enough absurdity to go around.

"Sir?" Sebastian clears his throat. "I think this might be your key." He points at the card poking out of Richard's shirt pocket. "If you'll allow me—"

"Get your paws off him." Darlene slaps his hand. "Kids these days with their gender fluid lifestyle. Thinking they can touch anyone they want."

Nic snort-laughs as Sebastian grabs the card.

"Here." He waves it in front of the scanner and a green light blinks. "Door's open, you can go in."

Darlene frowns. "Doesn't look open to me."

"Nope," Richard agrees. "Damn newfangled gadgets, always breaking down."

"For the love of—" Stifling a sigh, Seb grabs the knob. Nothing happens because, of course. It's been six years since he scanned the card. He waves it again. "Pull the knob now."

Richard grabs the card back and grumbles. "You don't have to be so pushy about it." Gripping the knob, he jerks it toward him. "You sure this is the right key? This technology is such bull-puckey."

"Please, sir, if you'd just—" Seb stops and forces a smile. "The key, if I may?"

He holds out his palm and Richard glowers. Looks at Darlene. "You think we can trust him?"

Darlene looks from him to Nicole. "You look like a nice young couple." Her gaze lands on Sebastian's hand, and she scowls. "You're not wearing a wedding ring. And you're together at a hotel?"

"We just got married!" Nic flings her hands from the pouch of her hoodie, displaying a ring Seb swears was just on her right hand. She must've switched it in her pocket. "We're newlyweds, so it's pretty modest. We couldn't afford one for him."

Darlene bumps Richard and smiles. "Isn't that sweet? Remember when we were first married? We lived in that little cottage over near—"

"Here we go!" Seb grabs the card and waves it at the sensor. This time, when the light blinks, he wrenches the knob and kicks it open. "In you go. Ladies first. Careful with the walkers. There you are, ma'am. Nice and easy, watch your step."

There's shuffling and muttering and a bit of cursing from Richard.

When the door slams shut behind them, Seb looks at Nicole. "Will that be us someday?"

Nic laughs and shakes her head. "I plan to be like Nondi. A septuagenarian coordinating hits. Or maybe Terri—under the radar, but a secret sly fox."

"Good plan." Even if it's not what he meant. He was thinking of growing old together. Of the pair of them sharing smiles and secrets and maybe gun mounts on their walkers.

God, he's a sap.

It's just sex. God knows you'd suck at anything more.

He drags in a breath and slides Nic a smoldering smile. "Wasn't I about to be inside you?"

"Smooth segue, Minty Fresh." She looks at the card in her hand. "Looks like we've got the room right next door." She points to the number, and sure enough—317 shares a wall with 315. A thin one, from the look of it.

Seb drags a hand through his hair. "Son of a—"

"Want me to get us a new room?"

"No." Grabbing the card, he waves it at the sensor. The light's barely lit when he jerks the knob and shoves the door open. "At this point, the bed could be on fire and I'd still fuck you on it."

There's a thud on the wall next door. "Language, son!" Darlene pounds again. "Honestly."

"Sorry, ma'am." Seb looks at Nic and whips off his wig. "Not sorry," he whispers as he flings it on a lamp. "Not even a little."

Nic giggles, tossing her wig on the dresser as she shoves through the door. "You're in luck. The bed's not on fire." Dropping her bag, she flops on the mattress and grins up at him. "Why are you still dressed?"

God, he loves her.

Not loves. *Wants.*

It keeps getting scrambled in his head. "One second." He snatches the do not disturb sign and jerks open the door.

Richard's standing outside. "Lost my goddamn room key."

He's frowning at the floor. "You haven't seen a silver metal key about yay big with—"

"Here." Seb plucks the card from the man's shirt pocket and hands it to him. "Have a good night." Looping the hanger on the knob, he shoves the door shut.

Turns to find Nic topless.

"Good God." He starts toward the bed as she twists her arms to unhook her bra. "Wait, no—let me."

"I dunno, pal." Grinning, she fingers a bra strap. "You can't even get your own clothes off."

"Evil woman." He pounces, pinning her arms above her head. She's warm and deliciously soft as she squirms beneath him. "Maybe I'll make you come just like this."

"You think so, huh?" Nic laughs and twines her thighs around him. "I'd like to see that."

So would he. Seb tilts his hips, dragging his hard-on up the seam of her jeans. He watches her face for the instant he skims her clit through too many layers of fabric.

"Oh." Nic's breath hitches. "That's not your keys."

"Nope." He strokes again, making her arch off the bed. "God, you're hot."

"Seb." Her thighs clench around his hips. "Do it again."

Like she has to ask. He's firmer this time, dick gliding up dampening denim.

Nic groans, her lashes fluttering. "You're seriously fucking me through our clothes?"

He answers with another thrust, hips grinding, circling, rubbing careful friction right where she wants it. He sees in her eyes he's hitting his mark. "You complaining?"

"Nope." Nic shudders beneath him.

With the hand not pinning her wrists, he unhooks her bra. "Your tits really are spectacular." He takes a nipple in his mouth, and she shudders again. "Fucking perfect."

The sound she makes isn't quite a word. Not one he recognizes. Something between a groan and a growl as she tilts to meet his next thrust. "Pants." She moans and arches again. "Off."

"Why?" She's closer than he'd guessed, which goes to show how unhinged they both are. Thrusting again, he lets denim's rough friction do the work. "This seems to be working for you."

Another moan slips out. "Not at all." Her breath hitches, eyes catching his in a challenge. "Not even when you do that circle thing with your hips like you're—*oh God.*"

He laughs and does it again. "I love how fucking sensitive you are." Not a phrase he ever hoped to say while dry-humping Nic Bello. Not until he had his mouth between her legs, his mind mashed together with hers. It's both things making magic.

"Seb." Her eyes squeeze shut. "It feels so fucking good."

"That's why I'm doing it."

She's not the only one losing it. If Seb's not careful, he'll come in his pants like a horny teen. Dipping his head, he sucks her nipple again. "That's it," he growls as she bows up to grind against him.

"Sebastian." Her thighs grip like a vise. "We really should get naked—"

"I can feel how wet you are." Arousal seeps through her jeans and into his. "How bad you want it."

"This is crazy." She works her hips, scrambling for purchase. She's close. He feels it in the strain of her spine.

"That's it, Nic."

"*Sebastian.*"

"Let it go." One more long, languid stroke, his cock connecting with her core as he drags it through her heat and—

"Oh, God!" She shatters beneath him, fingers raking his shoulders as his hips pump and he fights to hold on.

Cocky as he's been, he never thought she'd come like this. It's all he can do to hold back, to keep from embarrassing himself. For both their sakes, he needs this to last. What kind of man loses it while still fully clothed, grinding on a woman dressed from the waist down?

But he's that kind of man because she's this kind of woman. Nothing like he expected, and everything he's dreamed of.

As she collapses beneath him, he kisses from her chest to her throat. "Can't get you off fully clothed, huh?"

"Smug bastard." She blows hair off her forehead. "Maybe I faked it."

"Maybe." Seb moves his hips and she jolts with an aftershock. "Maybe not."

"Pig." She jerks her hands free, which she could have done all along.

They both know it, too. That's the beauty of what's between them.

As he kisses her throat, Nic jams a thigh between his to flip him on his back. It's a move he could block, but why?

Sebastian rolls willingly, gazing up like she's the moon and he's looking for direction.

"You've got two choices." Nic licks her lips, bare breasts inches from his mouth. "Lose the shirt, or I'll cut it off you."

"I'd kinda like to see that." He laughs and slides his palms to her hips. "Maybe if I—"

Riiiiiiiiip.

He blinks at the blade in her hands. Tiny and sharp, it juts from her key ring like a bright bolt of lightning.

Sebastian swallows. "Took your keys back."

"Yep." Nic opens his shirt like a book, peeling cotton pages to bare his chest. "Should I get your pants, or—"

"Not a chance." He flips her off him, and the keys hit the floor with a clink. Heart racing, Seb shucks his shredded shirt. "You're not getting near my dick with that pipsqueak knife."

"Chicken." She's smiling as she unhooks his jeans and shoves them down his hips. He'd offer to help, but he's busy pushing her pants off with her panties still in them.

Her nails spear his left butt cheek as she holds his eyes with hers. "I lied."

Seb blinks. "About what?"

"The blue teddy bear on my key chain." She tilts her head to where they dropped. "It's not a thumb drive inside."

"What is it?"

"Condom." Her expression doesn't change, but green eyes flicker. "Ask me when I swapped it out."

He pushes her pants to the floor. She's naked beneath him, hot and wild and perfect. "When did you swap it out?"

"The day I came to your house." She holds his eyes, asking him to read between the lines. "The day I trusted you enough to let you in."

The words coat his heart like warm honey. Not letting him inside her body, that's not what she means. Not even if he's inches from sinking into her.

His voice rasps out rough. "Why?"

Dumb question for a guy who stands to score, but Nic doesn't flinch. "Because I saw you with your grandma. I saw you as a human with feelings and family and hurts and all the baggage that makes you who you are. It's the moment I knew you were a good man and not a charmer with a store-bought smile." She's holding his eyes, and he wants to look away.

Wants to but can't.

Nic cups his face, so it's a moot point, anyway. She's forcing him to look at her. "You don't want to believe me, Seb, and that's okay. I've got enough belief for both of us. You're a good man, Sebastian LaDouceur. Fucking get used to it."

His heart burns his ribs. A thousand flippant answers scatter like ash and flutter out his ears. "Let me show you how good I am."

Nic shudders and drops her hand. Stretching an arm out, she gropes for her keys. "I can't quite reach—"

"Got it." He grabs the tiny teddy bear, off-balance for a fraction of a second.

That's all it takes. She flips him onto the floor, pinning him beneath her. Her thighs clench snug around his hips. She grins and grabs the keychain. "Thank you."

"You're welcome?" He barely sees her hand move, and she's rolling the rubber on him. "God, woman. Are you trying to kill me?"

"If I were, you'd be dead."

He doesn't doubt it. "We're doing this on the floor?"

"Haven't you seen the exposés on hotel housekeeping?" She shudders. "They wash comforters like once a year. They got in there with black-lights and found bloodstains and semen and—"

"Okay, okay." He stifles a groan as she squeezes his cock. "This conversation's kind of a boner killer."

"Hardly." Another squeeze. "I could pound nails with this."

"I'd rather you didn't." Hands on her hips, he notches himself at her entrance. "There's a better use for it."

"Oh? I'd like to—*Jesus*!" The words get lost as he sinks inside her.

"You were saying?

Nic groans and throws her head back. "Fuck! *Sebastian*."

"You are." He tilts his hips, letting her get used to him. Letting Nic set the pace. "You're so tight." He's never felt anything like this. Her slickness, her heat, how she rides him like she owns him.

He wants to be owned by Nic Bello. It's all he's ever wanted.

"My God." Her lashes flutter, and there's awe in her eyes. "How did I never know it could feel like this?"

She's got him there. "Not sure."

But he feels it too. Something electric snaps between them. She's lightning in his arms, a live wire. They'll burn up the carpet if they keep going, but he doesn't care. Not about anything but her.

As Nic rolls her hips, his thumb finds her clit. Her lashes flutter again. "You want control?"

"Nope." He wants her to use him. To take pleasure from his body. "Show me what you need."

Tossing her hair, she grins. "Gladly." She starts to move, her heat slicking his hand as she circles against him. She's got the pad of his thumb where she wants it as she moves again. "It's like you bought your cock from a catalogue."

He laughs and glides a hand up her waist. "Is that good or bad?"

"Good." The rhythm's getting quicker. "You've got this perfect curve that hits right where I—*oh!*"

"There?" He tilts his hips again, watching her break apart. Watching himself in her eyes, a man on the brink of exploding.

It's never been like this. Not once, not with anyone. For as long as he lives, he'll have this image burned in his brain. Nic Bello, lush and lovely, pink flush flowing from her breasts to her face as she throws herself forward and clutches his chest.

"Sebastian, *oh God!*" Nails rake his pecs as he drives up again, feeling her clench around him.

He tries to hold on, but there's no point. Not with Nic panting and squeezing and calling his name. Dynamite blasts his brain and a million bits of stardust rain around them as he groans and loses himself inside her.

Nic goes limp on his chest. He can't see through hair falling over her face, but her breath parts the curtain of blonde.

"Dead." The pale blonde flutters. "Gonna need a snatch transplant."

He laughs and his cock slips out, making her groan. Scooping her up in his arms, Seb gets to his feet. Turns and tosses back the questionable comforter. "Are hotel sheets okay?"

"Mmmhmm." She burrows against him, not fighting anymore. She's got her face in his chest and her legs hooked over his elbow.

She's warm and soft and completely boneless in his arms. "Anyone ever tell you you're pretty good at sex stuff?"

"Just pretty good, huh?" He tucks her in beside him, curling his body around her. "I'll add it to my resumé."

The truth? He's heard it before, this praise for his bedroom prowess. Once upon a time, he lived for it. Sought it out as his conquests counted orgasms.

The whole truth? None of it meant anything.

Not compared with what he just shared with Nic. As her breath brushes his forearm, he feels her go slack with sleep.

"Nic?"

She's dead to the world, snuffling in her dreams. He kisses her temple. "I love you."

He'd never say it if she could hear. It's his secret to keep. To take to his grave without burdening her. This can't be serious, he knows it. *She* knows.

That doesn't stop him from dreaming it could be real. Imagining a life where they fall asleep like this each night. Where he could have more than just her body.

"I love you," he whispers again, wishing it could be enough.

CHAPTER 12

*N*ic wakes with an arm draped over her eyes. It's not her arm, so that's... *concerning.*

"Morning, sunshine." Sebastian rolls over and kisses her temple. "Ready to get some bad guys?"

Blinking, she sits up in bed. "We really did that." Not the bad guy thing; that's minor. "We slept together."

"'Fraid so." There's a flicker of caution in his eyes. "That a problem?"

"No." Slapping the nightstand for her keys, she finds a tiny tin filled with breath mints.

As she shoves two in her mouth, Sebastian quirks an eyebrow. "Is that the poison? Because it really wasn't bad, and actually—"

"Can it, Minty Fresh." She thrusts the tin at him. "I have a weird hang-up with morning mouth, and I can't have this conversation with you until I know I'm not breathing fire."

Seb grabs the keys and takes two mints. Watches her with wary eyes. "What conversation are we having?"

"The one where we remember having sex and feel weird about it." Scanning his face, she hears his words from last night. The ones she wasn't meant to hear.

I love you.

He's not saying it now, so Nic licks her lips. "The conversation where we both get uncomfortable and awkward, and then we have more sex to forget we just banged the enemy." She tugs the sheet over her breasts. "Speaking for myself on that last one."

Sebastian nods and munches his mints. "How about we skip the first part and move to the second?"

Nic rolls her eyes, though the offer's tempting. "We'll keep it quick." The sheet slips, and she tugs it back over her breasts. "Does this change anything for you?"

Seb flinches. "Sex, you mean?"

"Yeah." She's not sure what answer she's wanting. The truth, maybe.

I love you.

"Well." Seb drags a hand down his face. "I don't really do serious relationships, so..."

"Right. Yeah." Nic swallows to keep her heart from wedging in her throat. "Got it. Yeah, same." She can do this. "So, we're in agreement."

"Yep." His charming grin turns to smolder. "We got that out of the way. You said more sex was next on the agenda?"

He starts to reach for her, but Nic jumps out of bed. "Wait." She spots his T-shirt on the floor and tugs it on, remembering too late that she made it a vest. "I need to take the lead on this, okay?"

"We still talking about sex?" Seb grabs the throw pillow propped on the headboard. As he hugs it to his chest, she's briefly jealous of a bolster.

"The job, Sebastian." She tugs his torn T-shirt together between her boobs. "I need to do this for Nondi."

"Define *do this*." His brow furrows. "Not a sex joke. Are you talking solo job or—"

"Not solo, no." Not entirely. "But it needs to be me bringing in DJ Costa. Delivering him to Nondi."

When he doesn't respond, she rushes to fill the silence. "This is my family legacy. My target. I need to be the one taking the risk. I don't want you storming in like some alpha military hero who—"

"Okay."

She blinks. "What?"

"I said okay."

It can't be that easy. And yet— "Why are you looking at me like I'm not nuts?"

Sebastian frowns. "It's too early to translate that. Are you mad I don't think you're crazy?"

"You don't?"

"Of course not." His smile sends something sloshing in her belly. "I think you're a strong, competent, professional operator who knows what she's doing. You might not need me, but I've got your back if you do."

"Seriously?" She lets go of the shirt. "It's that easy."

"Shouldn't it be?"

It should. But it never has been. Every man she's dated wanted control in some way. The TV remote, the keys to the car, the freedom to smack her if he didn't like the words coming out of her mouth.

Shaking off Clint, she stares at Sebastian. "You're really okay with this."

"If you are, yes." He props the bolster back against the headboard. "I was also serious about the sex." He pats the bed beside him. "It'll go a lot better if you're not standing five feet away."

Scanning his face, she sees the man she slept with. Sexy. Smart. Lethal. She sees the other Seb, too. Kind. Compassionate. Vulnerable. A little broken, but who isn't?

I love you.

In the echo of his whisper, she hears her own.

She also sees his lips quirk. Replays their last few lines of dialogue and sighs. "Go ahead and say it."

"What?" The alarm in his eyes says he's thinking of last night's whisper, but that's not what she meant.

"The dirty joke you're thinking," she says. "Need me to tee it up again?"

Seb's smile is almost relieved. "Yes please."

Her sigh this time is for dramatic effect. "I think my last line was 'you're really okay with this?'"

"And I said something sensitive before admitting I'm serious about the sex and that it'll go better if you're not standing five feet away." Seb's smile slides to devilish. "My dick's long, but not that long."

"And there it is." She tries to roll her eyes, but it's impossible to look at him like that.

And right now, she wants to look at him. And touch him. And tackle him on his back so she can—

"Hey, pretty lady." His smile gets bigger as she straddles him. "Come here often?"

"Not often enough." There's a cyclone in her brain filled with bullets and bombs and precise coordination of the job ahead. In her body, there's another sort of squall. One filled with hunger and desire and this strange sense of belonging.

Somewhere near her center, two storms collide to form something else. Calm. Peace. Certainty.

"Not often enough, huh?" He cups her ass and squeezes. "Better up my game."

Nic puts a hand on his chest to feel his heart thud through her palm. "Shut up and fuck me, Sebastian."

He grins and rolls her on her back. "Whatever you want, Rogue."

* * *

"That's the compound, huh?" Seb hands her the binoculars. "Nondi wasn't kidding about the lack of cover."

They're nearly a mile from Don Julio DeCosta's place—aka DJ Costa—and well out of firing range. Out of range for most binoculars, except these specialized ones Seb got from God knows where. He hasn't said.

Nic squints through the lenses. "It's huge."

"I get that a lot." The strain in his voice makes the joke fall flat. "You don't have to go in alone, you know."

"Yeah. I do." Nic scans the front door. The five-car garage to the left. The shack by the gate where an armed guard waits. "I need to do this for Nondi. For my family. For *me*."

"Sounds like a lot of pressure."

She looks at him. "More than I can handle?" Challenge seeps through her voice, and so does insecurity. "You think I can't pull this off?"

"I think you can do whatever the hell you put your mind to." No hesitation from Seb. "But it doesn't have to be solo if you don't want it to be."

"I want it to be." Does she? "I do." She's pretty sure, anyway.

"Okay then." A pause. "I'm here if you need me."

"I know." God, that feels good. Better than she wants it to.

Seb brushes some hair behind her ear. "You've got your earpiece?"

She nods and feels it shift in her ear. Jellybean sized, it can't be seen from outside. That's the hope, anyway.

Nic drops the binoculars and meets Seb's eyes. "How do I look?"

"Confusing." There's a slow head shake as he takes in her thick, dark hair pulled high in a ponytail. The prosthetic nose and cheekbones that leave her looking like a reality TV bimbo. Boobs thrust to terrifying heights by her bulletproof bustier.

"I like you better as normal Nicole," he says. "But is it okay to be turned on by this Nicole?"

"That's Amanda to you, bub." The code name Nondi picked for this mission.

"It was your mother's middle name." Nondi's face pinched in pain as she handed Nic a thin gold band with three tiny diamonds. "That was hers, too. An apology gift from your father." Nondi made a face. "The stones represent you three kids."

Came in handy with Darlene and Richard last night. As she twists it on her right hand, she hopes the luck holds today. "You did a great job with the makeup," she says to Seb as she flips down the mirror for one last look. "I barely recognize myself."

"I still recognize you." His smile goes tipsy. "In a lineup of a million women, I could pick you out with my eyes closed using only my dick."

Nic nods, not sure what to make of that. "That's disturbingly sweet."

"My specialty." Seb lifts a hand to straighten one of her big hoop earrings. "Seriously, though—you look good."

Fighting flurries of pleasure at his touch, Nic draws a breath. "All right. It's go-time."

A muscle ticks in his jaw. Seb looks deep into her eyes. "You're sure?"

"If you ask me again, I'll castrate you."

He puts up his hands. "Signal if you get into trouble."

"Yeah." Heart pounding, Nic grabs the door handle. "I'll be fine."

Doesn't mean she hasn't thought of six thousand ways this could go wrong. They planned through everything, practicing takedowns in the hotel room until Richard and Darlene banged on the wall. After that, they did mental drills.

What if DJ isn't home?

What if he's got five guards? Ten? Twenty?

What if he sees through this disguise and spots the scared six-year-old whose parents he shot?

A thousand thoughts assail her as she slips from the car. Whatever's to come, she's ready.

"Wait, Nic." He catches her wrist and squeezes. "It's stupid to say this, but… be careful."

"Why is it stupid?"

Seb shrugs. "Like you planned to charge the front door wearing a bunny costume until I mansplained the need for caution."

"Good point." Nic bites her lip. "Know what else sounds stupid?"

"What?"

"How they say in the movies, 'I'd die for you.' What good is that?"

Seb frowns. "Isn't that supposed to be romantic?"

"What's romantic about leaving someone alone?" Emotion swells in her chest, but she swallows it back. "If you love someone and they love you back, the last thing either of you wants is to lose the other." She's babbling now, letting his confession last night cloud her brain. It's the last thing she needs, this distraction.

Or maybe she needs to get this out. "Seriously—someone sacrificing their life so the person they love can survive? That's not heroic. It's just dumb. Dumb and cruel and pointless and—"

"You're right." He leans across the seat to touch her face. "Let's both stay alive."

Nic nods and takes another breath. "I'll be careful."

"I know." He drops his hand from her face. "And I'll be here if you need me."

"If I need you, it won't be here."

"Fair point."

She licks her lips. "Gotta go."

"Okay." If this were a movie, he'd say it now.

I love you, just like he whispered when he thought she was sleeping. Like a hero in an action flick.

But this isn't a movie, and she needs to leave. "It'll all be over soon."

"You'll do great."

She nods and exits the car, clicking the door shut behind her. Rounding the hood, she heads for the van. White and nondescript, it says Beth's Flowers on the side. A real flower delivery van, borrowed from a real florist in town.

Borrowed isn't the right word. But *hot-wired* sounds gauche, and besides, she'll take it back when this is over.

There are lots of things she'll do when this is over, starting with Sebastian.

Heaving herself into the driver's seat, Nic starts the engine. Draws another breath. "Here we go."

His voice hums in her earpiece. "I hear you loud and clear."

Nic nods and doesn't answer. They've agreed to stay silent. To keep communication to a minimum so they don't get distracted.

That doesn't mean she's not craving his voice. His presence in her ear, even if he's parked a mile away.

As she taps the gas, the van rolls forward. She eases past the rundown barn where he'll stay hidden. It's a half mile of gravel road to reach the highway, and Nic takes her time covering it.

There's a vase of roses in a box beside her on the seat. Sebastian's creation, assembled this morning in the hotel bathroom.

"What?" he asked as she watched him work. "You've never seen a shirtless man arrange flowers?"

"Not with a gun on his hip." She watched as he stuck a fern frond in the corner. "You're good at that."

Forehead creased in concentration, Seb poked a sprig of ivy between two buds. "Vase, wet foam, card claw, cardette—voila!" He stuck a last rose in the center. "Five bucks at the Dollar Store, a bunch of grocery store flowers, and you've got yourself a pro-grade flower delivery."

"Impressive."

And fancy enough to get her to DJ Costa. That's the hope, anyway. As the compound comes into view, Nic squares her shoulders. Watches a man rush from the guard station as she glides to the edge of the gate.

The guard grips a room broom, a Heckler & Koch MP5K. Nic tries not to see his finger on the trigger. She puts a hand up in a friendly wave and rolls down her window.

"Hey there." She laces her voice with the faint western twang she's heard on this side of the mountains. "Flower delivery."

The guard glares at her through the gate. "What for?"

She shrugs and feigns confusion. "I didn't read the card, but it's our top-of-the-line sympathy bunch. Someone paid extra for purple roses. Those cost more, you know."

The glaring guard definitely *doesn't* know. Neither does Nic, but the guy's keying in a gate code. That's what matters. It's for the walk-in gate, not the one for cars. She won't get that lucky.

The guard shoves through the gate. "We're not expecting flowers." He comes to the driver's side and frowns at her nametag. "Amanda?"

It comes out like a question, and she projects perkiness with her answer. "Yep! That's me."

"Why'd someone send fucking flowers?"

Channeling Sebastian, Nic gives her best smile. "I guess it's a surprise?" She pretends to squint at the bouquet. "It's a delivery for a mister—" She plucks the slip of paper from the box on her passenger seat. "—mister Costa."

"From who?"

Whom she corrects as she hands him the slip. "A Rosie...*Porecca?*" She says it wrong on purpose, but sees the guard's eyes flicker. *Good.* He knows the name of his boss's sister. Aunt Rosa, back in Dovlano.

The woman her father might've banged. Irrelevant to the takedown, but a useful bit of intel to get her through the gate. Few people know about DJ's reclusive sister. Nic's hoping that works in their favor.

"Huh." The guard glares at the receipt. Narrows his eyes, then starts a circuit around the van. He peers in the windows, hand cupped to the glass. His trigger finger never leaves the gun.

Nic holds her breath, glad she talked Seb out of hiding in back. Inspecting the van, the guard will see nothing but flowers. A dozen more bouquets, each as ornate as the one beside her on the seat.

The guard returns to her window. "This is legit?"

Like she'd say no? Nic shrugs. "I'm just the delivery girl. If you want, I can call my boss. Beth took the order."

"Yeah." He scans the slip some more as Nic lifts her burner phone. She's got Nondi on speed dial, just in case. Seb set it up so the florist's number goes straight to the burner phone. If the guard wants to check—

"Yeah, okay." He hands back the slip and frowns at her hands. "What's with the gloves?"

"Company policy." Another bright smile as Nic fans her latex-clad fingers. "Petals are sensitive to the oils in people's fingers. Beth takes pride in delivering fresh, unblemished arrangements for—"

"Yeah, yeah." He motions with the hand not holding the gun. "Hand 'em over. I'll give 'em to the boss."

"Sure, no problem." Nic draws a breath. "Is he home? Because my boss said to make sure he gets it. I guess that lady really wants Mr. Costa to have the flowers for a funeral or something."

It's way more words than she meant to say, and Nic prays she hasn't overplayed her hand.

The guard frowns. "Yeah, he's around. Busy, but I'll get 'em to him."

"Thanks." Grabbing the vase, Nic hands it out the window. "Careful," she warns. "Roses are really delicate. Please don't touch the petals, especially the white ones."

"Got it," he grumbles, gun hand grazing a pale-yellow rose. He tucks the vase in his arm like a football trophy. "Okay, go. Get outta here."

She could take him out now. Double-tap to the forehead, clean and neat.

But that's not the plan, and besides—he hasn't wronged her. Hasn't hit his kids or beaten his wife, to the best of her knowledge.

So, the man gets to live another day.

He also gets a nap. That's assuming the Lindalinium kicks in quickly.

Thanks, Nondi, for teaching me about poison.

For the charm on my keychain with enough to take out two grown men.

"I'm going." She hooks a thumb behind her and flashes a prosthetic-toothed smile. "Will you tell me if I'm gonna hit something? I can't see so great in reverse."

"Yeah, sure." He's already stopped watching, pivoting to punch the gate code. "Don't hit the boulders. We had 'em brought in special from Dovlano."

"From who?"

"It's a country in—never mind." He gives her a disgusted wave. "Just watch where you're going."

"Thanks!" She takes her time putting it in reverse as he opens the gate. Watches his back as she cranks the wheel. "Have a good day," she calls out the window.

He doesn't reply as he slips through the gate with the gun slung over his chest.

Nic goes slowly backing up. Keeps one eye on the guard, praying he returns to his shack. There's a plan for if he heads to the house, but it's easier if he doesn't.

She's backed fifty feet down dusty gravel when he ducks through the door of the guard shack. Tapping the brakes, Nic watches him set the flowers on a shelf. Sees him take a seat on his stool and—

"And you're out." She lets out a breath as he slumps to one side. His head drops to the counter like he's napping.

Nic darts a glance at the house. No curtains move. There's no one on the steps.

From start to finish, that took four minutes. She's on track.

"You good?" It's Sebastian in her ear.

Nic stares straight ahead. "Mm-hmm."

Shoving the van back in gear, she pulls forward. Stops at the gate and waits for Seb to speak again. "The gate code is 66489."

Score six points for the tiny camera mounted on her side mirror. "Thanks." She doesn't move her lips in case someone's watching.

"You're clear." His voice strokes her eardrum. "No movement at the front of the house."

Here's where it gets risky. She grips the wheel, holds for five seconds, and lets go. A relaxation technique Nondi taught her.

"You've got this." That's Nondi's voice in her head, for real this time. Her grandma's ten miles away, tucked in a desert hideout where she's spent part of the past year playing dead.

When this job is done, Nic has questions for her grandma.

She shoves the door open, sliding from the seat 'til her shoes touch dirt. Three quick steps, and she's tapping the gate's keypad with a gloved finger.

Seb speaks again. "How long 'til he wakes up?"

Nondi replies for both of them. "Lindalinium should keep the guard down for an hour. By drugging him first, we see how it'll hit DJ." A pause. "It has strange side effects for some folks."

"Strange." Sebastian doesn't ask more, but Nic knows he's wondering how Nondi defines that. *Strange* like anal leakage, or *strange* like dropping dead? Doesn't matter in the long run, but it could deny Nondi the chance to see this through.

"You're doing great," Seb murmurs. "Nice work, Nic."

She doesn't answer as she slips through the guard station door and checks his pulse. It's steady, like his breath. Snatching the magazine from the gun, she checks to be sure he's not packing more heat.

All clear, she takes zip-ties from her apron pocket and uses them to prop him upright. Rests his arms on the counter so he looks alert and ready. Even spares a second to wipe drool from his chin.

Nic steps back to admire her work. All set.

She checks her watch. That took three minutes.

Grabbing the flowers, she slips from the booth and hits the button for the big gate. "Vehicle entry point is open," she says with her back to the house. "It slides left to right and there's a sensor on the top left. You've got eyes on it?"

"Yep." Seb's voice, clear and steady. "You're in?"

"Copy." Back in the van, she glides through the entrance. Parks close to the house, scanning for cameras. She spots two beneath the eaves, so there must be more. They planned for this.

Her left ear itches, and she's dying to scratch it, but that has to wait. There's Lindalinium all over these gloves, and she can't risk swapping them out. Maybe no one's watching, but she can't take the chance.

Killing the engine, she leaves the door unlocked. Handy for a quick getaway. Clutching the vase, she grabs the delivery slip and slides from the van. Her shoes tap the pavers, thudding with her heartbeat as she mounts three stone steps to the raised entry.

Drawing a breath, she reminds herself to stay in character. She's a plucky, cheerful delivery girl with a love of false eyelashes and big cleavage. She can do this.

Nic lifts a hand and raps the door. Waits for the echo of footsteps. Her brain runs the numbers. There's at least one more guard inside. Maybe two or three, plus Costa himself and also—

"How the fuck did you get in?" DJ Costa stares and grips the door with blunt fingers.

Holy shit!

Nondi growls in her ear. "Since when does the asshole answer his own door?"

Since now, apparently.

Facing her parents' killer, Nic forces a smile. "Flower delivery for a Mr. DJ Costa?" She holds out the vase. "The guard waved me through. He checked the receipt and called my boss and—"

"Fucking flowers." Not a reaction Terri mentioned.

But DJ grabs the vase and scowls at the tiny envelope anchored in a clear plastic claw. "Goddamn Rosie. Always one for the sentimental schlock." His scowl deepens as he looks at Nic. "You did say they're from her?"

She didn't, so this could be a trap. "I didn't read the card, sir. I'm just delivering flowers."

It's his cue to grab the envelope. As Nic watches, he slams the vase on an entry table and rips open the card. "Haven't seen her in sixteen years," he mutters as he tears it open. "Figures she'd want to rub it in."

Leave it to a guy like Costa to see flower delivery as passive aggression. Seems best not to say anything, so she waits. To be dismissed. For the Lindalinium to hit him. For DJ to drop dead from the sheer weight of her hatred.

You killed my mom and dad, asshole. Wait 'til my grandma gets her hands on you.

His head jerks up. "You're expecting a tip, aren't you?"

"I—whatever you think is best." She tosses her ponytail and watches him through fake lashes. Prays for the poison to kick in. There's enough on the card to knock him cold in five minutes. How long has it been?

"Figures." DJ mutters something in Dovlanese. Curse words, from the sound of it.

"Okay, well." She takes a step back, conscious of the Glock tucked in her frilly florist's apron. "I'll let my boss know."

"Yeah?" DJ leers. "Well don't tell him this."

He lifts a fist and Nic's braced for a blow. But DJ crumples the card and shoves it in his pocket.

She takes a step back. "Sir?"

"Girlfriend's got a birthday coming." He picks up the vase to survey the flowers. "Guess she's getting flowers."

All right. Not a twist she prepared for, but it's fine. "Recycling for the win." She gives a weak smile and takes another step toward the van. "Oh! I almost forgot. I brought plant food. Let me grab you some."

"Huh?" He frowns as she steps off the porch. "I don't have time to stand around waiting for—"

"It'll just be a second." More like six, but who's counting? She's hoping he follows. Makes it easier to get him in the van when he collapses. Not that she'll mind dragging him down the steps if he drops right here. "You want the flowers to last for your girlfriend, right?"

"Like I fucking care." But he doesn't slam the door.

Nic jogs to the van, letting her boobs bounce. She feels dirty as DJ's eyes devour her, but it's part of the plan. As she opens the van door, she's grateful again Seb's not inside. DJ saunters down the walkway with the vase in his hands. "What'd you say your name is?"

"Amanda." She's perky and bright as she swings the door wide. Nothing to see, nothing to worry about—

"God damn." DJ spits another curse in Dovlanese. "That sandwich I had keeps repeating on me."

She swings back to look at him. "Sorry?"

"Gas." He farts in illustration. "Christ."

"I'm sorry to hear that." God, that's potent. Holding her breath, she grabs a packet of flower food and holds it out. "Here you go."

DJ replies with another butt blast. "I've gotta take a shit."

Great. What every woman wants when driving a killer to his doom. At least it won't last long. Not once Nondi gets her hands on him.

She almost feels guilty, then remembers what this asshole stole from her. From her family. From other people's families.

And now she wants to wring his neck. To wrap her hands around his throat and squeeze until—

"Nic?" It's Sebastian's voice in her ear. "We might have a problem."

DJ's frowning at his phone as he farts again. "What the fuck?"

"Um." If he soiled himself, he's not riding in the van. She'll tie him to the bumper if she has to. "I guess I'll get going now."

"Son of a bitch." DJ scowls at the gate. "Dana's home early. You're gonna need to tell her we're not fucking."

"Excuse me?"

DJ laughs. "You farted, too?"

Lovely. She's got a pubescent killer on her hands. "Why do I need to tell someone we're not... having relations?"

Would a florist say fuck? Better play it safe.

"Because Dana gets suspicious, that's why." DJ huffs exasperation. "Just—act like you're not hot for me."

"Okay." Not difficult.

But as the gate swings open, dread pools in her gut. Dana returning wasn't part of the plan. As the blue Mercedes slips through, Nic prepares to pivot.

"Nicole?" It's Sebastian again, his voice low and urgent. "Dana's in a blind spot. What's happening?"

She can't answer because DJ's talking. Talking and... um. Those sounds aren't coming from his mouth.

"Fuckin' A." He snarls another Dovlanese curse. "What in holy hell is wrong with my ass?"

She forces her face to look concerned. "Maybe you should go lie down?"

"And have the bitch thinking you just blew me? Not a chance."

Another foul air biscuit drifts past, and Nic's eyes water. She starts to step back, but DJ grabs her arm. "The fuck?" His fingers clench her bicep. "I don't feel so good."

As the man teeters, Nic snatches the vase. Silly, since flowers are the least of her concerns. The driver's side door flies open on Dana's blue Mercedes. As the gate grinds shut, a big-haired brunette leaps from the driver's side.

"DJ?" She frowns at the man dangling off Nic's arm. "Who are you? What's wrong with him?"

"I'm Amanda. I have no idea." She fights to stay in character. "He was like this when I showed up with your flowers. They're for your birthday. Here!"

Rolling with improv, Nic holds out the vase. Hopes there's enough Lindalinium residue to knock out Dana, too.

But DJ picks that moment to let out one last, lethal fart before collapsing to the ground.

"What the fuck did you do?" Dana drags a pistol from her purse and trains it on Nic. "Hands in the air, bitch. Now!"

Dammit.

Nic thinks fast. Lifts her hands with the vase, then lets it drop. Glass explodes as Dana dances back from blobs of wet foam spattering her shoes.

It's the distraction Nic needs.

Diving for Dana, she tackles her to the ground. The gun goes off, but the shot flies wide. Grappling for the weapon, Nic drags her knees through sharp gravel. Gets Dana in a chokehold and squeezes hard.

"Sorry, girlfriend." Nic shifts her shoulder to cut off Dana's airflow. The gun drops to the ground behind her. "Relax and I won't snap your neck."

She won't snap it anyway, but Dana doesn't know. She might be a terrorist's girlfriend, but that's not enough reason to kill her. As the woman goes limp, Nic grabs another zip tie from her pocket. The big kind, one large enough to cinch Dana's wrists together as she rolls the woman onto her belly and makes sure she stays down.

"Nicole!" It's Seb's voice, frantic in her ear. "Who's shooting?"

Breathing hard, she peels off her gloves and wipes sweat from her eyes. "DJ's down. Dana's out. I just need to—"

"Freeze, bitch!" Voices snap her gaze to the house.

Seven men, all armed to the teeth, point weapons at her.

There's a Colt 1911, a Walther PPK, a Sig Sauer P320 like she used her first year as an operator. Even a freakin' AK-47 gripped in the paws of a bearlike thug glaring daggers at her.

Nic draws a breath. Gauges her odds with a glance at Dana's little Smith & Wesson. Calculates how fast she can reach it. If the Glock in her apron makes more sense.

"Wait a minute." A man in a red flowered shirt holding a 9mm Ruger steps from the pack. "That's a wig. Some bitch in disguise."

Nic lifts a hand and yep—her wig's askew from the struggle. She starts to smile, to talk her way out of it. What would Seb do?

But the man with the Walther speaks first. "She's hot." Sneering, he elbows the guy with the Ruger. "Let's have some fun. Hold her down while we take turns giving her the ol' beef injection."

Gross. Gross and… alarming. Nic keeps her hands where they can see them. Her heartbeat hammers her skull. She can grab her gun in two seconds. Take out two or three thugs before the rest of them start firing. If she rolls behind Dana's car—

"Wait, I know this bitch." The guy who got the elbow returns the jab. "Hey, Bruno—"

"Kill her." The man who must be Bruno stares at Nic with cold eyes. "That's Issela's girl."

"Oh, Nic." Nondi breathes the word in her ear. "Don Julio's father. I—thought he was dead."

Not dead. But he definitely wants *her* that way.

The guy with the Sig Sauer scowls. "You mean Gordon and Anessia's kid?" He raises his gun.

Bruno doesn't blink. "Shoot her now."

Nic grabs her Glock, but she's too late. The shooter takes aim.

Sebastian screams in her ear. "Nic! I'm coming. Just hang on and—"

"Seb." She fires once, twice, knowing it's futile as she fires again.

As the bullet hits her body, she croaks her last words. "I think it might rain."

CHAPTER 13

*S*eb's life blinks before his eyes.

Not *his* life.

His father's life. Greta's life.

The most vibrant life of all.

"Nicole!" He shouts through the earpiece, hoping she can hear him.

Knowing she can't.

His camera showed the bullet strike. He watched her fall, saw her topple over Dana's body as blood sprang from a spot near her shoulder. Her heart?

Stomping the gas, Seb grabs his Beretta off the passenger seat. Shoves it in his quick-draw holster. In his earpiece, he hears DJ's men.

"Shit." One of them mutters in Dovlanese. "Someone see if Dana's okay."

"Dana? Who the fuck shot Dana?"

"No one, dumbass. The blonde bitch took her out."

Pedal to the floor, Seb steals a glance at the monitor. Six thugs, not counting the two Nic shot. Two goons stalk toward her body, while another crouches by DJ. Seb's heart squeezes as he jerks his eyes back to the road.

"Nicole." It's barely a croak as the engine screams. "Please don't die. Please don't die. I love you so fucking much."

What a moron, saying it when she can't hear. When it doesn't matter. If he turned back time, he'd tattoo it on his forehead. Scream it from the rooftops. Shout it in her ear before begging her never to leave him.

Please don't die.

The gate looms up ahead. Thick bars, likely steel. He knows the gate code, but getting out to punch numbers isn't smart. They'll pick him off before he gets a foot from the car.

Praying his seatbelt holds, Seb guns the engine. Aims for the spot where the walk-in gate hinges to the big one. Braces for impact.

Smash!

The smaller gate flies wide, metal shrieking as Seb plows through. The big gate bends, bowing at the weak point where the Volvo's hood strikes. There's screeching and grinding and screaming that might not be the car.

Yelling again, he stomps the gas harder. "Nicole!"

Gunfire erupts, and he's never been gladder for bulletproof glass. For the Hollywood skid class that trained him to carve a perfect arc. His tires spit gravel as the Volvo goes sideways, striking the men approaching Nic's body.

Seb rides the *thump-thump* of bodies beneath his tires. Doesn't flinch as a glance in the mirror confirms they're not getting up.

He hammers the brake, and gravel spurts behind him. Nic's to his right, limp in his periphery. His heart clogs his throat, but he can't look now. Not when he needs to protect her. This Volvo shield is the best he can do for the next few minutes.

Drawing his gun, Seb scans the porch. Five thugs stand gaping with weapons at ready, all aimed at him. Better than pointing at Nic, so he'll take it.

He prays she's alive. That there's a god who'd listen to a man like him. One who's killed for money, who's failed his family, friends. Failed the woman he loves.

Not this time.

He throws open the door. Bullets bounce as he braces an arm between the car's door and window. He's got his head behind the bulletproof glass as his finger finds the trigger.

Bam!

He picks off the first man, the one who ordered Nic shot. It's a clean strike, right between the eyes. "That's for Nondi."

As the asshole goes down, he fires again. "That's for my dad."

There's a gasp as the guy with the Sig Sauer drops. That's the man who shot Nic, and Seb feels nothing as he watches him slump down the steps.

Guy number three backs toward the door, but Seb's got a bead on him. "That's for Greta."

He fires, and the man falls like the others. He turns on the next guy. The one who wanted to hold Nic down and take turns—

"This is for Nicole." His vision goes red as he squeezes the trigger. The guy goes down and doesn't get up.

Alone on the porch, the last guy puts his hands in the air. "Come on, man." His throat rolls as he swallows. "I don't know any of those people. Your dad or Greta or whatever the hell a Nondi is—"

"Don't fuck up my scene." Seb takes aim. "I'm a Hollywood butt double. I know my goddamn lines."

"Huh?" He squints. "Wait. You're that actor? That phony ass charm boy who thinks he's better than—"

"Nope." Seb takes the shot. "Not anymore."

As the last man falls, Seb turns away. Springs from the car and flies to Nic's side. He falls to his knees in the gravel, breathing fast as his heart clogs his throat.

"Please don't die." He feels for a pulse and finds it. "Please don't die, Nic. I love you so fucking much."

Her skin's warm, but there's too much blood. Where is it coming from? There! Finding the wound, he grabs a handkerchief from his pocket. "Please don't die. God, Nic—I love you. *I love you.*"

Her lashes flutter. Eyes open, she squints at him. Tries to smile before she spits out her fake teeth. "Maybe someday," she croaks, wincing as she draws a breath, "you can say it when I'm conscious."

Oh, Jesus.

He chokes on a sob, fighting the urge to pull her close. "You're okay."

Nic winces again. "I got shot, Minty Fresh." She licks parched lips, "Pretty far from okay."

But she's alive. And he sees where gunfire hit her bulletproof bustier, leaving deep divots. She's got bruised ribs for sure, but the bleeding— "It's a shrapnel wound." No bullets lodged in her flesh. No gaping holes. "Thank God."

Wincing, she tries to sit up. "Best purchase I ever made." She inspects the bustier, wincing as she picks out a piece of steel. "Damn."

"I thought I lost you." His voice sounds hoarse, and he's barely holding it together. "I thought I'd never get to say it. I swear on my goddamn life, I'll tell you I love you every day, a hundred times a day, for as long as I fucking live."

"Yeah?" Her eyes meet his, and she smiles. "Watch it or I might think you're getting serious."

"You have no idea." It's all he can do not to hug her. To drag her to his chest and never let her go. He'd do it if he weren't worried about her ribs. "There's another thing."

"Yeah?" Nic holds up a finger. "One sec."

Snatching her Glock, she aims and fires. "You were saying?"

He whips around to watch another thug hit the ground. A

man near the garage with an Uzi in his arms and a brand-new shiny hole in his head.

Holy shit.

"Recognized him from some intel I got last week." She shrugs. "Three domestic abuse charges on his rap sheet. What did you want to tell me?"

Blinking back to Nic, he shakes his head. "Let's get you to a hospital." He's got training as a field medic, but no way is he trusting she's okay. "You need to be checked out."

"Sure, sure." Wincing again, Nic gets to her feet. Waves him off when he tries to help. "Throw DJ in the van, and I'll follow in my car."

"What?" They're not aborting the mission?

Pressing the cloth to her wound, Nic looks him dead in the eye. "If you think I'm going back on my word to deliver DJ to Nondi and get Beth her van back, you don't know me at all."

Right. "I know you." And she knows him, better than anyone. "Not as well as I want to, but—"

"We've got time." She squeezes his ass with a pained grin. "Plenty of time to play catch-up."

"Yeah." His grin turns big and dopey. "We do."

Brushing dirt off her pants, she bends to snatch the ring off Dana's finger. "Get the car, Minty Fresh. I've got plans for you later."

* * *

"That went well." Seb checks the rearview mirror. Sees the hospital vanish as he rounds the corner. "You're sure you don't want those pain meds?"

"We've got a wedding to get to." Nic adjusts her seatbelt. "You heard the nurse. It's just a flesh wound."

"*Not* what he said." He's known military generals less hard-headed than Nic. "You know 'flesh wound' is just a made-up

Hollywood term that lets the good guys keep fighting when a real-life human would be writhing on the floor?"

Nic rolls her eyes and checks her bandage. "Are you mansplaining my injuries, Minty Fresh?"

"Just saying." God, he's glad she's got so much fight in her. "If you hadn't turned so the shrapnel hit that big muscle pad on the outside of your shoulder, you'd be in a helluva lot of hurt."

Nic flips down the visor and checks the mirror. Wipes a smear of dirt off her cheek. "If our roles were reversed right now, I'd make a crack about you ogling my large muscles." She shifts in her seat, wincing so slightly he almost misses it. "I'm fine, Seb. Seriously. Just drive."

He bites back the urge to remind her she could have died. Or had countless other bad things happen, including getting stuck in a small rural hospital explaining how she got shot. As it happened, Dante's cop pal called in a favor.

Chief Dugan—a buddy from Ponderosa Resort—waved his magic wand to get them sprung from the hospital with minimal interrogation. Austin Dugan's the straightest arrow Seb knows, so there must be a reason he's got a soft spot for folks in the gray shades of the law.

He looks at Nic again. "You think Nondi's okay?"

"Oh, yeah." Better than that, based on the gleam in her eye when they left her in the desert with a gagged and bound DJ Costa. "She's getting some quality time with my parents' killer. It's the best damn day of her life."

It's a thing of beauty, he must admit. "You think she'll make it to the wedding?"

"In disguise, maybe." Nic shrugs. "I get it. Her youngest grand-kid's getting married. She doesn't want to mess it up by rising from the dead."

"Understandable." They're driving fast on the highway, headed back the way they came. It's still early, still six hours from wedding time, but it feels like six weeks have gone by.

The Columbia River glitters inky and blue, its surface churned white by a red and blue tugboat. At the edge of the shore, a family sits on a blue speckled blanket. A man and a woman with a baby between them, two towheaded kids skipping through grass.

Seb's heart squeezes. Before he can think, he's flicking his turn sign signal for the rest stop exit.

Nic frowns as he veers off the highway. "Need the bathroom or something?"

"Or something." There's a parking spot ahead, up near the rock wall overlooking the water. Seb steers into it, then kills the engine.

"You okay?"

"Yeah." He turns to look at her, and his heart beats faster. "You good walking fifteen feet?"

Nic looks at the water. "Are you having me walk the plank?"

Grinning, he gets out of the car. "Let me help."

He expects her to fight, but she surprises him by taking his hand. As he hoists her to her feet, he holds her arm for balance. Scans her eyes to be sure she's not woozy. "You okay?"

"Yeah." She smiles and tips her face to the sun. "The fresh air feels nice."

"Come on." Taking her hand, he leads her to the rock ledge. From here, there's a view of the craggy cliffs that line the gorge. Of the wide and sparkling river stretching east to west. Off to their right, the family starts packing up their picnic. The kids dance around the parents' legs as Mom and Dad fold the blanket.

Seb looks back at Nic. "I thought I'd lost you." His breath comes out shaky as he draws a breath. "You know that stupid expression about seeing your life flash before your eyes?"

"Yeah." She sounds wary, and Seb doesn't blame her. God knows he's made jokes at worse times than this.

"It wasn't my life that flashed before my eyes. It was yours." That's not entirely right. "It was mine without you in it, and I hated it. I fucking *hated* it." He squeezes her hand, not sure this is coming out right. "Nic, I can't picture living without you. Without your sunshine or your fire or you snapping at me for mansplaining or—"

"Hey, now."

"No, I love it." Drawing a breath, he holds her hand tighter. "I love *you*."

"Oh." Nic blinks, so maybe he's said something wrong. "You said you didn't want anything serious."

"I don't." Seb threads his fingers through hers. "I want to spend my life making you laugh. Trying to, anyway." His own laugh comes out choked as he grips her hand. "I want to get old with you rolling your eyes at my dumb puns. I want to watch you turn up your hearing aid because, deep down, you're cracking up at some silly joke with a punchline I've forgotten."

"That sounds... *wow*." The shimmer in her eyes may not be the river. "Seriously?"

"I'm seriously serious." As serious as he gets, anyway. "I'm nuts about you, Nic. Always have been, but it wasn't until I almost lost you that I knew I had to tell you. To *show* you."

He lets go of her hand and grabs his keys. Draws them from his pocket and slides off a keyring. "For the first time in forever, I'm picturing a future. One with you in it, and Nic—God, I can't tell you how good it feels. How much I love the thought of waking up with you each morning and falling asleep at night with you beside me. How I'm looking forward to touching you and kissing you when we're forty or sixty or four hundred years old."

"Count me in for immortality." She wipes one edge of her eye. "This sounds... kinda too good to be true."

"It isn't, though." Fingers steady, he takes the bullet off his keychain. Holds it out to her. "Here."

"Why are you giving that to me?" Her fingers curl around it as she looks at him.

"I'm done wishing for a way out. I don't want out. I want *in*. In your life for good if you'll have me." His throat's closing up, so he swallows a few times to get it working again. "If it's what you want, too."

"It is." A slow smile spreads across her face. She looks at the bullet, cold and hard in her warm palm. "What did you want me to do with this?"

"Anything you want. Get rid of it, keep it—it's up to you." His shrug feels sorta sheepish. "It's more symbolic. That doesn't actually fire."

"I know." She looks at the bullet. Looks at him. "To a future." Nic draws her arm back. Throws it at the water, sending the bullet hurtling through the air.

They watch together as it arcs toward the water. Neither speaks as it lands with a splash. Shimmering rings ripple out, then fade to nothing at all.

Seb takes her hand again. Slips his left one in the pocket of his hoodie. "I thought about buying you a ring, but we're not there yet." He is, but she may not be. It's fine, he can wait. As long as she needs to. "But they had this in the hospital gift shop, and I thought of you."

He pulls out the tiger keychain and hands it to her. "One for each of us. I left mine in the car. Seemed like a better symbol than the bullet."

"A tiger." Her fingers close around it, and she laughs. "I'll take it. And Seb?"

"Yeah?"

"I love you, too." She wraps her arms around him, wincing as the injured one stings. Worth it, though. "Never in a million years thought I'd get to say that. Not with you saying it back instead of cracking some joke."

"Give me a minute to think of one." On second thought— "God, Nic—I love you."

She giggles in his arms. "I'm glad we took a chance on each other."

"Same." So fucking glad.

For second chances.

For being wrong.

For having a shot at getting it right.

"I'm all in, Nic," he says. "I love you."

"I love you, Sebastian." She draws back and looks into his eyes. "Come on. We need to get going."

"You sure I can't convince you to consummate things with a backseat quickie?"

"Pig." She smacks him in the chest, hand lingering a while on his pec. "Later for that."

"Fine." He'll wait. Forever if he has to. Something tells him it won't be that long. Watching her walk toward the car makes his heart squeeze tight.

Ten feet away, she turns. "Coming?"

"Not yet." Is it wrong he wants to watch her call him a pig again? "Give me a minute with you naked and—"

"Sebastian." Nic rolls her eyes. "What am I going to do with you?"

He can't wait to find out. "I've got ideas," he says, and follows her to the car.

EPILOGUE

"I now pronounce you man and wife." The officiant smiles as a breeze whips the hair back off her face. Closing her notebook, she surveys the bride and groom. "You can kiss now." Her grin widens, and the bride feels her belly swoop. "You've earned it."

Tipping her snapdragon bouquet to the side, she beams up at her groom. "Don't mind if I do."

She barely gets the words out before he's bending her back with a kiss that makes her toes curl. "There's more where that came from, *wife*."

As the crowd erupts in applause, Matteo gets to his feet. Sticks two fingers in his mouth and whistles as Renee rises and holds out her arms. From his spot by the altar, AJ bounds over for his hug.

"Did you see, Papa?" He's shouting so loud the horses look up from the pasture. "I gave 'em the ring."

"Good job." Matteo high-fives him as Jen starts to stand.

Dante helps, since it's a slow process. She's seven months pregnant with twins.

"You did it!" Jen waddles into the aisle and throws both arms around Nicole.

Nicole hugs back, happier than she's ever been. With spring sun on her shoulders and her whole family filling the wide, grassy field, this wedding is everything she never thought she'd have.

The man beside her is the best part. She looks at Sebastian over Jen's shoulder and laughs. "We did it."

"Sure did," he agrees with a grin.

"Sorry, Seb," Jen says with her arms around Nicole. "I need to hug my sister just a minute longer."

"We've got time." He steps back to give them their moment and Nic's heart soars.

She's never loved him more, which is saying a lot. Clutching her sister, she rocks back and forth, breathing the scent of honey and hay. "Can you believe it? All three Bello kids got hitched."

"Amazing, isn't it?" Jen squeezes harder, pregnant belly pressing into Nic's spleen.

Wheezing, Nic draws back. "You could kill someone with that thing." She sets a gentle hand on Jen's belly and makes a mental note to research prosthetic ones. What a great disguise. "You feel like you're about to explode."

"I might be." Jen laughs and swipes her eyes. "My big sister's married."

Sebastian slides an arm around Nic's waist. "Married to a kickass dentist with excellent taste in women."

"Nice ego, Minty Fresh." Nic tips her head back to look at her husband. Her *husband*. Whose life is this? "You *are* pretty awesome."

Seb plants a kiss near her temple. "Is that how I scored the best wife on earth?"

"Must be," Nic muses.

They're only two feet down the aisle as their recessional

TAWNA FENSKE

music hits its halfway point. Nic doesn't care. All that matters is the man by her side. These rows of chairs filled with all the people she loves.

How freakin' lucky can she be?

"Let's see it." Renee rushes up and grabs her hand. "Oh! It looks great on you."

"Thanks." Nicole adjusts her mother's veil as Renee rolls her hand to make Nic's diamond flash. It's the first time she's worn their great-great-great-great-great-*great* grandma's ring for real. She still can't believe it's on her finger. That she got it back and it belongs to her.

To the family.

"Nice ring." Matteo grunts approval. "Doubles as a paperweight."

"Or a weapon." Dante rests a hand on his wife's shoulder. "Throw a punch and you'll put someone's eye out."

Not a bad idea. "I'll keep that in mind," Nic says.

As the music swells, she surveys her siblings. Their spouses and kids and this whole, happy, loving mess. "Seriously, guys— we're married. Who'da thunk?"

"Me." Sebastian plants a possessive hand on her back. "Aren't we supposed to be marching down the aisle or something?"

"You've got someplace to be, Minty Fresh?" She looks at him and feels her belly swoop again. "I could hang out here all day."

"I'm good with that." He lets his hand dip to her butt so he can sneak a squeeze. "It's gonna be awkward consummating things, but that chair looks sturdy."

"Pig." Nic laughs and lands a kiss at the edge of his mouth. "Control yourself."

As the song spins to a close, a new one starts. It's "Kill the Lights" by Alex Newell & DJ Cassidy. She doesn't remember adding it to the recessional list, so that must be Seb's doing.

God, I love him.

It's the thousandth time today she's had that thought. She'll have it a thousand more before the day is done.

Drawing back, she looks down the aisle. "Seriously, though—I guess we should cut cake or throw rice or whatever the hell people do at weddings."

"They kiss." Her husband draws her close and demonstrates again. "A lot."

"Get a room, you two." That's Matteo, but Nic doesn't care. She really could do this all day. Her whole life, really, which is what she just signed up for.

Oh my God, I'm married.

Giggling, she slides left to nip his ear. "Aren't you glad we did it this way? Without the bridesmaids and groomsmen and whatnot?"

"As long as we get the honeymoon, I'm good." Releasing her, Seb takes her hand. "I love that everyone came."

"Right?" Nic lets her gaze trail the crowd, the bright clusters of flowers, the swarms of friends and loved ones.

Dante's in his uniform from the Court of Dovlano. Renee holds a drooling infant in a tiger-print dress. The baby-sized gown was a gift from Sebastian, who bought it for Mandi to wear today. Their niece is so cute, Nic's ovaries ache.

Seb grips her hand as his eyes find his mother. He tenses as Greta waves. "You good?" Nic whispers to him.

"Yeah." Sebastian waves back. "I really am."

The reunion with Seb and his mom happened gradually. It began with a postcard from Nondi, inviting Greta to family dinner. Even for Nic, things felt stilted at first.

But the surprise of having Nondi back from the dead shifted something in the family dynamic. Adding another long-lost member seemed right somehow. With Nicole and Teo and Dante by his side, Seb eased into a relationship with his mother. It's still a work in progress, but they're getting there.

Nic's never been prouder.

A voice behind them shouts. "Smile, lovebirds."

They turn to see Nondi crouched in firing stance.

"Nice." Nic's grandma clicks a few shots on her camera. "I got a good one of that kiss, too." Rising to her feet, she slips back in beside Terri. "Quit checking out the flowers."

"What? I outdid myself with these." Terri lets go of the floral spray on the end of the aisle. Stretches on tiptoe to hug Sebastian. "I'm so proud of you, honey."

"Thank you." His voice sounds raspy as he hugs her back. "I think Dad would have liked it."

"He'd have loved it." Terri lets go and drags Nic into her arms. "And he really would have loved *you*."

"I hope so." Nic squeezes her new grandma, grateful for her expanding family. For the excuse to gather like this on a warm spring day.

At the back of the aisle, folks start shuffling toward the food. Nic doesn't blame them. This is officially the longest recessional march in history.

"Cake!" AJ tugs the hem of her dress. "Miss Nicole, we can have cake now?"

"Absolutely." She takes her nephew's hand, looping her other arm through Sebastian's. "You think it's okay to cut the cake before we serve food?"

"Why not?" Seb kisses her temple. "Our first task as a married couple should involve sharp objects."

Seb hasn't given up life as an operator. Neither has Nic, though she's slowed down. Too many abusive assholes for her to walk away completely, but she's not alone now. It's helpful having Seb as a backup, with Nondi pitching in when time allows.

Her grandma's trying to retire. She's even started knitting again.

"Hurry it up, you two." Nondi clicks one last shot. "I'm with the kid. Let's get some damn cake."

"Yeah!" AJ bounds to his great-grandma and hugs her leg. "Damn cake."

"Language, AJ." Renee rolls her eyes at Matteo. "It's pointless, isn't it?"

"With this family?" Teo shrugs. "Probably."

Nic smiles at her sister-in-law. "There are worse things than a cursing five-year-old."

She can think of several. A life without love, for starters. Lucky for her, that's not a problem she'll face.

"All right." She tugs her husband's arm. "Should we get walking?"

"Let's hit it."

They march the aisle with AJ skipping ahead. At the edge of a flower strewn arch, the boy stops and whirls by the table stacked with gifts. "Presents first!" he shouts. "*Then* cake."

Nic looks at Jen. "What's the etiquette here?"

"You're asking me?" Jen shrugs. "My wedding had a pig in it."

"Ours had a toddler peeing in the grass." Renee snickers. "Might not want to consult anyone here on wedding etiquette."

"You're experts from where I stand," Sebastian says, and Nic can't argue with that.

"The kid's right." Nondi shuffles around the gift table, picking up a package and setting it back down. "Cake's important, but maybe there's a knife wrapped up in here. Something to cut with, you know?"

With this family, Nic *does* know. As she surveys the table piled with wrapped presents, she spots several that might be weapons.

"All right." She reaches for an oddly shaped gift that looks like it might contain a gallon of ice cream. "Who's this from?"

"Oh, that's mine." Terri scurries forward with a smile. "Not *just* mine. I had help."

Intrigued, Nic peels the gift-wrap back. Whatever it is, it's heavy. Glass, maybe? She shucks the pink-speckled paper.

"A jar of peanut butter?" Sebastian lifts a brow at his grandma. "Someone's angling for snack time at our place."

Terri pats his arm. "Open it." She tucks a handful of purple hair behind one ear. "Not everything's what it looks like, you know."

Oh, Nic knows. As she unscrews the cap on the giant jar, she bursts out laughing. "You painted the inside to look like peanut butter?"

"Yep." Terri smiles at Seb. "Go on, look inside."

He sticks his hand through the mouth of the jar and comes up with.... "A book?"

"It's a recipe book." Terri takes it and flips open the first page. "My snickerdoodle recipe is right here. Dante added his elk chili, and Matteo gave up his cornetto recipe. There's something in here from everyone."

Nicole's eyes fill as AJ tugs the hem of her dress. "Corn-lettles are my favorite."

"Mine, too." Nic swallows hard, overwhelmed with the certainty that *these people* are her favorite. "Thank you, Terri."

"You're welcome, sweetheart." Seb's grandma nods at an enormous package hunkered beside the table. "I'm dying to see what's in that one."

Not the best word choice, but Nic's intrigued, too. "It's huge."

Seb's lips skim her ear. "Figured I wouldn't hear that from you 'til later tonight."

"Pig." Nic elbows him in the belly, but secretly? She can't wait to get him alone.

But they've got lots of time. AJ scurries to the big gift that's taller than he is. "I made it!" he shouts as he pats the side. "Nondi and me did potato stamps."

Nic moves around it to touch the brown paper marked with smeary paint hearts. She looks at Nondi. "Just like you did with us when we were little." Emotion clogs her throat and she swallows again. "I remember."

Nondi tousles AJ's hair. "He's crafty, just like you."

Seb must sense she's close to tears because he takes her hand and tugs to the other side of the gift. "Looks like we can peel back this edge and save the paper." He slides a knife through the seam because *of course* her husband has a blade at their wedding. "Oh, wow."

As the paper falls to the grass, Nic gasps. She looks at Renee in wonder. "Is that the dresser we saw at the thrift store in Portland?"

"Not quite." Her sister-in-law loops an arm through Matteo's. "That sold before I could get back there to buy it for you, so Teo and I had a better idea."

Matteo takes it from there. "We took a woodworking class." Arm around his wife, he nods across the pasture where the old shed stood. "We reclaimed all the wood we could find that wasn't burned or blown up."

"Look, Miss Nicole." AJ drops to his knees and yanks on a drawer. "It gots hidden places."

"Whoa." Sebastian squats beside him to admire a series of cubby holes. As his gaze lifts to Teo's, he grins. "I think we can find things to hide."

"Thought so." Matteo scrubs a hand over his jaw. "Congratulations, buddy."

"Thanks."

Nic throws her arms around her brother. "Thank you so much." She moves to Renee, hugging even harder. "I love it."

Next comes a basket filled with four bottles of wine. Nic pulls one out to admire the label as Jen sidles up beside her.

"It's a new line we're trying." Jen turns the bottle in Nic's hand to show a dark silhouette of three men. Three men who look... *familiar.* "It's called Good Guy Blend." Jen winks. "The artist worked from a picture we gave him."

A picture Nic knows well, since it sits on her mantle at home. She traces a finger over the shapes of Sebastian, Dante, and

Matteo. They're leaning against the fence at Dante's wedding, the three of them posed like brothers. "It's amazing."

"So is the wine." Dante turns a bottle at the back of the basket. "There's one for your first anniversary, one for number five, one for twenty-five, and one for your fiftieth."

Nic looks at Seb and sees all those years unfolding. "I can't wait."

He kisses her forehead. "Same."

"Speaking of photos." Nondi shoulders past Teo and grabs a silver-wrapped gift off the table. "This one's next."

"What is it?" Nic fingers a seam on the package, turning it over in her hands. "It feels like a book."

"Open it, Nicki." Nondi laughs as Nic shoots her a glare. "I'm not getting any younger here."

Seb slips his knife through the seam and cuts the tape. "It's not going to explode, is it?"

A valid question, and Nic moves slowly as she peels back the paper. "Oh—a photo album?"

"A new one." Nondi's eyes soften. "For all the new family memories."

Feeling her eyes fill again, Nic flips open the cover. Stares at the first photo in confusion. "A funeral?"

"*My* funeral." Nondi taps an image of Nic and Jen draped in black. They've got arms around each other and their heads bowed close. "You probably don't remember, but I hired a photographer that day."

She doesn't remember. To be honest, she's tried hard to block out that day. Her vision blurs as she studies the image. A dark October day on a drizzly Oregon hillside. Gray clouds fill the horizon as she and Jen huddle beneath a drippy oak.

Sebastian steps closer and squints at the image. "Is that Matteo?"

Nic looks and… *yep,* that's her brother leaning on the tree. "But—Teo wasn't there."

"I fixed it." Nondi beams with pride. "Got a friend who taught me Photoshop. I made sure Teo could be there this time."

Nic draws a finger down the image of her brother's arm. To his hand resting on Jen's shoulder. This is her family, frozen together in one of the toughest moments of their lives. Her gaze slips to the side and she frowns.

"Who's that guy beside us?" She looks at Nondi. "I don't remember him."

"That's not Photoshop." Nondi reads her mind. "That's *me*."

"What?" She blinks at her grandma. "What do you mean?"

"I was there." Nondi touches her arm. "Even when you didn't know it, I was always there with you."

Sebastian cocks his head. "You were a middle-aged Latino man?"

Nondi huffs. "You're not the only one in this family who's good with disguises."

Pride floods Nic's chest, mingling with love and joy and something else she can't name. "Oh, Nondi—thank you." Nic swipes her eyes. "It's incredible."

And most incredible of all—

"I love you." Sebastian slips the album from her hands and hands it to Renee, who turns the page and coos at a picture of baby Mandi. Jen's looking at the album, too, admiring an image of her own wedding as Nondi points to the spot where she hid that day.

But Nic's only got eyes for her husband. "I love you so damn much." Her eyes lock with his and she squeezes him hard. "Forever."

His lips skim her ear. "Ready to fill that book with more memories?"

"So ready," she says, hugging him harder. "Let's get started on forever."

· · ·

***

Thanks so much for seeing the Assassins in Love series through to the end! Since this book gave you glimpses of my Juniper Ridge world, how about a closer look? The series starts with *Show Time*, but each rom-com in the series stands alone. Let's hop ahead to Cooper Judson's story for a chapter with Seb's old Hollywood pal. Here's your exclusive peek at *Just for Show...*

YOUR EXCLUSIVE PEEK AT JUST FOR SHOW

CONFESSIONAL 961

JUDSON, COOPER (FAMILY FUCKUP)

WE ALL HAVE OUR ROLE TO PLAY.

I DON'T MEAN THAT IN A HOLLYWOOD SENSE. I LOST COUNT OF THOSE ROLES YEARS AGO, MOSTLY BECAUSE I SPENT MY ACTING CAREER BAKED OUT OF MY GOURD.

NAH, I MEAN FAMILY. DEAN'S BEEN THE MAN IN CHARGE SINCE HE SAT IN HIS HIGHCHAIR HAGGLING FOR MASHED PEAS INSTEAD OF SQUASH.

MARI'S HARD-WIRED FOR HEAD SHRINKING, AND LANA'S WHOLE SUNSHINY SCHTICK—NOT AN ACT, BY THE WAY—MAKES HER PERFECT FOR PR. GABE AND LAUREN HAD THEIR PLACE ON THE OTHER SIDE OF THE CAMERA, BUT ME?

[ADOPTS HOITY HOLLYWOOD AFFECTATION] TURN AROUND, COOPER. SMILE FOR THE CAMERA, COOP. HEY, COOPER—KEEP SMILING. SMILE BIGGER. SMILE LIKE YOUR LIFE DEPENDS ON IT.

[RETURNS TO NORMAL VOICE] IT DOES.

DID.

CAN I GET SOME WATER OVER HERE?

* * *

*T*here's a cow in my yard.

A calf, specifically.

In a past life I'd wonder if it's a weird hallucination, but I've been sober for years. Also, there's a ranch three hundred yards from here, so it's not so odd to have a baby cow peering in my bedroom window.

I blink a few times to be sure it's really there. The calf stares back, head tipping to one side.

"Meh-eh-eh-eh."

It doesn't moo like a cow's supposed to, maybe because it's a calf. The longer it stares, the more judged I feel. Swinging my legs out of bed, I address my guest through the window.

"I'm up, okay?" Glancing at the clock, I grumble some more. "It's six-thirty. My LA friends are falling into bed right now."

The calf looks unimpressed. Or maybe hungry. Or bored or accusing or… why am I diagnosing cow moods? I'm not equipped for that.

But I'm equipped to help get this big-eyed baby safely back home, so I throw on sweatpants with a T-shirt and drag a hand through my hair. Shoving my feet into flip-flops, I step out the sliding door and onto my back deck.

Breathing deep, I take a sec to appreciate where I've landed. The sun's coming up on the horizon, all pink and orange and glowy. Pine trees shimmy in the breeze, and the prettiest cliffs I've ever seen march the property line like they're coming to greet me. It's worlds away from where I was before. I slide out my phone to snap a pic, then dial my friend's ranch.

"Hey, Tia." It's her voicemail, but only because she's out mucking stalls or weaving hay or whatever ranchers do this early in the morning. "I think I have one of your pals. Big eyes and a skinny, twitchy tail. Red and white fur." Wait. "Do cows have fur or fleece or just a coat? It's a calf, actually. Call me."

I hang up and approach my visitor, half expecting it to bolt. I hold out a hand, moving slow and easy and calm. The calf bleats again, then stretches out to sniff me.

"Hey there." Its nose feels like velvet, and I take my time stroking the warm slope of its neck. "We'll get you back to your mom, okay?"

Its eyes are so trusting my chest hurts. Since when am I the guy someone's counting on?

Lifting my phone again, I tap the other number. The one I shouldn't call, but that doesn't stop me from dialing. I tell myself I'm calling because she's chief of police and knows about reuniting lost animals with owners. I watched her last week using ham from her lunch to lure an escaped dog. She crouched in the dirt, blond hair brushing her face as she murmured words that made my heart sit up and beg.

"Cooper." She answers on the first ring and my heart does its begging thing again. "Are you okay?"

I ignore that she probably thinks I've fallen off the wagon. She's hardly the first to assume that.

"Hey, Amy." I clear my throat when I hear it's rusty and sleep worn. "Hope I didn't wake you."

"I'm an early riser."

I know this. I know most things about the pretty police chief in this tiny town my family transformed from an old cult compound to a reality TV social experiment. I know she grew up ten miles from where I'm standing and that her laugh sounds like Christmas bells. I know she earned the top score at her police academy and that her right eye is a shade darker than her left.

"There's a cow in my yard." It sounds stupid when I say it, so I hurry to clarify. "I'm guessing it's Tia's, but I'm afraid it'll panic and get hurt or run out on the highway or—"

"I'll be right there."

She hangs up before I babble enough to leave her asking what sort of idiot calls the police chief to handle a baby farm animal.

Me. I'm the idiot. The idiot who looks for any excuse to see Amy Lovelin. I'm not proud, but that's where we're at.

Her Juniper Ridge police SUV glides to a stop beside my cabin and she gets out wearing slim black pants with a gun belt and a blue blouse that's freshly ironed. I add this to my list of things I admire about Chief Lovelin. Polished, put-together, and willing to wrangle livestock at sunrise.

"Wow." She pushes hair off her forehead. "It's really a cow."

"You expected a hedgehog?"

"Thought you might be pulling my leg."

Old Cooper might've joked that her leg's not the body part I'd like to touch. "Definitely a cow," I say instead. "Calf. Bovine. Juvenile representative of the organic cattle community."

Amy laughs and I try to think of more cow words to keep her smiling. She's approaching the calf, holding out a hand and deploying the same sweet voice she used with the dog. "Hey, sweetie. Need help finding your way home?"

A voice inside me screams *yes!* as I do my best to look calm and unaffected. I even ease back to give them space. "I can find a rope."

Amy looks up. "You have rope?"

"Not for bondage." I blurt the words before thinking better of it. "Uh...for a project. On set. For the show. Definitely not for tying people up."

Kill me now.

But Amy's smiling so I back my ass into my bedroom and slam the sliding door shut.

For the record, there's no rope in my bedroom. I find it in the kitchen junk drawer, along with a sturdy pair of shears. When I return to the porch, Amy's stroking the calf's neck and holding it by the halter.

"Don't worry, sweetie," she's saying. "We'll get you back where you belong."

"Must've wandered off from its mother?"

Amy bends to peer at the animal's undercarriage. She's down there a long time and I definitely don't look at her butt.

"Uh..." I drag a hand through my hair. "Do calves have addresses branded on their junk?"

She straightens with a smile. "Actually, it's a steer."

"Steer?" I should probably know what that means.

"A neutered male calf," she explains with more patience than I deserve. "Maybe eight months old, so he should be already weaned."

I ease closer, threading the rope through its halter. "How do you know so much about livestock?"

She catches the end of the rope, looping it neatly around a tree trunk. It's on the tip of my tongue to point out we make a good team. I doubt Chief Lovelin would appreciate the observation.

"I grew up in farm country." She ties an elaborate knot around the trunk of my favorite pine, then stands and dusts her hands on her pants. "I'm guessing my childhood lessons weren't much like yours growing up on America's favorite sitcom, huh?"

I want to be flattered she knows my career origins before I branched into cinema, but it's hardly a secret. By sheer dumb luck, I'm the Judson with the most famous face. The Hollywood hellion, the son whose movies rocked the box office and whose scandals graced a million magazine covers. Blockbuster action flicks, relationship flops, three Oscars, my regrettable, drug-fueled bullshit...it was all out there for the world to see.

Well, not *all*.

"I don't miss it." Why did I say that? "Hollywood, I mean. I'm not missing that life at all." I stroke the steer's nose and slide my gaze to the trees instead of Amy. It's easier that way.

"Not even a little?"

I shake my head, forcing myself to meet the clearest blue eyes I've ever seen. "Not one bit."

She studies me like she's deciding if that's the truth. "It's still so weird to me."

"What's weird?" My anxiety kicks into gear. *I'm* weird? My career? The fact that I'm standing here in sweats with no underpants hoping to God I don't do something dumb like pop a boner?

The possibilities are endless.

"You," she says, confirming my fear. "Not you, specifically. The fact that you could just walk away from being on the same plane as Brad Pitt or George Clooney or Ryan Gosling or Idris Elba or—"

"This is a fun tally of actors more talented than me. Should I get a pen?"

Amy rolls her eyes. "Don't be fake modest. It doesn't suit you."

I'm not sure what to say to that, so I settle for petting the steer some more.

"My point," she continues with a look that's just as pointed, "is that you gave it all up to come here and be a glorified errand boy."

"Harsh."

She cocks an eyebrow. "Give me your business card."

I look down at my sweatpants. No pockets. No second layer between my junk and the morning breeze, and I'm really hoping she can't tell. Why didn't I take two seconds to grab boxers?

"I don't have a business card on me," I point out.

"Okay, but if you did, what would it say?"

It's definitely a trick question. "Not 'glorified errand boy.'" I shrug. "All right, I *did* ask Mari to put that. Too many letters. It has a nice ring to it, though."

Amy snorts. "It says 'gofer.' Your card says *gofer.*"

Her gaze goes sharp like she's expecting me to crack under this ruthless interrogation. I'd be squirming if it weren't for the speck of a smile in her eyes. Also, it's kinda hot.

"It does say gofer." I sound way too cheerful for this early in the morning. "Not *gopher* with a *ph*, by the way. Honestly, it'd be a step up to go from Hollywood A-lister to rodent."

Amy's trying not to laugh. I see it in her eyes, and I wonder what it takes to nudge her over the edge. "All I'm saying," she says, "is that you walked away from one of the hottest careers in Hollywood to be the guy who gets coffee for people."

"Hey, now." I fold my arms and watch her gaze flick briefly to my chest. "I'm an equal opportunity gofer. I also get tea or milk or soda or—"

"I know what you do, Coop. We've worked together enough that I know there's a sizable brain in your thick skull."

"Thanks?"

She shakes her head almost sadly. "I understand wanting change. I just struggle to wrap my head around one so massive."

"Should I be flattered you've used both 'sizable' and 'massive' to describe me in the last thirty seconds?"

I expect her to laugh, but she blushes. Blushes and keeps her eyes on my face. It might mean she's trying not to look somewhere else, and I'm self-conscious again about my lack of underwear. I should make an excuse to duck back into my room. Maybe slink into bed and burrow beneath the covers to dream up an alternate universe where Amy follows me inside and slips beneath the blankets, her skin bare and smooth against my—

"You do seem happy."

I blink. She's not scanning my crotch, so that's good. "Thanks?"

"No, I mean…this life." She hooks her thumbs on her gun belt. "It suits you."

"It does."

Silence stretches like a fresh-laundered sheet tugged between us. I should stop thinking about sheets and blankets and anything to do with Amy in my bed.

"Giraffe!"

She blinks like I've lost my damn mind. "Excuse me?"

"You're right I don't know much about cattle, but I worked with giraffes filming *The Sahara Heist.*" Why am I sharing this story? "We were on location in Tanzania and these giraffes broke into my tent. Five or six of them. I chased one wearing my boxers."

She folks her arms. "Is there a punchline where I ask why the giraffe was wearing your boxers?"

God, I love her.

Not love. *Respect.*

"Funny you say that. I wasn't kidding." Also, I'm realizing I've steered this conversation to underwear, so she might notice I have none. "The giraffe stuck its head in the tent trying to get my beef jerky. Weird since they're herbivores. But it somehow got my boxers looped over one ear and I freaked out thinking it'd get caught on a tree and choke or something. I bolted out the door after it. Fully-clothed, for the record."

Amy frowns. "Did you catch it?"

"No, but the boxers fell off when it ran. The crew teased me for weeks about my kissy print underpants."

Amy's laughing and stroking the steer's neck, but curiosity creeps into her eyes. "Beef jerky? I thought you were a vegetarian."

"Yeah." I clear my throat, aware we're treading close to a danger zone. That the calf being here on my property conjures up stuff I don't want to think about. "I gave up meat years ago. Personal choice."

She's watching like she knows there's more to the story. No one else would do that. They'd just nod and shrug and figure it's a Hollywood fad diet.

Not Amy. She sees straight through me. Always has, and it scares the hell out of me.

I'm fumbling for a subject change when a familiar shout saves me. "Hey, Coop! What's with the cow?"

I turn to see big brother Dean jogging beside his CFO wife.

Apparently, crunching numbers and plotting TV dominance isn't enough to challenge them. Dean and Vanessa get up at the butt-crack of dawn to sprint in matching spandex.

"Hey, Ness." I high-five Vanessa since she's closest, while Dean's inspecting the steer like it's a set prop. "You guys are up early."

"Training for a half-marathon." She leans against the tree to stretch her quad. "My brother, Vonn—he's coming from Europe and wants to run some crazy-ass race. Gotta be sure I smoke him."

"Sibling rivalry for the win." I glance at Dean, who's still studying the steer.

He looks up frowning. "Seriously, bro. Why do you have a cow tied up outside your house?"

"That's not a dog?" I summon my acting chops and feign confusion. "The animal shelter has some explaining to do."

"It's Tia Nelson's." Amy steps in, since my smart-ass response isn't cutting it. "At least, we think it is. She raises Herefords like this."

Vanessa strokes the steer's neck and makes smoochy sounds. "Aww, and you found your way to Cooper. Animal magnetism, sweetie. All the girls love Coop."

I might be imagining, but I think Amy's eyes darken.

"It's a steer, actually," I blurt. "A boy with his giggle nuggets lopped off." I nod to Amy so I'm not taking credit for her smarts. "Chief Lovelin pointed it out."

"Interesting." Dean's still frowning. "We should do a segment on baby farm animals."

"Oooh, you're right." Vanessa's math brain takes off running. "Our advertisers loved the stuff on the animal shelter. You think Tia would let us film there?"

"I can ask." Tia's one of my best friends and isn't even technically part of Juniper Ridge. "She agreed to those PSAs on organic farming."

"Thanks to the legendary Cooper Judson charm." Vanessa winks at Dean. "Your baby brother could charm the shell off an egg."

"No doubt." Dean grunts. "He and Mari and Lana got the good-natured human vibes in the family. The rest of us are just surly assholes."

"Yeah, but you're *my* surly asshole." Vanessa stretches for a kiss on his cheek.

"Seriously, Coop." Dean slides an arm around his wife's waist, distracted by whatever she's whispering in his ear. "I don't know what you said to that investor last week to make her sign a two-year contract instead of walking away like she planned."

"It was nothing."

Nothing but a soul-sucking lunch date where I agreed to do a shirtless Zoom chat with her book club. I hate myself sometimes.

"Well, we appreciate you." Vanessa smiles. "You're the cog that keeps us rolling. I don't know what we'd do without you."

"Fact," Dean agrees. "As brothers go, you definitely don't suck."

I feel Amy's eyes on me and fight the urge to look at her. "I like to be useful."

Vanessa stops manhandling my brother and looks at Amy. "Do you have siblings?"

"I—yes." The hitch in her voice drags my gaze to her face and I wish I hadn't looked. Wish I didn't see the ache in her eyes. The rolling of her throat as she swallows. "I have a brother."

"Older or younger?" She's missing Amy's tension, but most folks would. Most haven't spent hours watching every flicker in her eyes, every blink, every tick in her jaw that betrays her careful cop façade.

"Younger brother." Amy licks her lips and glances at her watch. "I should get going. I'll stop by Tia's to have her collect this guy, and then I've got spin class."

"Oh! You should meet Vonn." Vanessa claps her hands

together. "My big brother? He's really into cycling. I'm trying to get him to move back to the states and I know he'd love meeting you."

"Sure, that's great." Amy's backing away, her smile not faltering even a little. "Give him my number."

I start toward her, then stop. The last thing she needs is an underdressed creeper chasing her. "Amy?"

She stops, fingers flexing at her sides. "Yeah?"

For an instant, we're the only ones here. Just the two of us with something sharp and electric snapping between us.

I break the link first. "Thanks." I shuffle back so I don't reveal how pathetic I am. "For showing up. For helping with the steer."

She nods and pulls her keys from her pocket, still backing away. "Don't mention it."

I watch as she gets in her car. As she revs the engine and adjusts the rearview mirror As she eases the car from its spot, hands at perfect ten-and-two on the wheel.

I'm still watching when her shoulders slump the instant she thinks no one's looking.

She drives away, gaze on the road ahead.

Just as she crests the hill, she lifts a hand and wipes her eyes.

***

Want to keep reading? Click to grab *Just for Show*!
https://books2read.com/u/4DxQRO

ACKNOWLEDGMENTS

So much stinkin' love goes out to my street team, Fenske's Frisky Posse. Y'all are the bomb, and I can't thank you enough for your extra heaps of support with this series. Thanks especially to my typo warriors, Erin Hawkins, Jennifer Becker, Tammy M, Becky C, MaryEllen W, Angela Pool-Funai, Rosie Burke, and Regina Dowling.

Extra thanks to Imari McClure, Judy Lynn, and Goldie for the photo album idea, to Jen Lundsten Williams for the wine idea, to Erin Hawkins for the recipe book idea, and Cheryl Sullivan Hastings for the reclaimed wood furniture. Your contributions made for the perfect happily ever after!

Bonus thanks to street teamer Tristan Roslin for suggesting many moons ago, "maybe you should have a female assassin with the code name Rogue..."

Thank you to editors Susan Bischoff and Lauralynn Elliott for your gentle guidance and occasional smacks upside the head. I'm damn lucky to have you.

High fives to my dentist, Andy Engel, DMD. Our running joke of more than a decade became one of my favorite romance heroes I've written, so thanks for making that happen (and for making my teeth nice and sparkly).

Thank you to Meah for your cheerful help and can-do attitude no matter how much I pile on you. And thanks especially for picking up extra slack when things went off the rails midway through this series release cycle. Love you so hard!

Much love to my family, Dixie & David Fenske; Aaron & Carlie & Paxton Fenske; Cedar & Violet Zagurski. I couldn't do this with you.

And (((HUGE HUGS))) to you, Craig Zagurski. Who'da thunk 11 years ago after your first date with a soon-to-be-published novelist that you'd end up reading sex scenes on video in our kitchen while zillions of pets yowled at our feet? I love our life together and I love YOU even more, hottie.

DON'T MISS OUT!

Want access to exclusive excerpts, behind-the-scenes stories about my books, cover reveals, and prize giveaways? You'll not only get all that by subscribing to my newsletter, I'll even throw you a **FREE** short story featuring a swoon-worthy marriage proposal for Sean and Amber from *Chef Sugarlips* in the Ponderosa Resort series.

Get it right here.

http://tawnafenske.com/subscribe/

ABOUT THE AUTHOR

When Tawna Fenske finished her English lit degree at 22, she celebrated by filling a giant trash bag full of romance novels and dragging it everywhere until she'd read them all. Now she's a RITA Award finalist, *USA Today* bestselling author who writes humorous fiction, risqué romance, and heartwarming love stories with a quirky twist. *Publishers Weekly* has praised Tawna's offbeat romances with multiple starred reviews and noted, "There's something wonderfully relaxing about being immersed in a story filled with over-the-top characters in undeniably relatable situations. Heartache and humor go hand in hand."

Tawna lives in Bend, Oregon, with her husband, step-kids, and a menagerie of ill-behaved pets. She loves hiking, snowshoeing, standup paddleboarding, and inventing excuses to sip wine on her back porch. She can peel a banana with her toes and loses an average of twenty pairs of eyeglasses per year. To find out more about Tawna and her books, visit www.tawnafenske.com.

ALSO BY TAWNA FENSKE